THOMAS FULLER

MONSIEUR AMBIVALENCE

a post literate fable

ISBN978-0-9859773-1-3

Cover and interior design:
Ingalls Design, San Francisco

First Printing, April, 2013

So we never live, but we hope to live.

Blaise Pascal, *Pensees*

One reader called Monsieur Ambivalence "an old fashioned experimental novel and a new fangled sermon or screed in which the individual is all-or-nothing, both a stranger in a strange land and all too familiar to himself."

The writer of this book thinks this a fair reading of the work, believing this early and innocent reader to be sensitive to the writer's intention, but remains open to the possibility of other interpretations and even welcomes them.

CONTENTS

Finally, let them recognize that there are two kinds of people
one can call reasonable; those who serve God with all their
heart because they know Him, and those who seek Him with
all their heart because they do not know Him.

Pascal, *Pensees*
194

Where am I? A good question, and much more
appropriate than the old baroque question,
who am I?

I'm right here at the moment trying as hard as I've ever tried to be here,
the abrupt first child of Mr. and Mrs. Jonathan Fuller, both deceased,
allegedly leaving the United States tomorrow to live in a village in the
middle of France with a woman named Helena. I like staring out of windows but don't do it enough, to take some alcohol every evening, first
something white and then red, and to write poems I never seem to finish.
I have a weakness for tv, and am moving to France without one. I read at
least 200 books a year, trying to read good books I don't understand, like
the book I'm reading now, *Pensees*, by Blaise Pascal. I'm either pleased or
displeased by my life or both, but there's very little about me I wouldn't
like to change at some point under the right circumstances.

Helena said France. It was a place where no one knew me and I knew no
one. I didn't speak the language, a real blessing it turns out. I'd have time
to read and think while shedding previous influences. I could say *yes* or I
could say *no*.

If I said, *yes, I'll go to France*, it was to see if I could sit alone in a room by
myself for one hour as instructed by Blaise Pascal.

If I said *no*, the answer would destroy the illusion I had about living in a
small village. I could start living my life over again, someplace far from the
people and life I'd known.

I must have said *yes* at some point for Helena and several others say they
have pictures: that I lived in the village of Montaigut and walked upstairs
to the terrace in the petit maison every morning for at least one hour to
write in the yellow notebook I bought at Auchan in Clermont-Ferrand.

If I say *no, I'm not going*, as I believe in retrospect I might have said, I would
not know what I know now, though what I know now comes close to nothing and was told to me in a language I have no hope of understanding.

YES SITS QUIETLY   As I'm in the habit of living my life in terms of what my life is not, a large part of me is French, for it is French to define things by what they are not. Pascal claims all the discord in the world arises from man's inability to sit quietly in his chamber, irrespective of one's ability to eat the bread and drink the wine of France. If I say *yes*, it's only to see if I can sit quietly in a room for one hour.

MAKING A PLAN   The plan: Helena and I will walk Paris for two weeks, bike the Loire from Blois to Angers, put the bikes on the train at Angers to Clermont-Ferrand, bike from the station to the little village. Jean-Claude will wait up for me, roll a cigarette, take me in to see Simone, his partner. Somehow we'll communicate. I'll be properly fed, the cheese of the Auvergne, especially Pavin and St. Nectaire, has many adherents and Jean Claude always buys good wine, Bordeaux's and Rhone's.

Only five people are concerned now that Teradact's out of the picture— Helena, Jean-Claude and Simone, Monica and Robaire (poor Robaire, robbed of his happiness and sent back to Brussels without cigarettes)— and all of them, except Helena, still live far away in a little village in the midst of the Auvergne, France, except Monica and Robaire, who haven't kept in touch since moving to Belgium.

TRUTH AS A SERIES OF ASIDES   Wasting time's expected of me—doing nothing, entertaining or being entertained, thinking about what time might be—it's what I'm expecting of myself. I'm supposed to be doing nothing in real life. I walk without thinking and I walk not to think. If a thought comes I think it, I'm looking for its truth.

Since Truths are few and farther from me than they once were, I have to start small. Helena and I eat well, and we share our food with others. Therefore I could be eating a tomato when I die, it's possible a tomato is the last thing I'll ever see. That's how death works, it takes away the person you thought you had to be all the time you were thinking about who you might be. When you die you won't be thinking about yourself, this much is certain.

The truth's easy once you start saying it, but difficult at first; you're not used to it. You see it's not truth you're thinking but you think it's truth, you think it into truth. Then there are the truths themselves, independent of the others, true because they contradict you. A truth like this either happens all at once or takes forever, depending on how smart you are or how open your heart is. It changes you a lot, and if you keep saying it and saying it nothing else is ever the same or as satisfying and you become a true listener.

At first when you start telling the truth you'll feel mostly dead, what being dead could feel like, and want to start telling lies all over the place. I didn't know what else to do. Other people seemed to know what to do, not me, I didn't. Other people seem to know everything. It's my fate to be ambivalent, it's as bad as smiling at the times you don't want to smile, or having to be around people you don't want to be around, or wanting a cigarette. Since I've started telling the truth I've had this thought more than once— *that truth is time, changing*

> Truth is time changing
>
> Truth is
>
> Time, changing

TRUTH

IS TIME,

CHANGING

> Truth
>
> is time changing

A comma can change everything! A comma's importance can't be overemphasized. Philosophers, poets, saints know a whole life can be devoted to nothing more than how one thinks about a comma.

PREAMBIVALENCE   Helena says I *always seem to be offended and put upon to do anything*, she says I *sigh* as I work and *complain constantly*. Not until later in the story does she say I'm ambivalent, and she has the right, she's right here with me.

If I go to France with Helena—I'm not saying I will—it's for silence, to receive the rewards of not-having to talk. Not knowing the language I can cure the garrulousness that plagues me.

Even with Jean-Claude and Simone, my friends, Helena takes care of the conversation. I sit and eat and drink wine and roll an occasional cigarette from Jean-Claude's tobacco, getting permission by a glance, by miming the gesture of rolling a smoke. Jean-Claude understands I like to roll my own rather than having him roll them for me.

I usually bring wine to his house, a bottle of white and a bottle of red, though Jean-Claude won't open one or the other, insists on walking down by himself to his *cave* to bring up three or four bottles of his own—usually three reds and one white, the red usually from the same maker and vintage, for he buys his red wine by the case when he finds what he likes. One month it's Bordeaux, the next Chateauneuf de Pape. He always buys from the maker himself, takes time with the winemaker, drinking a bottle or two with him, one of the very few times Jean-Claude travels anywhere, other than to drive to work at the tire factory in Clermont-Ferrand or to his sister's in Issoire.

We always start with white, starting with white is the right way to do things in France, the proper progression, an Aligote or a Sancerre, but we never start with the white wine I've brought. Sometimes he doesn't bring up a another white and we've already drunk the white I've brought, and we sit there looking at one another like we've made a mistake but have decided not to talk about it.

Jean-Claude's a great preserver of things, just short of a scavenger. The house he shares with Simone was once the GRANGE, (grange), a barn built in the 13th century, he says. (I believe him, Simone says it too and she was born in the house). It was was once her grandfather's, who permitted his son to turn it into a bar and a dancehall when Simone was a little girl, an occurrence that makes her cry every time she thinks about it.

The cave's such a legend in the village that no one's ever seen it. Peter the Dutchman, who speaks very good English and owns a ruin in the village, says Jean-Claude keeps a Volkswagen built by the Nazis in the 1940s there; he claims he saw it when Jean-Claude left the cave's wooden doors open on a hot summer day. Peter told Jean-Claude he'd seen the car,

Jean-Claude denied it, said the car was an Opel.

It was blue, Jean-Claude said to Peter. *You saw a blue Opel, Peter, that's what you saw*, laughed the whole thing off.

Peter's sure he saw a row of toy dolls neatly perched on a shelf and puppets hanging by their strings from the ceiling, but says he never mentioned this to Jean-Claude.

The relationship's different now. Peter thinks Jean-Claude is such a private man he felt violated by what Peter had seen. He worries about Jean-Claude's drinking, having found empty bottles of Ricard pastis in the weeds beside his house, claiming he saw Simone's poodles there and that *the dogs never went anywhere without Jean-Claude.*

PHILOSOPHY'S THE RIGHT WAY TO LIVE When someone asks, *what do you do?*— and they shouldn't—I say, *I do philosophy*. The philosophers themselves say they *do* philosophy, beginning with Wittgenstein, the Austrian, though it might have been Baudrillard or Derrida (Frenchmen). It doesn't seem possible that Descartes or Montaigne or even Pascal would have said that they *do* philosophy had they been asked, though they were philosophers. The question itself—*what do you do*—presupposes that one's identity is gained by how one makes a living, by what is done with the majority of one's time. I make it a point to never ask another person what they *do*. If I'm asked, I answer that *I do philosophy*, and I usually don't like the person who asks.

I've never been asked *what do you do?* in France, a big plus in its favor. Jean-Claude never asked, *what do you do?* The question wouldn't occur to him. He either already knows the answer or simply doesn't care, he knows what I do has nothing to do with who I am. If I said to him, *you know Jean-Claude, what I do is to do nothing*, he'd understand. But if I said to him, *philosophy is what I do*, he'd pretend he didn't hear me.

I learn a great deal by staring at someone's mouth as they speak, without fear they will notice I am staring, as what they are saying is paramount to them, so that it excludes me, the listener, to the degree it cancels any suspicion they may have that they are being inspected. I watch the way the words leave the speaker's mouth, especially the mouth corners, the position of the lips, the posture of the chin holding the lips that form the words they are saying...

...Helena speaks French, her feet on the ground in regard to language, she's as proudly humble of her ability to speak as I am of my inability. She's committed to France, there's no ambivalence. Jean-Claude speaks of her *peasant-like strength*, means it as a compliment. He might be talking about her body, it's possible, angular and solid, lean and sturdy, a functional artist, a potter and clothes-maker. Her friends don't speak French as she speaks, if they can be said to speak French at all, but speak it for some unspeakable purpose. They like the sound of it as they've heard it spoken by the French, but the minute they touch down in Paris they abandon the language, afraid they'll say the wrong thing. They must think language is a virtue toward which one aspires; hearing French spoken in France and not understanding a word, they never fail to give up trying to speak it.

I don't know what I'd do with the language if I had it, I'd have to Talk To People. I let French be translated, only knowing a word here and there, having no other choice but to let others do the talking for me if anything needs to be said. Helena translates, which stops the conversation a moment or two after it begins, then Jean-Claude picks out one or two of the several English words he knows and pounds them to death for my sake, a word like *perhaps*, which is now our favorite word together. *Perhaps* he says in English, *peut-etre* I say in French.

Would Jean-Claude learn English if he come to America? No! If I know any French I learned it from him, so I hardly feel any need to speak French at all. O, some words here and there with Jean-Claude in the privacy of his home, perhaps if we're drinking wine and goofing around, and then only for fun. I'm always expected to allow for his English more than he is to allow for my French; this is understood between us. Jean-Claude leaves himself undefined just like me, so he can go on ahead and become who he is.

I could learn the language I guess, but WHY? I like not knowing what's being said around me all the time, in not having language, as it may or may not give advantage to my experience. Pictures support me instead, and birdsong and a pieces of really good bread. When I break a piece of bread off the whole white stick, I want to write a poem about listening to birds while holding a bird in my hand and feeling along its throat as it sings. I could even twist its neck, it's just another few words.

I speak English and my sister is a boy, Jean-Claude says. I laugh, always laugh when he says something to me in French, it's like I'm speaking French to him when I laugh, he seems to understand. Otherwise I say, *ce vous plait* or something else in French and he pretends he understands.

INTRODUCING
MONSIEUR
AMBIVALENCE
We're staying in a little hotel along the Loire. I've registered as Monsieur Ambivalence. I'm trying to read Blaise Pascal in bed. Helena's asleep beside me.

Every night I try to read a little in *Pensees*, sometimes only one or two things, before I sleep. It's a habit—not that I understand or agree with Pascal when I do understand. I'm interested in him as the *other*, someone opposite, someone who knows more, whose knowledge is original. Knowing Pascal's a reflection on those who don't know him, there are far more who don't know Pascal than those who know him and far fewer who could say anything about him should his name be brought into a conversation, though it never is. Some of his entries intrigue me to the degree that I read them twice, three times; some are boring and I want to edit, reduce to one or two lines and make minimalist poems of them; some I skip completely.

Pensees was assembled after his death. I'm reading it by chance, having found a copy of the book in the waiting room of the airport. If I hadn't known Blaise Pascal until now, I should have. It was my mistake.

If somebody asks me, why are you living in a village in France, I'll say, To learn to sit quietly in a room by myself for one hour. That's in his book. Pascal thinks that all world problems stem from man's inability to sit quietly in a room by himself for an hour.

I've started to make notes in the margins of *Pensees*:

> How large France must have looked to Pascal, from the top of puy-de-Dome, how vast and in need of his thinking, which looks both focused and boundless—he invented the first calculator, among other things—and how small it all seems to Helena and I as we make our way through the Loire Valley toward the village that we did not yet know we were coming to.

Helena's still sleeping.

I haven't told her that I'd used her name for me—Monsieur Ambivalence. She seems to be looking at me in a new way, as if I am becoming a different person to her. Perhaps it's the biking, that I'm a follower, that it's a time when we can be both alone and have our own thoughts about each other, watching ourselves move through the countryside in black clothes. Our conversation's better, even the silences, and though we still disagree the spaces in our disagreements are becoming larger, more expansive, big enough for both of us to be together when we're disagreeing.

CROISSANTS FOR BREAKFAST   We discuss the route early in the morning, after coffee, bread and butter. She keeps the map in the pocket of her biking shirt, takes it out, spreads it on the breakfast table. *We're just outside Saumur, we'll be traveling toward Tours. If you want to stop at a chateau let me know now. I'd rather not, but we can if you want. There's lots of them, chateaus,* she says. I pretend to look at the map with her. She traces the route with her finger until I nod. It's like we're deciding where to go together, but really we're not, it's already been decided. Helena's a good navigator, she likes maps, she's able to open them and fold them back into the form they were opened from. I can't open and close a map properly and have given up. The whole idea of reading a map seems archaic, I'd rather just get going, even the wrong way.

At breakfast, Helena butters a roll and looks at the map of the Loire. I start talking about what she'd said about me, about being *French all my life*:

I don't disagree Helena, though I'm not sure what you mean when you say that I'm French. I think you say it because you want me to be French!

Keep in mind how disillusioned I was when I found Jean-Claude watching television, that he had a room dedicated to it in his old stone house and watched continuously!

He sits in his big round camp chair, with the yellow canvas stretched around blue steel supports, staring at the tv. Watches anything—soccer games, game shows, movies, old Joe Cocker concerts. He barely looked up when I'd come in the room. O, he'd sit up finally—seeing me there—and say hello, show some life, open a bottle of wine or roll a cigarette, but it was like I'd broken a spell.

Jean-Claude knew he'd ruined the image I had of him though I had no image, other than that of a man who knew what was proper, for 'proper' is his favorite word. A restaurant is either proper or it is not. A household is run properly or it isn't. He used the word 'correct' the same way. Jean-Claude is able to make a pronouncement without being judgmental. I envy him this quality. I wish I could be more like him, but I can't.

It was disappointing Helena, I swear to God. The glow of the tv in house after house, that coy, brutish blue light that only a tv can make, subtly seeping through the lace curtains and out onto the little streets. It was so incongruous that it was worse than being at home. They were supposed to be in those stone houses reading. Or fucking. Or having wine or coffees and sitting at wooden tables, talking, not watching tv.

Helena eats while I talk. She looks like she's already heard what I'm saying and knows everything I don't know. She looks at me like a writer who's stepped away from a piece of writing for a few minutes and sees what's wrong with it immediately upon returning

FINALLY, BREAKFAST ARRIVES *Her roll,* she calls it, as opposed to my roll which is separate and which I've not yet touched, a croissant to her French roll, is *good* but *would be better if it was heated up* a bit.

We're the only people in the dining room, so cold we see our breath. I put my hands around the coffee cup, wondering if there's any cognac around. She won't look at me; I know what she's thinking, she's reading her mind out loud to me! She's sure she's right, and if she's right then I'm wrong. She looks like she's always living real life. I hope one day I will become as sure of things as she is and look the way she looks.

She speaks of my *being French*, but I had such naïve ideas of what their lives were about, about what my life might become if I moved there. Inside, behind those stone walls, I thought everyone in the village was reading and thinking, I mistook quietness for inwardness.

I felt missing from my life, I'd come to France to get away from the life I was living, to read *Pensees* over and over again and to write every day so that I might better understand. I thought this was a place that had everything I didn't have, and I'd come to try to learn to sit quietly in a room by myself for one hour. At least I'd be doing something good for myself, the other things I needed in my life could come forward from that point. Maybe I'd take something I learned home with me. I didn't want to just drag my problem from one country to another, but what else could I do? The relationship I want with Pascal—to attempt to put into action the observation that all the world's problems come from man's inability to sit alone in a room, calmly, for one hour—may or may not be the right thing, admits to some self-sacrifice but seems like the only course of action I can take.

I thought everyone in the village was of the same mind, of similar spirit. But they weren't, they lived as far from themselves as I did, and farther.

I'M WHAT FOLLOWS   Almost always I follow, out of some false sense of wanting to protect Helena, to be there if she falls, not only to make sure she's going the right way. I'm de facto navigator, a back-up, I'm the one last chance of seeing a sign before it's missed. When she's up ahead, I can't help but think about the past. How short her hair was in the old days, how she'd changed from being beautiful to being ordinary the moment she'd cut it. I said I loved her then, and I had but I hadn't. And now her hair's long again and she's put it in a braid; I watch her braid as I follow her on my bicycle.

Helena rides so far in front of me that I lose sight of her and feel compelled to push myself forward, pedaling as hard as I can to catch up, as if it's a competition, and pass her and ride in front for a mile or two. I don't say a word when I pass, hoping she'll feel by not hearing a word that we are two different people, people so different as to be unknown to one another. Once I'm past her I wonder why I made the effort and drop back once again to the rear, to return to being the follower.

Helena often stands up on her bike, riding up one of the small hills of the Loire Valley like it's much smaller than the larger hills she rides at home. She's not large, but her energy is so thoroughly organized into its physical intention that she seems to be challenging the hill itself; there's not one millimeter of doubt in any motion she makes.

From a distance, I make a list of questions I'd like to ask her if we were riding together and she could hear me:

Is it the same here as it is there or is it perhaps worse here, since we expect so many things to change when we travel?

Am I giving my life away to you, or are you giving your life away to me?

I'm hungry, I want to get off the bike, take a nap in the sun. I'm always hungry in France, but a big meal at noon isn't a good idea. She thinks it's dumb to eat much while we're biking. A glass or two of white wine at lunch is out of the question. The wine will come later, at dinner I hope. Perhaps we'll order a second bottle and talk.

WINE
WITH DINNER

Now that I'm rich I want to be poor, I say to Helena at dinner.

She's listening, so I continue.

*All I can think of is not being here. I want to leave but it's like wanting to rest and hoping to go forward at the same time. What I really want is not to be bothered, to do nothing, to eat good food and drink good wine. Perhaps it's impossible, perhaps Aristotle is correct, I can't have one until I've eliminated the other—***The Principle of Non-Contradiction** *and* **The Principle of the Excluded Middle—most** *fundamental of starting points.*

Helena says nothing, so I keep talking.

Who knows whether it will be any different in France than it was back there? I don't. I'm sure I don't want the kind of life Jean-Claude and Simone have, living in the home of their ancestors, surrounded by stone walls so thick they break drill bits, living like they have to walk down to the cemetery every day to put a flower on a family grave. The French believe too much in a beginning, middle and end. I'm not that sort of man, Helena. I don't even like what I'm good at, for instance. I don't like to think that much. I only like the way I feel *in moderation. When I think I want to write, for instance, and when I actu-ally write, it feels like I'm reaching down into a trashcan until I touch the bottom.*

Helena responds.

You give too much thought to things, you care too much what other people *think. There's no need to say anything to anybody, you're under no obligation. If they ask, say you're going to France to eat the cheese and drink the wine. Tell them you're going to France to learn to rest. What's wrong with that?*

You've made friends much too easily here; you don't have to know a soul there. Here it's possible that you've surrounded yourself with people so incapable of introspection, as you like to say, that you've become one of them! It's fascinating to me that your need to be liked by others surpasses your need to love yourself. It's an illusion that you're loved here anyway.

Helena keeps talking, seeing that I am looking her in the eye.

I want to live in a place where it doesn't make a difference how much money I have or don't have, to live in a way that I don't have to worry about money or what it means anymore. It's time to see how little I can live on, not how much. And I can live on less there than I do here. I'm tired of being defined by who I know or don't know. I'm tired of eating steak, I don't want to eat steak anymore, I don't even like steak.

We'll take the petit maison. Remember how thick the walls are? I'll cook, you fill up the cave with wine. I don't mind, drink as much wine as you want. Go down to the cave every night. Find a nice bottle of wine, come up, cut a wedge of St. Nectaire or Cantal, pull apart some bread, sit down, drink the wine, and write in your yellow notebook.

Plot? All plot is a straight line that becomes a curve or a curve that becomes a straight line in regard to France. Here's the plot. Get out of the things you're in. Conclude things as quickly and as honorably as possible and leave. Can't you see? Where you are now isn't good for you!

Helena sees I'm listening, and continues.

Teradact understands; Jean-Claude gets it. You're brother gargoyles. I've seen you in the street with Jean-Claude, talking and laughing. I don't know how you do it, how you communicate without speaking French! Somehow you manage. It's a miracle! And they like you, every single one of them, even the women, Simone, Monica, Christiana, and the old lady who has the keys to the church...Marionette, yes that's it, the old lady who walks down the hill for bread every morning, the one who keeps the goat in her backyard.

We'll put everything in two bags, one black and one red. We won't take much. Just some clothes and a couple of books. "Pensees." I know how attached you are to that book. I don't know Why? There's no plot for godsakes. If there is one, show me. Please show me! I've looked at Pascal's book—in the original—and I didn't see a plot. As far as I can see it's a nice book of sayings, of observations. Pascal? Isn't he the one who said that the last thing a writer finds is the beginning of the book he's going to write? Pascal has that right, I'll give that to him. You know, don't you, that he was born in Clermont-Ferrand, not far from the village? And take Montaigne too, he'd be good for you now.

Helena doesn't stop talking.

You think it's impossible? It's time you fell off the face of the earth! *Can't you see that's why Teradact chose to live here? Now there's some real information for you. And if you must have a reason, say you're going to eat the cheese and drink the wine. And don't smoke. You must promise, no smoking. That was absurd, smoking those awful French cigarettes until you made yourself sick.*

It's my turn to say something, it must be my turn as there's the silence that has to be filled by the person last spoken to:

Helena, let me see if I understand. You want to live where it no longer matters how much money you have or don't have. You want to fall off the face of the earth and not eat meat. I am a meat eater. Steaks and chops, boudin, veal, chicken and rabbit in mustard sauce, terrines, pates, those kind of things. As to smoking, I suppose I could smoke if I smoked only those cigarettes I rolled from Jean-Claude's tobacco, and only on special occasions.

This is not to say I'm going to live in France. There are complications in my case that are not in your case.

Perhaps I'll flip a coin. A coin flip is legitimate, in the spirit of the thing. Blaise Pascal wasn't averse to gambling; Marcel Duchamp made life decisions based on a coin toss. Pascal said it was better to bet on there being a God than to bet on there not being one. Duchamp tossed a coin to decide whether he should leave Paris for New York, whether to make a certain piece of art, where to hide from the Nazis and so on...

Helena, you believe I've said yes when what I've meant to say is maybe, or perhaps.

Ordering a bottle of Loire Sancerre, Domaine Durand, at the nice little bistro near Autun, Helena drinks two glasses more than she usually drinks, which is usually one glass, and says something like,

Poor man, she says, *close your eyes. Imagine you've been walking from village to village, through the fields and over the hills from Solignant to Collanges. It's late afternoon, you're tired, you need to rest. I push on the door of the little church in Collanges—you're not sure I should—and to your surprise the door opens. There's no one inside. It's cool and empty. You walk into the church and sit down and close your eyes and you meditate, of all things you meditate. For the first time in years you hear yourself, you hear your heart beating, you hear your breath. Hearing yourself, you hear how mad, how stupid your other life has been, that part of your life you were living away from this place.*

You see, Helena says, *you've been French all your life.*

YELLOW NOTEBOOK

Late at night in a small hotel along the Loire, one of the places we'd find along the way when we were tired of biking, choosing a place for its price and the quality of its beds, I begin to write in a yellow notebook I bought in the Auchan department store in Clermont-Ferrand when I lived in France:

The Church in Collanges

It's exactly the way silence likes things—only some stones that have stayed together for centuries and a couple of windows for light— but it's not really architecture. Nothing's already happened here, nothing's happening again. You can't be afraid to open the door. Push, push, it doesn't take much.

CIGARETTES

Every evening Jean-Claude smokes hand-rolled cigarettes, leaning out over the bottom half of the Dutch door, looking out at as much of the village as he can see, which isn't much and is therefore all he needs: the old main road of the village before the main road had been relocated down below beside the river when automobiles took over, the white and blue ceramic Michelin signs from the turn of the century still posted on the sides of buildings down there (nothing that anyone other than a tourist might notice).

Jean-Claude knows everybody. He waves from the doorway, exchanges greetings with passersby, laughing and smoking, even when there's no one there, as there so often isn't. Not that he could see everything from the door, the street was narrow and the outlook from the door cramped, really no view at all other than that of Peter the Dutchman's restored ruin and the vacant ruin beside it. People do come to Jean-Claude every so often, the news always gets through. You can see him now, leaning out over his Dutch door, smoking, his eye-glasses on a chain around his neck.

I don't know if Jean-Claude even reads, or can read for that matter, though I suppose he must. He has a job, he has to be able to read. The books in the house belong to Simone, picture books of The Auvergne, its mineral springs, mushrooms, the old churches and abbeys...the closest I'd come to see Jean-Claude reading is when he uses the local newspaper to roll cigarettes on, to catch crumbs of tobacco. ...

...Ok, he doesn't read. The local paper maybe, old Tin-Tin books. He watches tv and smokes and drinks red wine, Simone says he watches for hours. If he isn't watching tv, he's thinking of watching tv. Jean-Claude disappoints me, all of them watch tv, continuously. Every night I walk down the hill from the petit maison to the river and every night in every house I pass I see the glow of their televisions bouncing off stone walls. If there's one image that preserves the spirit of the VILLAGE ANCIEN, it's blue light as seen through lace curtains.

If I say *yes, I'm going to France,* I'll say it because I'm committed to learning to sit alone in a room by myself for one hour.

BOOK TWO

I cannot judge of my work, while doing it. I must do as the artists, stand at a distance, but not too far. How far, then? Guess.

Pascal, *Pensees*
114

BEGINNING
TO GET RID OF
THE GREAT NEED
TO BE RIGHT

What to take, to leave behind? I've forgotten something I've remembered. No, I've remembered something I've forgotten. Yes, I've forgotten something; yes I took too much. No, I took too little. No, I've not forgotten after all; yes, I've remembered.

I am right that I was wrong and you were right more often than I. I denied your rightness from the beginning in direct proportion to my wrongness from the start. You are right more often than I think you are; I don't yet know after our time in France why I always think you wrong from the from the very first thing you say, since you are so often right from the beginning.

You said *turn here*, not long after reciting the poem by Verlaine—the one about the moon—trying to teach me the language by saying French poems and songs. I saw the castle and the church; you saw the sign to the *village ancien*. I followed what you said, driving up hill into the heart of the village.

It's the right time of evening to arrive.

The village smells of fresh milk, a roasted chicken, goat cheese. I see the village as a foot inside a shoe, that it fits into what's meant to be hidden.

They're all there at the beginning—Jean-Claude and Simone, Robaire and Monica, Peter the Dutchman, one or two others—standing in the square beside the old fountain in the evening, visiting. I didn't know them then, didn't know they were standing beside the fountain as they did every evening when it was warm and tolerable. It's in my notes, in one of the yellow notebooks. I even remember the clothes Jean-Claude was wearing—a white tee underneath an unbuttoned long-sleeve denim shirt, black Levi's. I was sure he wore an earring but I was wrong, it only seemed he wore an earring. Jean-Claude stood out, more dangerous than the others. I could imagine him carrying a knife and he did, as I discovered later. He had the most presence.

Well, I tried to keep quiet that day, didn't I Helena?
I tried to be a different person.

Bonsoir was all I said, a good French word. But *Bonsoir* went right past them. They stared, not as if I'd said the wrong thing but as if I spoke a foreign language!

I was so used to doing the talking. Perhaps that's why I wasn't understood...*bonsoir*, how hard is that to say? How hard is it to understand a word like *bonsoir?* Perhaps those who heard me that day were protecting their territory by not understanding.

I learned then to be quiet if I could, silent if at all possible. Such a stance might permit me access to become a philosopher.

PSYCHOLOGICAL PROBLEM   God I resent hearing English in France, in a restaurant or a hotel or on the radio...is it wrong that I hate hearing English spoken in France when English is all I can speak?

...the deep psychological problems of mine Helena identified in Brittany might be addressed if I only listened.

Buy sunglasses she suggested in Brioude after that terrible incident with the waiter. *This is a culture*, she said, *that directs itself to the male. If you don't wish to be addressed, avoid eye contact.*

MONIQUE'S RESTAURANT   Helena and I walked the village, top to bottom. It seemed to have everything each of us wanted and needed, it affirmed that our wants and our needs were good for us. It smelled like it was being cooked in fresh butter.

We ate dinner in Monique's restaurant on the road at the bottom of the hill. Monique was so proud of the place, a plain storefront on the main road below the village, *L' Table de Monique.*

She'd designed a little cocktail bar of river rock where three people could sit. Helena and I sat there and she poured us each a glass of Cahors without asking, then sat down beside us—though she shouldn't have, she should have put all her energy into her restaurant—and told us her story: born in Sapchat, two or three villages up the road, joined the circus and left for North Africa, (an acrobat or juggler, one of the two). Returned to France, settled in Marseilles, then Paris, learned to cook. She had dark circles around her eyes, indicating either instability or deep unhappiness, or both, though in retrospect I knew nothing of her problem at the time.

Monique insisted we order truffade, the dish of the region, made of potatoes, milk and cheese, the specialty of the house. I asked her if I'd be able to sleep if I ate such a rich dish. *You will if you drink enough wine*, she said.

There were only three other diners in the restaurant, a couple and a single man. The man had his head down on the table-top like he'd had a heart attack. I asked Monique if an ambulance should be called and she said no, that he ate there frequently and always put his head on the table after he ate entrecote. *He'll wake up soon*, she said, *or else we'll lock him up and he'll sleep here all night*. Monique treated us like Helena was a queen. Monique understood Helena, they all understood Helena, everyone, wherever we traveled in France. In the Ardeche she'd had trouble with Patois, but we weren't in the Ardeche we were in the Auvergne and she talked with them, not a lot as she was still so new, but enough for them to remember her and talk about us later.

In any case, Monique's gone, drowned in the river, a *suicide*, Jean-Claude says. The restaurant's dark now, though if you stand close enough to the window you can see the tables, the little bar, the river rock. I swear that you can see all Monique's hopes and dreams sitting there behind the dirty windows, whether you know her story or not.

THE RESTAURANT IN FISME WHERE I SAID I COULD LIVE IN FRANCE

In the restaurant in Fismes I said I *could live in France*, giving it a sacred dimension.

We ate there twice, *The Golden Door*, some name like that. I'll never forget the food: grapefruit and basil sorbet, a whitefish swimming in my mouth as if it was still in the sea, the pistachio soufflé. Helena seemed happy I'd said I could live in France, like she'd won a game of cards.

After dinner we walked through Fismes—a village in the north, a little grimy, at odds with the magnificent restaurant—for we were always on the lookout for the place we might live, for the place where we could *fall off the face of the earth*. Helena and I were progressing away from the state in which I must say something after she said something or she must say something after I say something, about to enter the place in our relationship in which nothing might be said and yet a great deal communicated. My own views that night were in flux as I walked through Fismes,

I couldn't wait to get back to our hotel to write down what I was thinking. Fisme—pronounced FEEEM—is where I felt that I might be able to live in France, though it might have been in the village to which we would eventually return and meet once again with Jean-Claude and Teradact and the others, since I never lived in Fisme. Fisme's too close to Lille, possibly the ugliest city in Europe.

—Why does anyone love anyone? Is love that quality between two people in which one is listening to the other only in the hopes of being listened to. AND in that listening there is an understanding AND in that understanding one's able to see, however briefly, who one really is; and in that seeing is something that must be accepted just as it is, without it being altered in any way...

–or—or or is it the desire to be beautiful to one other person in particular but to others as well, to be beautiful primarily to myself, to be correct with Helena first as a test of what might be considered correct for the rest—Jean-Claude, Simone, Robaire, Antonio, Christiana and, most certainly Teradact who has evolved into something of an ideal—so that I might live peacefully without being consumed by any worry about how I am looking to myself or to others...

{Well, they're just notes but notes can add up to something someday.}

It's believable now as it wasn't then, that it was in Fisme I said to Helena, *if I was to live in France it would be like living my life all over again.* In any case, it's in the village we would eventually settle in that I first meet the fabulous Teradact.

INTRODUCING TERADACT, THE KING I worshipped Teradact from the beginning, from the moment I first saw him in the village. Not enough can be said of his improbable and fantastic movement, each step of which was approached with the possibility that it would be his last and that his last step would find him *falling off the face of the earth.*

How's it possible that a man could manage to look like he'd just been born, having been born in the previous century? It's said that Teradact never had a child and so remained one, that not having children may be more bittersweet than having them, though Teradact did have the dogs, the spaniels, one right after another right up to the day he died. He also had Madame Teradact for whom he did everything, serving her for eighty years, forbidding her any work in which she might be forced to face a world more unpleasant than the one in which she lived (it is said that at the end of her life Madame Teradact did not know how to operate the washing machine or pay a bill and spent her time watching tv, only those programs which Teradact himself sanctioned, travel shows mostly, an occasional movie, a western or a mystery).

Every morning other than Monday, Teradact descends the fifteen stone steps from the front door of his home at the very top of the village (on the same little lane as the petit maison and Jean-Claude)—takes the next six, sometimes seven steps to the Peugeot, ignites the Peugeot, no small matter considering the unsteadiness of his extremities, the quaint small-ness of the car's key and the tiny aperture the key must negotiate—and drives the steep and narrow road from the top of the village down the hill for bread, a caronne and a baguette.

I've watched Teradact many times on his pilgrimage, from beginning to end, taking up the better part of my day watching. Teradact holds the bread in the crook of his left arm, the good arm that is, closes the door of the boulangerie, after exchanging a minimum of two and a maximum of eight words with the blonde behind the counter, the proprietor, a woman who is estimated to be anywhere from one-half to one-quarter Teradact's age and who has a locally noted and demonstrable preference for men much younger than herself, walks to the Peugeot to ascend the hill to his home.

Once up the hill and parked, Teradact removes himself from the car with great effort but not before re-setting the handbrake, aware that the parked cars of less attentive drivers have careened driver-less to the bottom of the village more than once for lack of a final inspection of the handbrake.

Restoring the round caronne and the jaunty baguette to the crook of his left arm, Teradact extracts himself from the car, leaning on the cane whose point must find the firmest ground (there have, Jean-Claude says, been missteps and Teradact left stranded, nearer death than such a great man should be, by the side of his car, prone and with soggy bread. He allows for no assistance other than that of Thierry, the drunk who lives alone in the house across the lane).

When at long last upright, Teradact takes the smallest possible human step to the left and lifts his cane into a position in which it might close the car door with the slightest push. He breathes deeply, assessing the next stage of his journey, the six or seven steps from the car to the ascending and final fifteen steps to the front door of his village, the thrusting of the key into the lock of the door, the hand on doorknob, the removal of key from lock, and the entry into the kitchen where two wood carving blocks, and Madame Teradact, await the bread.

Teradact is, however, not yet at his arrival space.

I must watch carefully, Teradact moves only the tiniest bit, one bread crumb of movement after another, for from the side of the garage closest to the corner of the wall of villa, where the initial step ascending to the villa begins, to the wall's absolute corner where the corner turns away so that it is properly described as the other side of the corner, a corner that cannot quite hide a body (as some turned corners can) even a body as sleight as Teradact's. For even now he has not quite turned the corner and become unseen.

Teradact is not unlike a piece of ice melting in cold water; his countenance dissolves with impeccable slowness, his being, its material substance, progressing toward the corner under observation, the said corner, the distance toward which Teradact takes each step, closer to not only the corner's far side but the first ascending step to his villa.

Fifteen steps loom—I've counted them from where I could not be seen—from the corner around which Teradact now peers as he moves forward and upward, although one watching must be satisfied by the assumption that once around the corner Teradact will successfully climb the fifteen steps, bread under his arm, for Teradact would never believe he was being watched, and deplores assistance.

It is known to those in the village who care to know, though I am not one of them, having never witnessed the actual event, that Madame Teradact, a great beauty, two years older than Teradact himself and not yet legally blind, is waiting every morning just inside the door for Teradact to return with the bread.

GENEALOGY, PARIS, AND ME

Teradact never hoped to be from Paris, he had no choice.

Born near the Bois de Boulogne, I can't imagine his parents. They must have been small, there are lots of smaller people in Paris. I know he had fun as a kid but couldn't wait to leave, not liking the way people lived. That's what I know, otherwise information about Teradact is highly controlled. Someone whispered he'd represented a family company that made photographic supplies, that he sold their stuff. Now when he goes to Paris only the food brings him back, he takes pride in knowing shops and restaurants no one else knows, having them to himself before others find them. He's antique, faithful to his wife, likes to read Pascal and drink good wine. He can't imagine his parents either.

He met his wife in The 11th arrondissement, it's where he became a man. They lived in 11th all those years, he told Jean-Claude who told me. Mrs. Teradact disagrees not long before her death, saying they'd lived not in the 11th but in the 20th, in the far east. *It was not so expensive there*, she said. She always spoke so softly

It's clear from the beginning—knowing the feeling of being in a place like Paris where I'm not wanted and don't belong because I'm not wanted, of being underground even when walking surface streets—that the village puts person before place. My memories of Paris deflate me, like some sort of syrup had been poured over the streets centuries ago and all I'm destined to see is preordained by dead people better than me. In Paris, sight is purely physical and I have trouble with time. I've never been so lost in my life, so lost there once late at night that I'd come around a street corner and seen THE PANTHEON all lit up, seeing all of a sudden how hard it is to be a real human being, that a human being is only a body wandering around in the hope of having something to see.

VILLAGE LIFE, A
FIRST FEW MEMORIES

ONCE WE FIND THE VILLAGE and settle into the petit maison, I sit on the terrace and listen to the women talking in the square in the mornings, learning the sound of Simone's voice and Monica, and Marionette the old lady who owns the land where the lambs live. I listen without knowing what they're saying, writing about the first morning we stayed in the village and walked out past the square and into the countryside, in one of the yellow notebooks I've bought in Clermont-Ferrand. Helena wants to walk, Walk, walk, walk once we find the village. Walking's like life to her. I walk much less, watch for Teradact, wondering what Paris meant to him when he lived there so long ago, what it means to him now that he's given up on being young.

It rained the first night. By morning the village smelled like a boulder in a cold river.

At first light, we walked the "D" road toward Gourdon and Olloix, walking in the middle of the road.

How quickly you walked ahead of me, Helena! I watched you bend to pick up apples, cherries and nuts that had fallen from trees by the side of the road until you disappeared onto the road that runs toward Olloix, near the wooden shack where the tail of the animal was pinned to the door with a piece of white paper on which a note was written announcing the *first kill of the season*. You looked through the window, you said you saw rifles, jackets on wooden hooks, a card table, two bottles of Jack Daniels.

I thought maybe we could break in, sniff around, maybe take a souvenir. You talked me out of it and we kept walking further and further out until we reached the lambs. I fell in love with the lambs and stayed behind to watch them in the field, you kept walking until you disappeared.

I waited for you beside the field of lambs. An hour passed and then you came. You'd taken off your jacket, stored the fruit and nuts you'd found in it and wrapped the jacket around your waist.

We walked back toward the village, together.

Suddenly you stopped walking and said, *what's that sound?* hearing something new in the air. I heard it too, but after you.

It sounds like a large bird flying away from a tree or a small bird hovering above an open blossom — whose wings are made of water and stone, the lightest possible heaviness and the heaviest possible lightness, thin pieces of silver wire through which a heart must continually pass to pump blood, somewhere behind a tall row of junipers at the edge of the village.

We stopped and listened, we could hear all the way to Issoire, 15 kilometres away. I said, *we've out-listened the music.* It was time to stop, so we walked back toward the village, the castle and the church coming closer and closer as though they were walking toward us.

It would be a year before Helena and I knew what the music was, who was making it, where it was coming from.

We'd only know if we returned to the village.

DECISION POINTS, A SPEECH BY HELENA, AND MARCEL DUCHAMP

Might flip a coin—to go or not to go—Helena: to France or not. Two out of three, three of five, six of ten, fifty-one of one hundred. There may be no end, for the result I foresee changes moment by moment and the answer is the misfortune of the question, as the Frenchman said.

I'll go. No I won't go. If I go, you lead and I'll follow.

No, I don't have the time to go. No, I don't have the money.
Yes, I have to go.

We should go together, we shouldn't, we should go where we shouldn't.
We have to go. I have to go with you and you with me.

Why stay in America if I am in France, why go to France if I am in America?

I'll never go back to America, never. I'll never own a car again, why own a car, you have to be stupid to own a car. Should I go back to America, I'll write a book about living there without a car, a best-seller.

It's simplest to leave everything, the house, the car, the furniture, my golf clubs, my yellow notebook, my credit card, pots and pans. I am French or I am not, either *jus soli* or *jus sanguinis*, of soil and blood.

If I go to France, no more entrecote and frites, no more lemon tarts in rue Buci or rue Moufftard, no more black coffee and carafes of white wine, no more Gauloises cigarettes. Following is something I must go through with, I must no longer mind following.

It's absurd to think I could live here, not knowing the language in the least, in a place turned as inward as this. Everyone here—Teradact, Jean-Claude among them—lives like they're living behind stones. The village seems like a tomb in the hour before and after noon and from darkness on...

...I've made a copy of the speech Helena made in the hotel room in Rouen. The place is a dump, a purple room with high ceilings and walls painted over so many times they're sagging like an old man's face . It's a drug dealer's room, perfect for not worrying whether or not you'll wake up in the morning:

> There is meaning in what happened that can't be misplaced by either of us—the meaning of what it means to be civilized. To be civilized does not only mean to be able to read and write and to appreciate reading and writing. It means to communicate and to appreciate, ie. to value communication. It means to listen, to have humility enough to actually listen and, once listening, to respond accordingly with love and with truth. That's civilized. You can read and write all the poems you want, look at all the pictures and sculptures, visit museums and galleries ad nauseum, but none of it will ever make you a better person, will contribute one bit to the well-being of the world if you aren't listening. To be civilized is to listen and to listen is to tolerate and to tolerate others is to be civilized.

The words sound like music, deserve to be in a composer's hands.

VISITING DUCHAMP   Doesn't matter if it's my idea or Helena's, when inspiration's everything the weather's always fine: to visit the birthplace of Marcel Duchamp in Blainville, Normandy, not far from Rouen. I think it's my idea, that I talked her into something for once, as I was interested in Duchamp, the great artist. I'd over-thought Duchamp for years, particularly *"The Readymades,"* as a man to art as Einstein is to physics, though I'd met a woman in New York who knew him and said he lived *like a dog* there, going to his studio every day and working very hard , having very little money and telling everyone he'd given up his art.

Blainville's not on any main road. We went out of our way, arriving at a reasonable hour. Driving to the center and not finding memorialization of Duchamp, perhaps the most crucial artist of the century and a mem-ber of a family of well-known artists, I thought I'd come to wrong place, or that the lack of memorialization was a purposeful manipulation, a Duchampian trick, that there might be another Blainville, village names in France often being repeated from region to region.

I parked the car and walked into a café in the center of town, immediately encountering four or five people and questioning each about the *"family Duchamp"* as they ate French fries and drank their beer.

"Duchamp, Duchamp ," they replied, shaking their heads. *"No, no, nothing,"* each of them said, two men and two women of the place and of an age when they might have known Duchamp and his work, if not that Duchamp was born in Blainville, then at least that he and his father, brother, and sister were artists of stature.

It didn't occur to me until much later, far away from Duchamp's birth-place, that visiting the cemetiere of Blainville might have been a good thing to do, but we hadn't, we moved on. Why hadn't I thought of this in the case of Duchamp, a man of whom it was said that his greatest work of art was how he used his time?

THE INTERNAL RETURN TO THE VILLAGE, WALKING TO THE RIVER ALMOST EVERY NIGHT, AND MEMORIES OF MONIQUE   My status is of a possible traveler, a man who's been where he's thinking of going and is thinking of going back to where he's been to see if he can be there again, before everything changes and he has nothing and no one to follow.

It's not entirely clear whether I should or shouldn't return to the village. I only have ordinary ideas these days, spend most of my time picking apart the present and looking for little clues there—built as they are on the past—to see how they might point to a future.

To go to the village again, to return to the scene where my quest had taken place and had, at best, been inconclusive and at worst failed, seems like such a gamble. There's the great possibility that I'd lose everything I have here, that in my absence everything might change at home, that I'd forfeit whatever place I currently enjoy or give my life away completely to Helena, who continues to live with such incredible certainty.

So many good things happened in Montaigut, the little village of accident and choice, though I did very little of substance there other than walking out to the terrace almost every day and writing in the yellow notebook. The village was good to me; the place led me to believe that it might be possible to sit in a room all by myself for at least one hour, quietly, as Pascal had advised.

If I go to France again, it's possible I'll go as someone new, rename myself, or pretend not to be who I am. I won't smoke or eat red meat or all that cheese and bread. *Three dots can make a face*, Pablo Picasso said, one of the few things he said that lacks pretension.

I walk downhill from the petit maison to the river each night, a habit I substitute for cigarettes. I have the river to myself, stand beside the dark water—like a black cat who knows everything's spooked by it—feeling that my life's both behind and in front of me, I stand by myself beside the river that took Monique, noting the shallows, the relative smallness of the river itself, the glints of light that show on the dark surface of the water.

Monique had to try very hard to die in this river, submerge with real purpose, not simply trusting the force of the river itself but forcing Her Self downward and trusting the desire for death completely, seeing the river as going somewhere she wanted to go.

She's long gone, the restaurant's closed, and all the nice little things she did for Helena and I—letting us eat a meal and pay later, the gifts of pates and terrines, the glasses of wine she never charged us for—are memory. Memory's as close to Monique I can come, a little reward.

Her girl friend did her in. She was fat and looked like a man, everything changed when she took over the kitchen as chef. They'd sit at a table in the middle of the room like they were the customers—Monique and her girlfriend/employee/lover—and smoke cigarette after cigarette. They may have been taking drugs. Whatever, it became a problem, neither of them made much of an effort. The fat woman sighed whenever anyone came into the restaurant, like it was an inconvenience, and Monique got dark circles under her eyes. *Big problem*, Jean-Claude said, *big big problem*, no one in the village has dinner the there

I should have said to her, *Monique, DO NOT associate with anyone incapable of introspection*, I'd had the experience of doing business with a person so empty I felt like I was with no one when I was with him. Finally, not able to go on anymore with what was not a relationship, I ended it as quickly as I possibly could.

Now I watch the river closely and see it two ways, as abstraction and reality. The river's personal until it passes the mill, then it becomes just an idea, joining the larger river. Standing beside the river the lights of the village sparkle on top of the water, reflected in the window of Monique's restaurant, image and abstraction., I can see the river flowing but it is a reflection, image and abstraction of image <::::::::::::::::::::::::::::::::::> When I think of Monique, I see her in the river as if she's drowning all over again, abstract, taking herself away. Her restaurant's empty.

The river's more like me than Helena. Helena's a hill and trees and grass. Together we cover the earth and look good in graveyards.

GRAVEYARD JOKE   Helena looks good walking around the old stones—walking right up to them and reading them—and I look good making up stories for them.

We don't know the dead, that makes it more fun, we can be with them for an hour if it's nice outside. I like graves that have no flowers or ribbons, where there's nothing but the stone itself and maybe a photograph of the person's face behind a glass frame. Have I ever known anyone better than I know Mathilde Beufalleuf? I stay at her grave for an hour, making her life up. It's something Helena and I do together, we're full of ourselves, we make jokes about dead people and god. *No matter what time it is when I'm in a cimetere, I feel like I should have brought a flashlight. Or that I don't believe in God until there's an emergency*, and so forth. A graveyard brings out good things between Helena and I, we're grateful, appreciate the atmosphere and the architecture, the way families are brought together @///////html.com.

Walking down the big green stony hill behind the village of Olloix, Helena asks if I'd *like to see the church.*

Perhaps we can have a meditation there, I say hopefully. I like to mediate now in the small empty churches of the Auvergne.

The church of Olloix was padlocked and we can't get in. If a church is padlocked in the Auvergne it's a sign of some fundamental problem with the village itself.

With no alternative other than walking back in the direction from which we came, we walk toward the Olloix cimiterie.

Would you like to see it? Helena asks. *I thought you'd never ask*, I say, and we walk through little Olloix's graveyard, in the shadow of the padlocked church, stopping before almost every grave to read the names of the deceased and the dates. Even in the day, I feel like I need a flashlight.

I ask Helena, *why we like to walk through graveyards*?
She says, *because everyone's so happy to see us.*

MY BACKPACK   I'd worn a backpack full of sentences I wanted to write as soon as I got back to the petite maison, but most of the words fell out of the pack and were lost. I ask Helena if she remembers any of them and she says there are two—that

If I was to see us together, I'd love us

We have to get there first before we know what it's like

—she said she picked them up when they fell out of the back pocket of my jeans, that I'd written them on a piece of white paper.

WALKING IS MEDITATION,   Helena walks, she's the walker I'm not, she leads
A PRAYER OF MEANING   by walking, walking leads her, she walks like she knows where she's going. Though she does and does not know, she doesn't know I know she often doesn't know, but still I follow.

Walking from village to village, I often have to make my own way; by taking a real road and departing from it to cross a field, thinking the crossing of the field will yield a shorter distance, following the signs, the next sign in what has been a series of signs, is not there, does not confirm what I've been led to believe, does not state the name of the destination I'm seeking, is a different sign in a different color with a different style than the signs I'd followed, so that I come to believe I have been following the wrong signs and that I'm lost. From Antoinght to Maureghol, from Maureghol to Chalus, from Chalus to Solignant, from Solignant to Vodable—itself rising on a luminous mound of earth in which the chateau of the dauphines may be seen—I'm often out of step, two or three steps slower than Helena, or far ahead of her as she is often distracted by what has fallen—fruit and nuts from the trees, little stones that catch her eye—and stops walking.

In Maureghol I become empty for the first time, meditating in the little roman church in the perfectly square village. The church door looked locked, but Helena pushed it open. She really pushed the door, gave it a good shove. I was proud of myself for not telling her that she shouldn't. We had a good half hour of silence in there, sitting far enough apart so we couldn't hear the other breathing. I sat down in front, she toward the back, the minutes passed as everything else was passing, the inventory I took of the church itself, chunks of the fading blue frescoes of angels and prophets falling off the walls, the lacework covering the alter, the small triad of stained glass windows, the pre-occupation with Teradact. Toward the end of the meditation I was all there was, there was no church, no pews, there was only me. I realized the danger, pulled myself back, as if on a brink of becoming non-existent, and went back to being who I thought I was again.

I should pray every day, it wouldn't hurt me, certainly I'd have a better life if I prayed. Not that my life isn't good, I'm old enough now to know how good it is, though its goodness might be improved if I prayed—the urge to pray in France influenced by the feeling that my life is more mine here than it is there. I'm offended by almost everything in my own country, but delighted in France by almost everything that once offended me before I prayed.

I'm easily seduced by differences, especially opposites. The place opposes me, and I must learn to live in its opposition. That one cannot buy fresh bread at the boulangerie between Sunday noon and Tuesday morning, that

meat is better bought and much more cheaply on a late Sunday afternoon prior to the charcuterie's closure two consecutive days, there being good cuts of beef, pork, and lamb at half price or better, as presented by Yves Chevalier, the butcher who's left his wife for another woman.

In France I'm attracted to things that have no meaning, things whose meanings are hidden from me, particularly things that may have no meaning at all or that mean something other than what I think they mean as long as they're attractive?

MR. TIMIDITY   I stop watching for Teradact, sleep later and later without thinking of rising until I know Helena's in the kitchen making coffee. I smell the orange she peels, hear her sigh as she sits on the side of my sofa bed or on the stone hearth of the fireplace, sipping her coffee.

By not watching, by not taking the steps up to Teradact's front door and knocking, I'm defined by what I couldn't do. I couldn't approach Teradact, I wouldn't have known what to say, or he to me in all likelihood, and so I re-play many of the times in my life I've gone forward and been disappointed, not finding what I'd sought or finding something so different it was as if I'd not searched at all.

I'll always regret not going up Teradact's stairs and knocking on the door, introducing myself as his neighbor when I had the chance. My regret reigns supreme, I'll never get over it, not even Teradact's death could make it better. In fact it makes it worse! I'm only consoled by thinking that he would certainly have been very different from the man I imagined and therefore a disappointment.

Teradact's *too old to replace the light bulbs in his house*, Jean-Claude says, *too proud to ask for help from Thierry*, who Teradact trusts for some reason and who would do anything for the old guy. Accordingly, Teradact lives without proper light, other than the floor lamps upstairs in the bedroom and downstairs in the dining room.

Simone swears it was only last summer, in the very last of the warm nights when certain insects rub their legs together to make a ruckus before they die, that Teradact chinked, with wet concrete, the spaces between the stones of his villa where he believed the insects lodged, in the hope that it would stop the worrisome late summer chorus of ceramic clicking that kept he and his wife awake. Simone insists she saw Teradact climbing up and down a tall wooden ladder with a small bucket of cement and a trowel, and her story's no more absurd than Helena and I becoming lost in a small village yesterday, somewhere not far from Brioude.

LOST AND ASHAMED We drive toward the village, seeing the spire of the church from a great distance, arrive near its entrance, waving to the old fat man wearing suspenders and a beret tending vegetables in the front yard of what we presume is his home, very near the ancient arch signifying entry to the village. While he hadn't returned the greeting he should have been giving us, we proceeded, parking the car near the arch.

It took little time to find and inspect the church and the chateau, then to wander into the square, deserted, as it was near noon, to eat the bread, cheese and apples we'd packed and drink our water near the fountain.

Thinking we'd toured the whole village, we agreed to make our way back to the car but did not, becoming lost in the narrow lanes of the village, losing even the church steeple and chateau. The village pressed us between old buildings, and we were unable to see what was right in front of us. Perhaps the old man we'd passed could help us...but where was that man, or his house we'd passed only moments ago?

I've never been one who can just stop, I have to go in circles and see for myself that I'm going in circles before I trust another to tell me I am. Helena shares this with me. And so we walked around the tiny village for almost an hour, finding our way back to our car at last, only by accident.

Helena reasoned the square must be in or near the center of the village, that radiating in any direction from the square would bring us toward some resolution, and I followed her, noting several mis-directions—the square itself re-emerges from different angles more than once—until at last I saw the ancient arch denoting the village entrance and we walked to our car and drove Northwest.

Overwrought, we stopped in Solignant at a small bar near the middle of town and drank two beers—drinking's something we could succeed at, to atone for our failure—then walked around that sweet little village for about ten minutes. Helena took some pictures and I wrote in the yellow notebook while I sat waiting for her in the car:

The Red Door of Solignant

There's no reason for the door to have made the impression it made, for it was only a small, if vividly colored, door that hung on an old stone hut in the square of the village.

Of the village itself, there is little to recommend. The door of which I write is only modestly photographable, has a mildly intriguing symmetry, a soft grace that has caused a select few of us to consider it with some curiosity, as if the door exists only to prompt questions from a discerning visitor; otherwise the door is unlikely to be thought of as an image with any real purpose.

When the door does catch one's eye, some questions arise: what is the purpose of the door? If there is something behind the door, what is it? Who placed the padlock on the hasp, and who has the key?

About the color of the door there is some discussion. Some believe it to be blue, others red. Red or blue, blue or red, the controversy continues among those who've seen the door. Red seems to be the truth, the door is painted red and not blue as some say and continue to maintain. It's possible that the door has been repainted over the years, from blue to red and from red to blue, so that those who maintain the door is blue have seen the door when the door was indeed blue, and those who swear it is red have seen a red door.

What's behind the door? Behind the door are all the words to this story in exactly the order they will appear once the story is written.

LANGUAGE AND SILENCE   Not speaking the language, I walk around in the silences of not knowing who I am. I keep to myself in ways I never have, semi-confiding only in Jean-Claude who accepts me and of whom I could ask, *should I live in this village, should I stay here for awhile?* I find new freedom in not knowing the language, allow things to be translated for me.

Not one of my friends in the village seem to mind the way I'm thinking or acting, which is new to me. They never see me for the stranger that I am. Each of them comes forward to tell me what I can't understand—and would never know—except Teradact, who remains out of reach.

THE BLIND MAN I NEVER SEE AGAIN At the party to celebrate the new paintings of Antonio_____, I meet the blind man. He'd been a guide at a lake in the mountains. Both his eyes are completely open and sparkle so brightly they look like they are seeing.

His last official duty is to escort President Mitterand on a tour of the countryside and the lake. It's a hot August day and a high honor, not just anyone's chosen. He was the CHOSEN ONE, but I can't remember his name. *I'm sorry, tell me your name again, please monsieur.*

He says he knows the moment he became blind, that showing the President the lake he looked too many times and for too long at the water—the intensity of the light was magnified by the water and caused his blindness. I suppose it's possible, he doesn't seem the type to look for sympathy, he looks like a pretty competent guy, with big hands. And Mitterand's never mentioned again.

I couldn't ask why he hadn't worn sunglasses, taken precautions he should have taken to protect himself, having worked on the lake most of his life. He must have known the danger. I suppose it's pretty new information, how sensitive the skin and organs are to the sun, how much radioactivity and other stuff is in the air, even in rural France. He looked at me like I shouldn't ask, but that might have been just the way his glass eyes looked.

When he spoke I could see right through him, sunlight and water poured in and out of him. I suddenly knew I was in my right place, a place where anything could happen where a blind man could talk so brilliantly and look at a painting as if he could see. I felt I belonged in France for the first time. And all I think to ask, *did he know of a good restaurant in the region?*

The restaurant at Lac Chambron is worth the drive, he says. He knows the owner. The chef did things the right way, the menu changed every day, there were some specialties, *everything is fresh*. He wanted to write the name of the place and the chef's name on a piece of paper for me, and wandered off to find a pencil or a pen. I've never seen him since.

As I moved through the old stone house like I wasn't there, the party happened around me — among faces that did and didn't look familiar. The pleasures of hand-rolled cigarettes were being explored, the cigarette tips making fiery yellow finger-prints in the dark. A small group gathered around the bread and cheese and wine in the center of the room, as people do all over the world. People spoke to one another without excluding me; though I couldn't understand a word they were saying I seemed to be part of the conversation.

I drifted along a white wall, looking at Antonio's paintings—small deftly rendered landscapes in oil that struck a pleasant balance between painting and photography. Many of the scenes looked vaguely like the village—not enough to say that *this is the fountain* or *this is the gate*—but transformed into images of their own, of an imagined place.

Suddenly the room became silent as a painting. It wasn't that people at the party stopped talking; they hadn't. If anything, the party had grown louder. But I didn't hear a thing. Standing against the wall under Antonio's paintings, I thought how strange that I'd gone to France without language and even though I said nothing, or very little, I was listened to. I was transfixed by myself, standing in a room filled with paintings, watching people walk up to the blind man and talk with him, listening to him talk through his glass eyes, possible not to for me to speak.

For the first time I could actually picture myself sitting on the terrace, not having anything to say, all alone for as long as 1 hour, all by myself.

HELENA TRYING
  TO LISTEN, ME   Hello, I'm listening to you::::::::::----------------
TRYING TO TALK   --_____------ Go ahead, speak.

I'm not saying I'm returning to the village. I'm not committing to living

in France for even a little while, and am I saying I'm not returning. If I lived in France I'd live here, not the village near Brioude where we'd been lost, Augnat, a village even smaller than the one we lived in. I know I have to decide, make up my mind. I should say *yes* or *no*, live in France or do not live in France.

But the present is uncertain and all questions are fragile {{{{{{{{{{{{{{{{
{{{
{{{
{{

,the present can never be reconciled with its opposite—the past—which is to be certain of things. Act accordingly, no matter how much time it takes.

There's always time to be patient, patience has as much time as it takes.

(((((())))))   )))))))))))))))))))(((((((((((((((((((((
((((((((((((((((((((((((((((((((((((()))))))))))))))))))))))))))))))))))

What price can be put on the value of living in the petit maison again?

Hidden away on the terrace, writing in the yellow notebook the things I
wrote then—the red door in Solignant, Jean-Claude's cave, Teradact making his way up the stairs of his villa, how the village sounded at noon, as if
the buildings themselves were asleep—looking at the words later, wondering if all I had written had happened, and if what had happened would
happen again?

CLOSING MY EYES,   When I close my eyes I can't quite see what
  I GO TO FRANCE   Teradact looks like. I know he's small enough to
walk beneath the trellis in front of his chateau, the one I've seen a child
have to bend down for, and that he has white hair. I see the silver Renault
clearly and Teradact dissolving at the corner of his house where he turns
to walk upstairs. Jean-Claude's standing at his dutch-door. He doesn't see
me, I have to see him. When he sees me seeing him he laughs, waving his
cigarette. I think he thinks I'm pathetic, but also that he likes me. What a
great guy, and funny.

I'm trying to keep myself hidden on the terrace and make a friend out
of myself. I sit on the terrace for hours at a time, scribbling in the yellow
notebook, I drink good wine, eat fresh bread and nice cheese.

How was I to know that if I traveled to France, what did happen would
happen?

BOOK THREE

Nature has set us so well in the center, that if we change one side in the balance, we change the other also. This makes me believe that the springs in our brain are so adjusted that he who touches one touches also its contrary.

Pascal, *Pensees*
70

Helena insists on "D" roads, marked in green on the map, the old roads of France, holding the map on her knees as I drive. She says she's taking *as much time as it takes*, will not rush, believes it's the right time in her life to take the time she needs to be lost.

Being lost is constant in the Massif, how we came to Monique's restaurant in the first place to eat truffade and drink the Cahors of hers. The wine actually looks like what the guide book said it looks like, like blood. This could have happened in the Ardeche or in Gorge du Tarn where there's always another village and another and another—wherever Helena looked, there is always one more little village, always in the distance, and each different from the other and each of them the same.

We didn't tell anyone tell anyone about being lost in the village near Brioude, or that I reported on it in the previous chapter.

The place confused us the moment we saw it and we felt trapped. Following our confusions we were like children in school holding petrified rocks for the first time, passing the rock to the next child who's just as stunned. We passed our lost-ness to each other. It could have happened to any visitor to a small village in the Auvergne, but it wasn't funny at the time.

I park the car at the entrance to the village and we walk under the archway toward the spire of the church. The buildings lean in, to confine us or lead us astray, like they're hoping to know at least one of us. The lane's so narrow we can't walk side-by-side. The closer we come the church the less spire we see, until finally it disappears.

Helena sits on a wooden bench in front of a row of old stone houses, one connected to another so that they all look the same, like nothing will ever happen to them.

When I sit beside Helena I'm sorry I'm lost in my shame of being lost. I can't take my shame and try to shake it off, it is and isn't a feeling or a thought. All my self-consciousness is inside me to the degree that the only other living creatures in the village are two doves. They've flown in out of nowhere, landing like they don't have wings. Pecking at the cobblestones BENEATH my feet, the birds strut, making motions that could be interpreted as both male and female. I thought of the thousand times I'd made love to Helena, how we'd sleep together later, if she'd DO it, wondering if she wanted me as much as I wanted her since we'd come to France, or before or after. It's possible I disturb Helena by sometimes acting sorry that I'm not alone.

When the church bells began ringing in Augnat, Helena stood up and looked down at me. She smiled like she'd known where we were all the time.

OUR VILLAGE, EXACTLY AS I REMEMBER IT   The first impression I have of our village (*our village* we called it to distinguish it from villages like Augnat in The Auvergne) is that it's a place where everything's already happened.

Jean-Claude stands at the top of the road, in the square beside the fountain, smoking. I can't remember who spoke first, who began the relationship. It was like cream entering coffee.

I was wearing my sunglasses. Jean-Claude's foot was up on the low stone wall beside the fountain that separates the lane the petit maison fronts, opposite the other lane, the lane where Thierry high-centered his car when he came home drunk one night.

Doing philosophy, as I was at the time, I used Wittgenstein's statement that *meaning is going up to somebody* and I went up to Jean-Claude without fear. From the beginning, I knew that Jean-Claude was the kind of man with whom shaking hands would not be the thing to do, that if I thrust my hand toward him he would not take it and I would never be friends with him from that moment forward. Walking toward him in a direct line, as if he was the only one there, was more than enough.

Look, look he said, *big fish have swum into the village.* He pointed to the fountain where the village drew its water and the women once washed their clothes. I looked into the fountain to see he was pointing to a group of tadpoles, just visible beneath the blooms of lilies and other water plants, lithe little protoplasmic shimmerings.

Then the women—Francoise and Monica— started talking to Helena in French as I stood beside the fountain in which Jean-Claude had indicated there were fish, seeing none but pretending that I had for his sake.

Jean-Claude and I loiter beside the fountain, say nothing but look into the water as if everything that might be said is beneath its surface and hopes to stay there. As the women talk with one another, several other men, friends of Jean-Claude I presume, walk by or stop to look into the fountain, saying nothing, staying or moving on.

Two men, Robaire and Thierry, are introduced by Jean-Claude, standing as he stands, each with his right foot on the low stone wall beside the fountain. They are replicas of him, staring at the water, smoking, making a comment from time to time and letting the words sink silently to the bottom of the fountain if that was their fate. There's no compunction among them to speak, a relief to me, not knowing the language, giving me time and space to concentrate on Jean-Claude.

JEAN CLAUDE EXACTLY AS I REMEMBER HIM In the beginning I saw Jean-Claude as the amused center around which the circumference collects. He alone looks outwards toward whatever may be beyond the little village; he alone believes others should be looking where he looks, though he seldom travels. He says he loves Paris, but he doesn't. He says there's a big problem with Paris, too many people. *I never know quite where I am in Paris*, he says, *whether I am above ground or below.*

I am the King of the Street Jean-Claude says. *I speak English and my sister is a man. I am very pleased to meet you,* looking at me as if I am the only person in the village. I shake hands with the other men, thinking it will signal to them that I am going to walk away, but it doesn't work. So I slink off, fade away, be sure not to look back, make a small wave to Jean-Claude.

Dinner at Monique's restaurant consists of me saying to Helena, *Jean-Claude feels like an old friend*, that it was like she *already knew Simone and Monica*. Helena says, *yes, of course* and laughs, though it wasn't possible, we'd only just arrived in the village by accident.

We could have made a joke with Jean-Claude, I say, a*bout being lost in the village of Augnat. He would have understood*, though by the time we'd met him we had forgotten the name of the village in which we'd become lost, and anyway Helena and I agreed to keep the story to ourselves.

Jean-Claude might have understood, though he'd probably say, *well, you could have flown in and out of Augnat like you can fly in and out of Chazoux* and flapped his arms like he was flying a jet. *There's an airport in Augnat with direct flights to Paris and Lyon* he could have said, an expert in the Auvergne who never misses a chance to make fun of another village's smallness.

Everything's a joke to Jean-Claude, serious to the degree of his seeing the negative side. Helena and I swore each other to secrecy to be on the safe side. If Helena told him we'd been lost in Augnat, possibly the smallest village in the Auvergne, he'd think differently of me, our friendship would be altered in a way disappointing to us both.

Helena and I agree to say we visited a charming village in the hills near Brioude, that the church was pretty and the fountain nice and we'd walked all the streets at least twice. We both forgot the village's name, only knowing it started with the letter *"A"* and was somewhere near Brioude. Jean-Claude said it must be the village of *Augnat* and asked if we'd seen the grounds of the chateau as the gardens were *beautiful*.

The middle of France fit Helena from the start, she's more capable of living with the past which surrounded us wherever we looked and traveled. The past is just the way things are, it's all hers to look at and wander around in, nothing's wrong with what's hidden or old. She's had the gift from birth of being content with her life, not wanting to change things, while I want to change almost everything I see.

Helena was born deep. I am seeking depth and so her being born deep is a rebuke to me. My striving for depth sometimes seems dear to her, sometimes ridiculous. She doesn't really understand why I'd want to try to sit in a room by myself for one hour in the same way that she doesn't understand the word, *"try."* You *"try"* to climb a mountain or *"try"* to throw a pot—you could always turn around and come back down a mountain or re-wet the clay and start over. That's as close to *"try"* as she'd ever come. The words, *"I'm trying to write a poem"* or *"I'm trying to do what a great philosopher said was necessary for a person to make a better world"* meant nothing to Helena. I said to her once when she asked me what I was doing in France sitting in a room by myself for one hour that I was *"trying to do it without restlessness,"* and she said that was *"only a metaphor and that The Bible is full of metaphors like this one."*

I know one thing—the things I'd done that I didn't want to do outnumbered the things I did that I wanted to do. This is sad to me, as it is to learn of chefs in France who commit suicide when not recognized by certain established, official institutions for the quality of their cuisine, a topic in the local news.

Things are always in the midst of falling apart in the village, right in front of my eyes; small ruins of stones and bricks, piles of wood stacked against a long unfinished wall, an old tractor rusting beneath the rotting beams of an abandoned grange. Scenes get all mixed up between chaos and order, progress and decline. It looks like the place is trying to prove that the past can live with the present, in some sort of haphazard belief that harmony might be achieved. A man as fastidious as Robaire leaves his tools outside, open sacks of cement. Weeds grow up along the sides of houses in the spaces where cement breaks free of stones, making the houses look like old men with nose hair.

I sink into odd uncommon feelings, delighted to see the thick stone walls of the houses, how the walls are made to keep everything inside that needs to be kept inside, so impenetrable that one could scream in them and not be heard outside, but be dismayed, knowing the inside could never correspond to the outside no matter how hard it tried. Time's all I think about. Everywhere I look the past threatens to overwhelm me, stone houses fallen into a heap look me in the eye like I've done something wrong. I see that I wasn't taught how to live properly , that before it's too late I have to teach myself. Maybe I have a starting place in the Auvergne, more than I could have hoped for.

Slowly, more slowly than once thought possible, incrementally, without the awareness that what was happening was happening, I begin to build small resistances to my old life. I walk around the village alone, wasting good time, or sit quietly on the terrace, writing in the yellow notebook. I waste time that's mine to waste. I LIVE THE WAY I ALWAYS WANTED TO LIVE, with no preconception other than to let time pass as it passes in a small village in the middle of France.

LE PETIT MAISON

I'm not sure I'd live in the petit maison again. It's a little hallucination of a place, like living in a four-layered rock, a mine shaft with furniture. The ludicrous front door opens directly onto the street. *Street* is the wrong word and *lane* won't do

either, though lane is closer to the spirit, it being no more than four steps from the front door of the petit maison to the front door of the house across the street owned by the Belgians, Monica and Robaire. The cave's below, stairway up to kitchen, bath, living room with fireplace with stone hearth, up another flight of stairs to sleeping quarters, and outside to the terrace.

It's impossible now to believe I ever lived there, to imagine myself walking from room to room and calling the place my home.

Helena likes the house. I could hear her from down in the cave, tromping around up there in the kitchen putting away her mustards and lentils, making it just the way she wanted—she sounded happy through three layers of stone. I'd gone to the cave to see what was there—a stack of firewood, some old photographs and postcards, a calendar from 1968 advertising a pig museum in Tourzel. Wine too, two cases of Chateau Tiregrand, a nice Pécharmant. Madame Rochet said it was ours if we wanted it.

I walked upstairs to take a shower. It was too tight a fit. When I dropped a bar of soap I had to stop everything, turn off the water, step out of the shower so that I had room enough to bend over, pick up the soap, turn on the water, and start over again. I've never figured it out, not even the toilet which had a mind of its own. No tv, no internet, only the little radio our landlady Madame Rochet is so possessive of, a chunk of brown plastic in a leather case that sits on top of the fireplace. Teradact's villa is next door, Jean-Claude and Simone two houses down the lane...

I saw almost from the beginning the house would make many things difficult. The bed was too small and hurt my back; the stairway too narrow and easy to scrape a knee or hand on the stone walls. I sat on the edge of the bed as if I was an old man catching his breath, looking toward the terrace, which I did not yet know was there as the door was closed and the curtains drawn. Helena was still downstairs in the kitchen; I thought I could hear her drop something, perhaps she was chopping onions or celery or sharpening knives. The space from where I sat on the bed to the door seemed to crowd me, leaving me so little space that I was forced to be with myself.

AS EVENING CRAWLS INTO BED   Broken pieces of evening light crept into the bedroom, crawled beneath curtain bottoms. I spread the red curtains apart, see the terrace for the first time and what is beyond—that two white cars traveling in opposite directions on the little road to Reignant across the fields have stopped to talk.

It's nearly night. Almost as soon as the red curtains are opened, it's time to close them, pull them across the doorway that leads to the terrace. I sit down on the bed. As usual I look for a book. *Pensees* is downstairs somewhere, packed up in the red traveling bag. I want to cry but can't get the tears to start happening and nothing comes out of my eyes.

THE TERRACE OF IMPORTANCE   *A little square of total privacy*, that's the terrace. I sat out there, shirtless on warm days, at the table under the Stella Artois umbrella, looking out at the green hills toward the villages of Clemensat and Reignant, seeing the gangly arthritic tile roofs of the old homes of the village as they saunter downhill, writing in the yellow notebooks I bought at Auchan. I've never been so alone, before or since.

On the second day in the petit maison, I'm confirmed as *Monsieur Ambivalence*. It's good for a
laugh, Helena likes the name. I expect her to keep it secret but know she
won't, at least for very long. The name will come out of her when I least
expect it. I'll ask her to keep it secret when she's in a good mood or at a
dinner with a bottle of wine and she's drinking a second glass, if she ever
goes that far.

I used the name at the hotel in the Loire, in the little room in Saumur, the
place with the ersatz ceramic pitcher on the wash basin meant to mimic
a Van Gogh, where I confessed to Helena that I'd made the commitment
to go to France as many times as I unmade it and that I was wrong. *Here I
am*, I said, *I am here in France. Can you see me*?

At the airport I'd whispered the wrong thing in her ear. I said, *I don't know
if I should go. I have a premonition*, etc. etc. And I did have bad feelings. No
one other than the pilot wanted to get on the plane. We were in coach,
having tried for an upgrade. Helena knows how many times I said I'd go
and hadn't, she can count.

I said to Helena at the airport, *I'm sorry for taking so much of your time in
the past. No matter how much I wanted to be free, it just wasn't my time.*

Two large problems loom, needing to be worked out:

    1) I've never made a self
    2) I've not inhabited a self other than the self that others have
       accepted as me.

(It's possible this is why Jean-Claude and I are able to pass our lives back
and forth to one another without language. We're instinctual creatures,
rare men. The understanding between us is that we've accepted the
selves others have accepted for us)

From a long line of hiders, generations upon generations, the past's
mounted upon me as it is on Jean-Claude—the only escape is to forget
the past or to change. I'm stuffed to the gills with the past, but everything I've suffered from it I've suffered privately; I prefer it that way. No
bemoaning, no reward in bemoaning , some release maybe, some sleight
feeling of righting a wrong I suppose. Yes, I complain—IT'S MY RIGHT—
but only about the smallest injustices, nothing in-between, and only to
those who know me. (Note: reality can't be faced without complaint.) I

try to spare Helena discontents, she doesn't like them, but she often enters the space where she can't be spared. **Then Things come to a standstill** as they did on the bed that night when I faced the wall in the dark and saw my life as no more or less than it was.

Gradually by degrees, from time accruing and me permitting it to, little by little, stepping twice on each stone while crossing a stream, tap, tap, tapping the stone with the tip of my right foot first before committing to it completely, not trying to change or to model myself on the past or on my personality but to stare straight ahead toward whatever's at bottom. Going along like this I can't be anyone other than who I am, though it's treacherous, painful, and takes nearly all my time.

Helena's no help, calling me *Monsieur Ambivalence* as if my identity is some kind of little joke between us, a pet name for a central weakness she considers both my charm and a disfigurement. Ambivalence is so foreign to her nature, *she can't understand how* difficult it is for me to break the habit of diversion in all its forms—reading, writing, drinking, helping out in the kitchen, having sex, requesting a cigarette from Jean-Claude.

I present these problems—the problem of either making a self or refusing to inhabit the self others have made for me—upon my arrival in the village.

SLOW REVELATIONS
OF SELF BECOME   By now you'd think the self would be revealing
SLOWER AND SLOWER   itself, yet all I see are the others—Jean-Claude, Robaire, Simone, Teradact. They're all so charming, each one of them much more themselves than I am myself.

For example, I see Simone in the street yesterday and ask where she's going. She says, *going for a walk.*

Where? I ask.

Wherever my heart takes me, I understand her to say in perfect French.

She thought I didn't know what she'd said, since I didn't understand French she could say anything she wanted. I understood her to say that her walking had no purpose other than to follow the feeling of where she was going at the time she was walking. I wanted to hear Simone say she was *walking wherever my heart takes me* because I wanted to live in a place where people said things like she said them.

In France, I try to let myself be led, especially at the beginning, I trusted I'd be led to the right place. It was a theory, not a game—to be able to live like this, like I'm being led, not by a person but by a place.

I sit on the terrace, writing in one of the yellow notebooks morning after morning in utter privacy. I'm a writer in France, nobody can see me, I have nothing else to do. I buy more yellow notebooks than I need at Auchan, the huge store in Clermont-Ferrand, I believe that by taking the time to write my life will come to me as it's meant to come.

For the first time in my life I see clearly it's impossible to ever become what I'd once thought of becoming, that there was no more or less to my life than this moment—looking out of a small stone house in a village in the middle of France—and that the moment of which I speak had already become the next moment. I'd just have to live with it, have to start with the past as it's all I have. It's abnormal perhaps, being sorry for not living more in the time I'm part of, hiding away to avoid things until they've been resolved and then delve into the consequences.

I stop going to Clemont-Ferrand for the newspaper, *The International Herald*. The news is a nuisance; the five copies available sell out by noon and there's much less news in it than there is in Pascal or in simply walking around the village. Walking in Clermont-Ferrand I walk with my head down, as I do in every city I walk in, tilted earthward, as opposed to walking in the countryside where my head is lifted as far as it can lift from my shoulders, my eyes following an upward arc. I tire more easily in the city, and stop for coffee or wine or at a park bench where I rest and watch the people pass by, as if they are worth watching. I become determined to walk uprightly, seeing myself in shop windows in Clermont-Ferrand and looking to see if I am maintaining correct posture, if my uprightness is not only proper but not being influenced by all the large meals I am eating—the cheese, Pavin and Tome and St. Nectaire, by the red and white wines I drink at night, by the good bread, the foie gras, the terrines. I ask myself, seeing a reflection in a shop window, *who is this man?* and walk by. The figure's dark and non-descript but shaped like me, and I wonder if a reflection can feel anything of the object it's reflecting, be either happy or sad, but the idea goes nowhere. I can't wait to get back to the village and the petit maison, to walk out onto the terrace and read or write in the yellow notebook.

READING *Pensees*   Anywhere I open the first 112 pages of *Pensees* I find something I can read, only reading between page 1 and page 112. I never read programmatically to progress from beginning to end, but randomly, picking the book up and reading wherever it opens. To read from beginning to end is much too Christian; I couldn't get through Pascal like that. I tried but saw from the start that it must be picked up and opened by chance, and then only read a little at a time. Not much, a paragraph or two is all. Besides, Pascal's book is the only book I've brought to France. I read it like that it's the only book in the world. Teradact apparently agrees. He still reads *Pensees* when his eyes permit it, according to Jean-Claude.

Jean-Claude whispers to me, he doesn't want anyone else to hear. He's preserving the edition of *Pensees* that Teradact bought in Paris years ago, keeping it with his knives and other little treasures in his cave. The leather looks expensive, the writing on the outside is in gold. Jean-Claude thinks it's worth some money, though pages are missing, which might reduce its value. Teradact must have cut out the pages regarding the fundamentals of Christianity, taken an X-acto knife to the pages from 150 on, leaving the index and back cover. Jean-Claude shows me the book but I can't touch.

I tell Jean-Claude I know a man in America who'd begin to read a book of philosophy and underline passages in green ink, making notes in the margins so that anyone picking up the book at random and looking through it would see his notations and believe the book to have been read by an intelligent man, which is what the man wanted. I wonder if Jean-Claude ever reads Pascal, or if the book's only an artifact.

THE BED SPLITS
US IN TWO   Helena and I sleep in separate beds, say goodnight in a brand new style.

I come to her bed, in the bedroom upstairs in the petit maison, beside the terrace where we both used to sleep, before the bed began to hurt me and I moved downstairs to the sofa bed, and we talk. Our talk is The Nile or one of the smaller rivers in France, the Monne or the Couze. The conversation is not within the will of either of us and is therefore a genuine conversation—not a synthetic, conducted conversation and therefore without horizon as the philosopher Gadamer says a true conversation has to be.

I hold Helena more than she holds me. It's sort of sad, though by holding her more I am allowed to see more of her than she sees of me. I watch her fall asleep, it's like she's reading her mind out loud to me.

As soon as she's asleep, I walk down the stairs to the first floor of the petit maison, unfold the sofa bed and read *Pensees* to put myself to sleep. I start and stop, start and stop, start again, reading from front to back. I go forward when something's been understood, never retreat, getting to a certain point and stopping when enough's been understood, reading in the manner in which Pascal might have written them. I read until the lights go out in the village, either 10:52 or 11:52p.m. —one night it's one time and the next night the other—or until my eyes close by themselves. I lie on the sofa bed, tilting my head back and read as if I am drinking a glass of red wine with the intent of drinking the majority of the bottle; other nights I only read a line or two, unable to hold one idea.

HELENA SHOULD READ *Pensees*   Helena should read *Pensees*. I tell her reading an entry in *Pensees could last her a lifetime* (if she actually read it.)

I see her pick up the book, then put it down. *It's not something she needs* is all I can think. Almost every night she asks me what I'm reading and I always tell her, *I'm reading Pensees*. If you can call my reading, reading, for it's not really reading, it's not reading the Way Helena Reads, from beginning to end. She's smart to only keep one book by her bed, a mystery usually, written by a woman. The women she's reading now writes a series of books with the same main character, a man. I tell Helena that philosophers are fond of reading mysteries; she *hadn't known*, she says

She asks, *and what are you reading?*

The same thing, I say.

In bed I tell her about *Pensees*, that Pascal's first entry is a clear declaration of the differences between the mechanical and the intuitive mind, a message to the reader, *'You'll need both of these minds if you're going to read my book'*.

—That the 4th pensee—*'to make light of philosophy is to be a true philosopher'*—is almost clear, not quite unless you grasp the spirit.

It's how I read the book, I say, *from the beginning to a certain point. I try to*

be random and precise, within a range. I want to please her, to say something that employs her mind.

I make notes in my book, underlining small passages that I read in bed at night , thinking about them the next day on the terrace or out walking. I'm doing philosophy in order to trust my thinking, to bring something forward enough to see, at least enough to share with Helena, and not to test Pascal

SOME NOTES
IN THE YELLOW
NOTEBOOK

The desire to be beautiful, for example, or if not beautiful, then acceptable,

since it seems that to be beautiful to Helena

I must first be beautiful to myself, which seems a contradiction.

Should I not first consider her beautiful and in that consideration find my beauty,

as I might the others—Simone, Jean-Claude, Antonio, and most of all Teradact, who while being absent now from living consideration has evolved into something of the ideal—

so that I can live successfully and at peace in the petit maison?

STROKING
HELENA'S HEAD

Helena's finally beginning to get gray. I noticed the other night as I stroked her head. She let me after all these years, she rested her head in my lap and I stroked it like she was a little child. She closed her eyes and yielded, she trusted me.

Well, there were some gray hairs in there, a few, not many, but once I saw one I'd see another and another and another so that it was like she was turning gray in front of my eyes. Or was I turning her gray? Was there something in my hands I was unaware of, a transmission I was making, giving her age and worry and the beginning of some brittleness. Was that my gift?

Perhaps the hairs I thought were gray were blonde...perhaps...anything's possible. She'd put something on her hair. A gel, a dye? Not that she was vain, she wasn't; she only wore a little makeup, spent a minimal amount of time in front of mirrors.

She senses her head getting heavy in my lap and shifts, so that I can see a different side of her hair, the left side from just above her temple to behind her left ear. It seems to be the same story—a few gray hairs getting into the mix. The hair's stealthier on this side of her head, maybe it was the way the light is, the particular slant of it, but it seemed as if the hairs I thought were gray were hiding behind her younger, more lustrous hair, which was the color of dark honey, of a jar of dark honey being held up to the sun, for the sun loved her hair, the sun showed her in the best light, blonde and cinnamon brown, a glint or two of gold, flecks of red.

Nor was it that she loved her hair! She liked her hair, I think, she wore it long most of her life except for those times she did not, those dark times, those times when she was trying to change and didn't know what she wanted to change into, cutting her hair short. The fact that she was wearing her hair longer in France and looked so beautiful made me believe that she liked living in France very much, whatever her hair looked like to her.

(She'd promised to grow her hair out in France if I stopped smoking and I had stopped, as far as she was concerned, smoking only the cigarettes that I hand-rolled from Jean-Claude's tobacco and never in front of her.)

Holding Helena this way I look deeply into her scalp, beginning at her forehead. Where her hair began growing there was no gray. I try to trace a hair from its root to its end, but have no luck. The gray, if there was gray and there wasn't much, seemed to come earlier, at the beginning of her hair or near the end.

(There was a time when I wouldn't hold her like this, she wouldn't let me. Things weren't simple between us, we were man and woman, it was presumed that we had differences and that our differences were very great. But now in the midst of whatever action I've taken, I withdraw, rethink, do something else, or do nothing, paring myself down to one, sleeping separately, wanting Helena to come to me all on her own, holding out hope that I will not have to call her, but that she would come on her own, alone late at night, not wanting to be alone, and that we will be joined first by her desire, then mine.)

I should shave, but don't; Helena can take another day of stubble. We've held our faces close this way before, her smooth face to my rough one. She's never said she minded. She touches my face when it's rough as if she's pleased that I have stopped doing what I normally do, like she wants to say again, *this is why one comes to France, to eat cheese, drink wine, read Pascal, to hold someone they love.*

She's sleeping. I don't know how she can sleep so well, like a child. It wasn't always this way. Once, I was the better sleeper.

I don't touch her hair while she sleeps, it might wake her if I did, though she's a cast-iron sleeper. She probably wouldn't mind being wakened, she doesn't know she's asleep so it wouldn't be like she's losing something. The place a half-inch under her right ear is quite sweet. Whenever I was angry with her or hurt by her I would try to conjure up the image of the half-inch under her right ear, or actually touch her there if I had enough presence of mind and she would let me. That place seemed innocent, untouched, free from anxiety and all other human drama, so smooth and soft that all that I could think of was forgiveness.

Now she's come awake again, but barely, her head still in my hands. She's just turned her head again, so that it fits perfectly in my lap, and stretches out full length so that I'm a sort of cradle for her. For a moment she looks up at me and smiles, but of course it's an upside-down smile. From this perspective what I see mostly are her eyelids, then her nose and the rest of her to her feet, which rest against mine at the edge of the bed. Her hair spreads out now over both sides of my thighs, and I'm almost sure she's sleeping once more. I take a handful of her hair; it is various, complicated, difficult to source, though for every gray hair there are ten to twelve the color of dark honey. I thought that I was making her old, that I haven't loved her the way she was meant to be loved; but neither have I hurt her to the degree that might have caused her whole head to turn gray so that she becomes a person I don't know.

Now that Helena's asleep, I go downstairs and tuck into the little sofa bed, having assembled it just so the two pillows are plumped against the wooden frame and I can read *Pensee*s half uprightly. As I read, I gradually slump into a prone position and read until the street light goes out, putting the book down as my eyes go to sleep. When I can't read anymore, I close my eyes and try to go to sleep. It's rare that I don't find the book open on my chest when I wake.

Helena says I *should write a book for Americans
going to France, full of good counsel, making
clear the virtues of choosing the smaller cities and towns, finding the
center, parking, the correct restaurants and
hotels, the places not in the guidebooks
that no traveler could find.

Call it "Confessions of a Travel Writer"
she says.

Nothing more than a book of little stories, she
says, *composed of advice for foreigners, how
to properly open a bottle of champagne,* for
instance, as Jean- Claude demonstrated the
other night by sticking a metal knife down
the bottle's throat once the cork's ejected
from the bottle, which lessens the champagne's tendency to excessively overflow
from the bottle upon its original uncorking.

For example, *did you notice that Simone
started to cry the other night when he
did so,* the action of the champagne and
Jean-Claude's knife seemed to unearth a wellspring and she began to
speak of her father, long dead, a drunk who moved from room to room
in the house across the lane (the ruin now being renovated by Peter the
Dutchman) moving out of one room when it was filled with empty bottles
and into another until every room in the house was filled with bottles and
he died.

Simone is, however, crying for her mother, not her father, according to
Helena, with whom I'm beginning more and more to disagree. It's clear
to us both, however, that after opening the champagne, Jean-Claude held
his thumb and forefinger close together and said, *Simone's family were as
poor as breadcrumbs,* rubbing his two fingers together so vigorously it's as
if he's rubbing out the past.

Writing in the yellow notebook, I start looking at things as though there's
nothing there. When I finally see something, it's not me looking for whatever I'm looking for—the door from the bedroom to the terrace, the chimney of Robaire's house, the green hillside near Clemensat—but someone

else who has no consciousness separate from what he's looking at. On the terrace I keep going into this feeling of not knowing what I'm getting into, filling up the yellow notebook with whatever words come to me. I no longer love or don't love myself, I am no longer conflicted about any choice, any matter of my life, whether I should go to France or should not. There are things I can pray for and things I can't. I can't pray for or against France, I can't pray to know whether I should go or not go. My story opposes me. There's no place without meaning, whether I'm here or there.

Helena wants me *to write a book for people traveling to France?* A book for travelers? So what's the story? And what happens? Am I going or not going? She believes I'm going, I believe I'm not. I believe I'm already here, she believes I'm not, that I don't spend enough time with her or myself in what she calls '**the present**'. I explain that the present is a hard place for me, like a stone house, soundless, empty, impossible, a place that can only be lived in alone. If I didn't have the terrace, I wouldn't have come to France at all.

All decisions are fraught with the possibilities of their opposites, the past is indecisive about the present and the present about the future. There's nothing to be done about it, other than to eat the bread and cheese, drink the wine, and walk until you can walk no more. That's the story and the book.

WALKING SONG   Walking in the countryside, every village I walk into asks me to live in it. The older the home, the more ivy growing up the side of the stones, the more I go inside and make it my own, mostly because I don't know what's there.

Most French songs are walking songs, Helena says, who often sings as we walk through the countryside. I wish she wouldn't, I prefer the silences of the countryside, the small expanses with nothing in them but trees and weeds and red and brown earth. *Do you hear the walking in the songs?* she asks when she sings, walking ahead of me. No, I hear myself thinking! That it's possible the act of walking precipitated the act of thinking, preceding the notion of rational thought.

Helena and I have walked seventy-three villages—three one day, eight the next—and are of the belief now that we know the Auvergne at least as well as Jean-Claude, if not Teradact himself.

It's strange, I say to Helena as we walk in the fields near Ludesse, *that we both love things that are old, like these old villages, old stones, doors. But we don't love our bodies as much as we become old.*

Later, having reached Ludesse, admiring the composition and colors of the doors of the homes in the village, the wood rotting away on some of the doors of the outbuildings, kept in place by shiny new steel hinges, the exposed stone arches with plaster missing and a porcelain rooster sitting at the very top, Helena says, *I know what you mean about our bodies. It might be a good idea too to love our bodies even more, to celebrate them, to see they still work and are beautiful.*

WATER AND BEDCLOTHES, A SECRET SPRING Often in other villages on nice days, never in the village we occupy but in the villages of Vodable, Ronzieres, Villeneuve, especially Villeneuve and Villeneuve Lembron, and other villages alongside the river Couze from St. Floret west, seen but not noted, bedclothes, sheets, pillowcases, but mostly bedspreads, are to be seen hanging out of the second story windows of some of the finer homes.

That the windows are open is one thing and that bedclothes are being exposed to the fresh air of the Auvergne is another, the most hopeful of images, as inspiring as the lambs in the fields between Gourdon and Olloix. I've yet to see bedclothes hanging from an open window in our village and have to look elsewhere, to Perrier, Montepeyroux, Vic-le-Comte. On fine days I look for this image in every village I enter, other than my own.

The fountains in village squares used to hold this sway (I'd considered making a book of them until I'd seen Simone's coffee table edition of the **Springs and Fountains of the Villages of the Auvergne,** though Jean-Claude destroyed the allure, showing me the tadpoles breeding in the fountain of our village. He and Robaire sometimes tossed smoked cigarettes into the water where women had once done their wash, reenacting some male ritual).

Jean-Claude's solicitous toward the water. It's with pride that he takes me one day to see the spring, treating it as a secret, as if no one else in the village knows it's there. He's brought an empty wine bottle, filled it from the spring and insisted I take a drink. The water is cold and clear, as new as morning and as full of antiquity as Paris itself.

Jean-Claude's secret spring is in a small cave cut beneath the road up to the *village ancien*. Few in the village seemed aware of the spring, though I don't know how they were not. Certainly Teradact knew, and Marionette, and the old farmer Pepe who sold fresh milk from the grange beside the square. They all must have known. Jean-Claude insisted that only he knew about the spring and considered it his secret discovery. He show it to me as if it's a place only he knows, and is therefore his own.

AT SOME POINT, A WRITER COULD BECOME PRE-OCCUPIED WITH TITLES TO THE POINT OF NEVER WRITING ANYTHING BUT TITLES   If I wrote a book about living in village in the Auvergne, I would name it

I Am and I Am Not

or

A Guide to France That Won't Tell You Where You Are

keeping in mind Descartes' notion of *the objection of objections*, that all knowledge, even if clear and distinct, might be about nothing outside our own mind and have no contact with reality, other than with god, god being the absolute most we could hold in our mind at any one time. Were I to try to write a book in the spirit in which Helena asks, I would write that the whole art of travel is in seeing what's been left behind.

DOMESTIC ROUTINE   Nights we stay in. Helena cooks, going to the market almost every day to buy what she needs for dinner. I make sure I drink a bottle of water for every bottle of wine, keeping track by carrying the bottles down to the cave every night and standing the water and the wine bottles together so they correlate.

After dinner I walk by myself to the river, each night finding a different path, a new lane, a variation of descent. I know every home and where every dog lives in the village.

When I arrive, the river always looks the same, like a black cat running under trees on a starry night.

On warm nights I sit on the little bridge beside the abandoned mill, a large concrete lump of a building with broken windows that looks like an exaggerated sack of flour a pop sculptor such as Claes Oldenburg might create.

I think and don't think, stare and don't stare, permitting whatever wants to come to come, invoking a poet of my acquaintance who said *he'd rather stare than think*, arriving more often than not at the memory of the last time I saw Monique in her restaurant, sitting at one of the tables late at night with her lover chef, smoking and drinking wine, both of them looking sad but not caring how they looked.

Beside the river, late at night, I have the village to myself. Seeing stars it's possible to believe I'm the only one seeing them. When time's up, I'm either tired or cold or want to get back to the petit maison before the village lights go out.

I walk up hill a different way, in an effort to get past the temporariness of being a tourist, doing the work the saints swear by—to take a different way back home. Quietly, in the spirit of living with less and less, I stop when the moon's bright to see if I know any of the names on the stones in the cimitiere. The walk back works into my heart, which is what I want, I want my heart to work my lungs, my lungs to feel like they are pushing past themselves. It's good for me, for all of us.

MARIONETTE, THE
SOUND OF OTHER'S VOICES,
ROBAIRE'S PAINTINGS AND HIS
POISONOUS COUGH

Marionette's a model for old age aging well, the shepardess, keeper of the church keys, walking down hill and uphill twice a day, once in the morning for bread and once in the afternoon to put flowers on her husband's grave.

This isn't a small hill to walk, top to bottom, bottom to top. Marionette won't take a ride, though I've offered twice. When I'm out driving and stop the car alongside her, she stops walking, shakes her head and smiles, no matter what the temperature, then walks again, not looking my way. What could be clearer than stopping the car beside her, trying to make eye contact, reaching across to the passenger side and opening the door? Helena says she doesn't like me because I don't know the language. *Old bitch*, I say, trying to make Helena laugh, *I think she's a sinful woman.*

She's in the rearview mirror, trudging uphill in her heavy black shoes, black scarf around her head whatever the weather, wearing the same blue dress and dark blue sweater, costume of the old countrywoman in the Auvergne

I come to know people by the sound of their voices. Monica is clever, Simone an innocent. Jean-Claude sounds as if he believes he knows all he needs to know. Robaire's a romantic, a man who thinks of himself an artist. His paintings look nothing like him, a small man made of wires and silver hair, a former gymnast in Brussels, totally committed to hand-rolled cigarettes, like Jean-Claude.

When Robaire shows me his paintings he tells me, *the imagination is all there is to life* and then he says, *to my life*, making clear the personal aspect of his project.

Helena asks me what Robaire's paintings are like, whether they're anything like Antonio's, a man who makes his living painting, I say *take a quick peek at the moon when it's nighttime, then close your eyes tightly and keep them closed. What you see through your closed eyes are Robaire's paintings.*

Robaire's coughing is becoming quite a concern. When I ask him the best time to be in the Auvergne he says, *now, right now, springtime, ah the air of the Auvergne is so...* taking as deep a breath as he possibly can to emphasize the freshness of the Auvergne air, waving his arms and coughing wildly.

Monica laughs, so we all laugh, and looks at us as if she cannot understand how we could possibly laugh at Robaire's condition. She'll put Robaire in the hospital soon, it's only a matter of time, forbid him cigarettes, and move back to the big house in Brussels. Jean-Claude, his best friend, whispers that he's seen Robaire walking up and down lane in front of their house in the evenings, that he only talks to himself and not to the others when he's in this state.

If I return to the village, it's possible that Robaire will not recognize me, will have completely disappeared. The last time I saw him he gave me the last painting he'd made: a bright orange ball of fire in a dark blue field. It looks like the sun is about ready to drop into the sea and set it on fire.

I FAIL FRENCH AND FRENCH FAILS ME   It's my fault I haven't learned French, only three lessons with Madeline, a Frenchwoman who moved to America after the war. She wasn't the right one to teach me, came to my house unprepared and out of her element, lacking energy and arriving late for every meeting. I'd stand behind the window, watch her cruise up to the house in the old Buick, waiting for her because she was late. She parked the huge car awkwardly, bumping the curb, gouging the super-sized tires on the curb's sharp edges like she was lost, and once the car was stopped and the key taken out of the ignition, powder her face in the rear-view mirror. Madeline emerged, walking to my front door as a fashion model. I just had to kiss her, ask if she'd like coffee.

Sitting at the table, she just sat there. She'd brought no textbook, no paper, no pen, only two big leather purses. She seemed to feel there was all the time in the world for me to learn French, that it was all my responsibility.

I told her where to start. *Perhaps with numbers*, I said. We did nothing but numbers the first session.

Helena listened from another room, delighted in the way Madeline said things. Helena liked the sound of her voice, that she was old and French from Nantes and still making her way in the world.

She's teaching me next to nothing, I said. *I'm not getting my money's worth*

She speaks very very good French, Helena said. *You can't do any better. You're lucky to have found her.*

I called Madeline the morning after our third meeting in the hope she wasn't there, to leave a message without having to talk with her. I shouldn't have worried—she's never there when I call—but she picked up the phone. I lied, mostly for my sake, not wanting to tell either of us the truth, told her I'd been transferred to another city for business.

Helena said *I'd given up, that Madeline could have taught me beautiful French if I'd only had patience and discipline to sit in a room alone for at least one hour. The last thing I want to do is learn French*, I say. *I can't even speak my own language.*

APPARITION IN THE VILLAGE One night near the summit on which the petit maison rests in the heart of the *village ancien*, I think I see Teradact in the lane not far from his villa. It's after midnight, the village lights doused, and dark.

I have a feeling I'm seeing Teradact, though he's even smaller than I thought, whoever he might be. The farther away I am the closer he becomes and the closer he becomes the farther away I am from knowing who it is I'm seeing. Everything comes in twos here—Simone and Jean-Claude, Monica and Robaire, Christiana and Antonio—so it's strange to see just one man as I seem to be seeing.

Doing the thinking I'm doing, doing philosophy on the terrace and committing to write at least a sentence or two of what I do by hand in the yellow notebook, I deal with the differences between thinking and feeling.

> I feel I'm seeing Teradact, but thinking it can't be as he sleeps from sundown onwards, does not walk other than from the villa to his car for bread etc. etc.

> I am, however, feeling that Teradact is there on the lane in the dark.

I walk toward what I'm seeing, the unmoving figure, slowly, keep close to the stone houses that line the lane on its right side, walk into a great mist, some atmospheric element that suffuses the village at night, a blissful charade of infinitesimal particles as if the middle of France is a metaphysical entity. I choose feeling I guess, concluding that while one does not necessarily have the privilege of choosing, my preference is for feeling. The struggle's all in the thinking I think, in the necessity of un-acknowledging thoughts one by one, so not to let thought take shape.

The figure in the lane if turned sideways might disappear like the sculpture made by the man who saw man as man was seeing himself, a true artist whose work is now well known around the world but who worked in solitude…

…I'd visited his studio in Paris, walking there by myself one morning from my hotel in the 11th arrondisement to rue d'Alesia, imagining him still alive inside the building where he worked and lived for years, a small street perpendicular to rue Alesia. (I was smoking in those days and smoked a cigarette in his honor on the sidewalk in front of his atelier, then found the Metro stop nearby, returning to the hotel before Helena woke).

Am I, I ask myself walking slowly along the far right side of the lane so as not to frighten the figure I think I'm seeing, *equal to the task of seeing what I'm seeing?*

God knows I've had practice, all the thinking, all the looking at art, the venerations, pilgrimages, the reading and the writing, the museums, the graveyards...yet there's more than a little foreboding in my pursuit of confirmation that the figure I am seeing is or is not Teradact.

Perhaps it's best not to approach, if indeed this is Teradact, as the approach and confirmation may prove disheartening. Gourmand, dog breeder, connoisseur, student of Pascal, philosopher, deifier of age, it is possible Teradact is incapable of living up to the idea I have of him.

Yet Teradact invites obsession...

...just yesterday he pulled off another miracle I'm told by Helena who was told by Simone, hauling a veal chop, a terrine, olives and a round of St. Nectaire cheese up the steps of his villa in the late afternoon, a time well past the time he goes for bread.

By chance, Jean-Claude stood behind Teradact in line at the Ecomarche in Champeix as he made his purchases. He made Jean-Claude promise not to tell Madame Teradact how much he'd spent, as he bought only the finest, most expensive cuts of meat, cheese, condiments. *I'll end up feeding most of it to the cats,* Teradact said to Jean-Claude.

[What I really want at night is someone happy to see me or, failing that, to exchange *bonsoirs* and keep walking. The petit maison is not far. Helena's probably already asleep or reading a mystery in bed.]

It's either Teradact or it isn't I'm seeing in the lane.

Can't force it, can't try to think, I must approach the problem as if it's not there or stop thinking about, abandon it the way things are abandoned in the village, like the rusty metal bucket left on the wall of a ruin with the word 'FAÇADE' hand painted in white. I come closer the figure I think is Teradact without appearing to force myself upon him. Perhaps it's better not to see him like this, up close, better for me to watch without him knowing I am watching, stand still or inch along, taking the little lane to the left to avoid confrontation though the descent is steep and I would have to walk back up the hill once again.

I can't move any way but forward, moving as if against my will and against Teradact's, if indeed it is Teradact, with a slowness foreign to me, but perhaps not as slowly as it seems, curious that the closer I come the smaller the figure becomes, so that I see only the thinnest shrouding of a human being.

I smell cigarette smoke and keep walking, what else can I do?

I keep walking along the dark lane until I walk into Jean-Claude, walking his poodle, the smaller of his two dogs, smoking a cigarette. He's dressed in a white shirt, dark pants, wearing a tie with the logo of the company he works for in Clermont-Ferrand. He's night watchman there; it says so on the badge pinned to his white shirt.

Hello is all I can think to say. *All the time I thought I was seeing Teradact, and it's you, my friend Jean-Claude,* I say. (Jean-Claude behaves like I've discovered him doing something he doesn't want me to know he's doing. But if I've discovered him why did he not avoid me, why did he not walk away?)

The Teradacts are away, he says, on *a trip to Bergerac to look at spaniels.*

Overnight? I ask, amazed++++++===========amazed not only that the Teradacts will need a hotel, food, gasoline but that they're traveling at all. Therefore!!!!!!!!!!!!!!!!!!!!!!!!!!!!!!

Jean-Claude throws his cigarette down to the ground. *Bonsoir* he says, happy to walk away from me, going home to watch tv.

IT'S NEVER TOO LATE TO TRAVEL   Teradact continues to amaze. The image of the two of them, THE TERADACT'S, negotiating the stairs of a strange hotel, the restaurants where they must eat, finding their way around Bergerac, a city of 26,000, is as astonishing to me as having found Jean-Claude in the lane instead of Teradact.

They've had spaniels forever, Jean-Claude says, *though not since the last was stuffed and mounted in the attic of the villa Teradact. The last spaniel's been dead for at least ten years.*

A new spaniel at this late date and Teradact to do all the work, for Madame Terdact has nothing to do with the dogs whatsoever!

Perhaps Teradact's misleading Jean-Claude; there won't be a spaniel at all! Bergerac is one of their annual getaways, a three or four day diversion.

Teradact drives, Madame navigates on an as-needed basis. Not much is said between the Teradacts when they travel and everything that is said needs to be said twice. One hears just enough of the other to ask *what did you say?* What was said is then repeated at least once, but never more than twice.

Do they travel in the Auvergne? I ask Jean-Claude. He doesn't know that they do or do not. He thinks they *prefer Brittany, then Paris where they once lived, then The Dordogne. There's family in Sarlat* he thinks, *perhaps a niece or a nephew.* When he travels, Teradact only tells Thierry, the drunk, where he's going. Thierry tells Jean-Claude and the news stops there. The Teradacts always leave early, stopping for bread at the bottom of the hill.

Jean-Claude stays in the village, considers Teradact's traveling a bad habit. "*Paris is very nice,*" he says, "*but it has a very big problem...too many people.*" Clermont-Ferrand has too many people, Millau, Vichy, St. Flour, too many people. Jean-Claude likes the crepes in the farmhouse restaurant above Bourboule, he'll go up there in the mountains *to eat the crepes* Simone says. That's as far as he'll go.

THE LANDLADY ROCET   Madame Rocet finally coughs up the walking tour of the village she promised, part of the agreement Helena made with her when negotiating for the petit maison, long delayed by both parties. We agree to rendezvous at mid-morning.

She meets us by the fountain, *Le Tallient*, dressed in black gabardine pants and a long cashmere jacket lined with fur.

Since she's late, the tour commences with silent negativity. We feel misled, having been led to believe by Madame Rocet herself that she was *of the village* and finding out from Jean-Claude and Simone that she's not.

The first question I ask—what the inscription **'Le Tallient'** *means on the fountain in the square*—she can't answer. *I wasn't born in the village, I was born in Compains on my father's farm,* she says.

We follow her to the church. It's locked.

Perhaps we should find Marionette, Helena says, *she has the keys.*

Madame Rocet presses on, as if the church isn't there and isn't part of the tour, as if not hearing Helena. We continue following her, not knowing what else to do.

This is the four, she says. *It's being restored as you can see.* We look inside the little stone building. The walls are black from floor to ceiling. *This is where they made the bread for the village,* Madame Rocet says, speaking of the four as if it was the church.

Neither Helena or I know what to say, having already become well-acquainted with both the church and the four.

As we round the corner, Madame Rocet appears lost while trying to avoid appearing so. *Is there anything else you'd like to see,* she asks, looking at her watch.

Helena points out a little hut made of stone and wood beside a small square patch of dirt that looks as if it had once been tended but is now overgrown with berry bushes and vines.

That belonged to Georg, Madame Rocet says. *He lived inside the hut for sixty years, grew leeks for the market in Clermont-Ferrand.* She's sure of her story and tosses her head back proudly as she tells it.

We walk around the hut and its tiny grounds. Madame Rocet lights a long black cigarette, makes a motion with her wrist that we can take as much time as we need.

Helena thanks her for the tour and her time, asks Madame Rocet *would you like some coffee? A drink? We have Salers and ice up at the petit maison.*

Some other time, Madame Rocet says. *We'll do this again. There's so much more of the village to see.*

We watch Madame Rocet walk back to her car, parked in the square by the fountain she'd not known the name of. She opens the door of a gold Mercedes, flicks her cigarette into the fountain and drives down the hill like she knows where she's going.

That was amazing, Helena says, *especially the response to your question about the fountain. It's not that she didn't know the name,* Helena says, *it's that she didn't know what it meant, that she couldn't translate* **Le Tallient.**

I think we know as much about the village as she does, I say.

No, we know more, Helena says.

It was interesting, though, what Madame Rocet said about farmers, that nobody now will marry a farmer for the work's too hard and no woman wants to do it, Helena says. *That was valuable information for your book.*

You know how the Surrealists walked in the early days of Surrealism when it was all about having fun? I say to Helena. *Andre Breton and his friends would walk out of Paris, east or south or west, leaving early in the morning after getting drunk or taking opium and walk until they were exhausted, and then write or have visions that were at first somewhat pure, then get fuelled more and more by drugs and alcohol. The idea was escape. "Drop everything", Breton wrote somewhere, "drop your wife, drop your girlfriend, park your children in the woods, drop your comfortable life...take to the road."* It was about being outside your own country, about arriving *somewhere new for the first time, having your senses wired with wonder and anxiety.*

Surrealism still sounds so good but it's become so passé, quaint, a wooden ritual, and Breton had so many odd fetishes. He tried to make religion out of dreams and had a great time dreaming for awhile.

SEEING THINGS AS THEY ARE, I SEE PEOPLE AS OTHER CREATURES   I've lived in the village long enough to come to the place where I'm seeing people as creatures.

The phase begins with Jean-Claude who's gargoyle. He stood alone in the street one evening, looking away from me, while the light surrounded his profile in such a way that he became a pet in the big zoo that is the world. Marionette is one of the sheep she keeps, Robaire's a lynx, Simone a salmon.

Seeing people as animals occupies me for a month. I can't shake myself out of it, no matter how much time I spend in church meditating. When I see Jean-Claude, a gargoyle approaches; Simone's s a salmon swimming against the current. If I'm introduced to a person I've never met, they are transformed into their animal the moment I meet them, stay that way whenever I see them. I can't believe how real it is. The harder I try to see the human man or woman they are the more animal they become.

The rule: there can't be two of the same. Though it's tempting to see two lions, three foxes etc. in the five faces and beings of ____, _____, ___, , _____ , as each insists on its individuality. It's wrong to see them as animals, so I give up and go back and see them as human.

UPSIDE DOWN COW   The lambs are long gone, Marionette's had them moved to fields she owns near Chazoux, but I walk out to their old pastures like they're still there, taking the long way around the group when they've gathered in the square to talk.

Wine bottles stack up in the cave.

Sometimes it's too warm or too cold to walk and Helena and I drive the car into the mountains. Most of the villages up there look beaten down, the wind and rain mess them up, they're very sad, like children's toys left out in the rain, but at least the weather's honorable.

In Chassagnes, the smallest mountain village in France, the temperature drops 15 degrees, the rain's cold and violent. I drive in one end of the village and out the other in the flick of a dog's tail. Just outside the village a cow's fallen, sprawled on its back in a wet culvert.

I stop the car, roll the window down and look at the cow laying in the ditch, covered with mud and grass, legs up in the air. The cow can't bring itself upright. It looks at me as if I'm another animal; there's nothing in its eyes, no question, no plea, no struggle, no attempt to change, no acceptance or rejection of its situation.

I don't know what to do, the cow's upside-down, it's too heavy, the weather too miserable. This isn't the France I know, it's acting like some other downtrodden place, but there's meaning here. I must face the problem with finesse, a mixture of compassion and detachment, if that can be done. If that can be done the situation will work itself out without taking action, and therefore without me.

Helena and I sit in the car, looking at the cow as the cow looks at us, at impasse. The possibility of taking some action and of that action's consequence is too uncertain, so we sit in the car looking at the cow like cows. It's said The Buddha says that enlightenment is achieved only when one becomes aware of their own physical being, but Buddha seems far away and I can't summon Pascal.

France places me in a Christian position, a pilgrim without believing I'm one, wanting to believe the best in things, wanting to believe someone's praying for me. It's why I came to France, made the commitment as many times as I unmade it.

As there's nothing I can do for the cow, I reason that non-action is in fact action, action contrary to natural impulse, which is to act, to do **Something;** that not expecting the miraculous from myself a true miracle might occur and the cow become upright before my eyes.

At the moment of seeing there's nothing I can do, a tractor drives toward the car through the mist and rain. I see the farmer behind the tractor wheel, dressed in a tattered lime-green sweater and the blue workpants of the Auvergne, coming to fetch the cow. From the heightened position of the tractor, from behind the tractor's window, the farmer shakes his head like he's having to see a bad movie five times in a row. This isn't the first occasion he's fetched this cow from a ditch, and it won't be the last.

I jerk the car out of the way of the farmer, continue to the next village.

ROBAIRE WALKS
LIKE A SURREALIST,
BEGINS TO GO CRAZY Robaire acts strangely, pacing the lane in front of the petit maison at night, just as Jean-Claude said. He no longer walks with Monique to poubelle, the plastic bag tucked neatly under his arm full of the remains of their dinner, a used coffee filter or two and a crushed up cigarette pack, her left arm linked in his free arm as they promenaded elegantly evening after evening halfway down the hill to put the garbage into one of the cans as if they were delivering roses to a Queen.

I hear him talk to himself down in the lane—it's never a good sign when one talks to oneself unless one's a philosopher, and then one must walk with one's hands clasped behind the back and not as Robaire walks, with his head down and hands by his side—though I can't understand what he's saying. All I know is that he's given up cigarettes, so perhaps he's grieving.

He's stopped making paintings, giving them away or taking them out of their frames and dragging them downhill to poubelle, stacking the little canvases against the large green container. The painting he's given me, the one that looks like the sun falling into the sea, loses its old meaning in front of my eyes; the more I look at his painting the more the imagination Robaire talked about with such reverence disappears, and I see more of what I think must be his ego or pure delusion. There's nothing more or less to Robaire's painting than the same old glorification of the artist, the self-glorification of someone who thinks he's doing something selfless when what he's doing is the opposite. Perhaps by giving up painting, by giving the paintings away, he's giving himself a chance to become the artist he already felt he was. It's possible this could be what he's talking to himself about as he walks back and forth in the lane.

Robaire's never spoken of his painting as such, never talked about *his work as work*, as so many artist's do, of his *oeuvre*, as if the work is something bigger than the artist himself, is a body of work that exists in a realm that exceeds the being of the man or woman making the work.

That he hasn't spoken of his work as work is to Robaire's credit, no matter the current renunciation of his own painting, for what is art but a high-quality diversion? Duchamp himself, who is said to have had a proper relationship with his own art, said that he *'lived the life of a waiter'*, and those who knew him in New York say he worked like a dog, but in secret.

IF YOU CAN'T TALK TO YOURSELF, WHO CAN YOU TALK TO?   Robaire dwells in the unresolved, as does every abstractionist, putting the pressure on the viewer, invoking Duchamp who claimed the viewer is as much the maker as the maker whether they know it or not.

At the moment Robaire gave me his painting, it was I who said it was *the sun*, I'm the one who does all the work once Robaire gives me the painting. Perhaps it's not the sun at all or the sea, or the sun falling into the sea, that he's meant to show at all, but something else, some other abstraction that has no relationship at all to the painting I've made of his painting.

It's the same with his utterances in the lane; that we want to understand him, for him to be as clear as possible. But he's speaking only to himself. By the sounds he makes, he must be looking toward what no one else can see, toward what he didn't do with his life... or perhaps he is in pain physically because of what he did do, waking up in the morning not feeling like himself at all, unhappy but not knowing why he's unhappy.

Speaking only to himself, late at night, walking back and forth in the little lane that separates his house from the petit maison, making the strange utterances that now constitute his language, which no one in the village seems to understand, utterances devoid of anything any of us could possibly interpret as *meaning*, should someone hear him speaking to anyone other than himself, Robaire paces well past the time the lights go out in the village, but quietly so that no one in the village complains.

Seeing things from another's perspective can be a problem. It's the problem with art now, art like Robaire's art, that it sees only from the perspective of the one seeing it. Art made this way is limited to only one perspective, and so one painting looks like another painting, and art becomes such a common vision that almost everyone seems to be making it. Accordingly, I take my head in my hands when on the terrace, instead of walking or pacing with my hands behind my back, which I'd once done as a philosopher, not walking as Robaire walks in the lane, in his madness, with his hands by his side but with my head in my hands, when I philosophize.

I've taken Robaire's painting down to the cave. Where I once saw the spirit of a man who gave all power to the imagination, the creator of a great orange sun falling into the sea, I now see a small man from Belgium who's so miserable without cigarettes that he's become another man.

Surely the painting's still down there, preserved in the underground temperature that's perfectly calibrated for keeping old wine, wallowing away in all the nice memories I have of Robaire.

I CAN'T DO
WHAT I SET OUT
TO DO BUT DON'T
QUITE GIVE UP

Sitting on the terrace, doing less and less, having not wanted to go to sleep, not liking the sofa bed, looking at the bed as if it were an enemy, having listened to the voices in the street below nearly all day, growing to know whose voice is whose but not knowing what anyone's saying, writing less and less in the yellow notebook, I contradict the goal of sitting quietly by myself for at least one hour and begin to pace violently from one side of the terrace to the other.

For the time being, I've tired of the days and stay up too late to make of anything out of them, finally falling asleep sometime just before morning, far too weary when I rise to be at peace with myself and sit quietly alone in a room as advised by Pascal. Instead I invent little projects for myself until the daylight is done away with and I can open a bottle of red wine.

SLEEPING IN THE DAY   I become a royal, sleep in the day if I feel like sleeping, crawl like the lizard I am from the terrace to lay on Helena's bed, keeping the yellow notebook by my side.

When I sleep in the day I start my sleep on my back, which differs from night sleep, which I start on my right side facing away from Helena, the one I typically begin my sleep with, though that's changed since I've moved downstairs to the sofa bed where I sleep alone most every night. I begin day sleep on my back with my head on the thinnest possible pillow, sinking into the bed in a way that is different than night sleep. In day sleep I trust that whatever the bed's made of will hold me as I fall. Day sleep sounds like the quiet of villages Helena and I walk through, the houses made of stone and people sleeping somewhere inside them.

Waking in the day on my back, I do things I've never done.

I pull everything out of the red bag, spread everything out on Helena's bed, and see that I'm not living with much at all.

Two pairs of the essentials—shirts, socks, pants, underwear, shoes—a black jacket bought on sale in Issoire. Everything is in the one red bag, even the books, the three of them, with enough space for two or three of the yellow notebooks if and when my writing fills them.

HELENA SAYS TO *widen my search*   For most of the day Helena and I hardly see one another. Our talk, if we talk, is only a few words, nice enough, nothing if not nice, solicitous certainly, each word said with the intention of fulfilling the basics of an intimate relationship.

She leaves the house by early morning, walking with Simone or one of the other women she's met, whose faces I can keep straight but whose names I can't, out enjoying the countryside. A group of them does yoga in Champeix, another goes to farmer's markets twice a week. They have coffee, go into Clermont-Ferrand for VO American movies, live very nice lives, not talking about taxes or politics or sports as the men do.

Helena thinks I should *widen my search*. I've come downstairs from the terrace, hearing the door open in the narrow hallow below, thinking it's my right to see how the day in France had been for her, to listen to details, nuances, should she wish to share, to take a demonstrated interest in something outside the terrace. She senses this, believes there is some sincerity on my part, not thinking that I'm happy in my quest on the terrace, as single-minded as it appears to her. *You need to get outside and expand* are her words. She says this as if I'm sad, knowing I am defenseless against sorrow, wanting things to be happy.

We're locked in a battle of sincerities, me—on the terrace for increasingly long periods of time, paying attention to the self I've so long neglected, but for the greater good, with the promise that if I learn to sit quietly by myself for at least one hour I will have made something—and Helena, who has no such need, whose need is met differently than mine, which is her right of course, going about her life in France without me, as if in an idyll. She's sincere, no doubt, though one must be thoughtful to differentiate sincerities — and rank them on a scale from one to ten.

When Helena says I should *widen my search*, part of my identity starts to come apart in the manner of a fraying. I'd rather she bite my neck and suck my blood. She's taking the misunderstanding I have of myself to a new extreme.

My *search* as she's phrased it can't be any wider. Yes there are happy and unhappy, satisfying and dissatisfying moments but the whole of it is beyond me and much larger than is my ability to achieve. Helena sailed past her initial encouragements and now doesn't even give lip service. I don't know what to think, seized by speechlessness, as is often the case.

{{{{{{{{{{{{{{{{{{{{{{{{{{{{{   }}}}}}}}}}}}}}}}}}}}}}}}}}}}}}}}}

{{{{{{{{Untalkativeness creates grave danger. An impasse is reached—I SAID, AN IMPASSE IS REACHED—constituting a crises. We've made unsophisticated assumptions, all couples make them, then carry them forward until impasse is reached. What we think we do for our own good couldn't be worse for us.}}}}}}}}

Dialog with Helena, once it begins, begins like this:

Me: Did you have a nice day?
She: Yes.

Me: Would you like to have sex ?
She   Let's have a glass of wine first.

Me: Ok, I'll get a bottle from the cave.
She: Perhaps you could get put on some dry boots and blue jeans

Me: Put something nice on?
She: Yes, reveal something less.

Me: I'm glad to have provided you so many memories, dear,
that you know that what I like is what all men like.

Then we sleep, the place where almost everything's solved.

It's time to say the words, *We live in a stone house in a village in France.*

I LIVE INSIDE ON THE OUTSIDE AND SHE LIVES FAR AWAY

It's time to say, *we're as far from home as two different people* are far from one another. I live on the terrace, trying to become someone I've not yet become, she lives more and more outside and with others. We assume we'll be together wherever we are, we live with this central assumption, France notwithstanding, that a crisis is always a crisis, best met by silence which dissolves in time like a pain pill.

I'm more convinced of the rightness of the past than her, I'm able to look and look away. I see the past become different day by day. She likes what she likes to see, what she sees is substance. Sometimes I know and don't know at the same time; she knows much more of the time. She tells me things; I sympathize. She shows me things I've never seen; I show her my seeing.

It's time to be quiet, silent almost, to trust we're never far from anywhere other than where we're from. I know that time needs at least one more person to really become time, that real time can't be kept by one's self. I don't know that she knows that.

SOME WORDS ARE LITTLE STONES   In the morning, the yellow notebook is open and lies on the floor beside my bed. I see I've written a little something—yes I have—

> I should have talked to you last night, but I didn't;
> I was concerned that my words might hurt your feelings.
> Now it's too late, and the moment when I knew that what I
> had to say might save us—even if my words were difficult
> and might have turned a lover and a friend into an enemy—
> is past.

> I must have known the truth, but said nothing; instead I
> remained silent, thinking there would be a time when I could
> speak openly. Sometime in the night, what I hadn't said
> woke me and I thought I heard you saying that what
> I'd withheld had real meaning.

The words look like hard little stones that are being thrown at me as I read them.

BOOK FOUR

Man must not be allowed to believe that he is equal to either animals or angels.

Pascal, *Pensees*

LINGUISTIC
EPIPHANY
In the empty church at Ronzieres I feel closer to god than I have in years, and decide to call god *'gof'* instead of god, or *'got'* or *'gor'* or *'get'* or *'got to'* which all seem closer the spirit of the thing as far as I understand it.

THE RED CAR
OF ALCOHOL
Thierry's drunk again, though no one knows how drunk until morning.

In the morning, no one believes he raised himself from the car, that dangles now on the precipice, and then walked up the lane into his home. He hasn't been seen since, is presumed to be asleep upstairs in his home.

He put the car in a vulnerable, unduplicatable position, centered exactly on the short wall separating the lane on which the petit maison resides from the lane below. The wheels on the left side of his little red car were not touching the ground, could gain no traction, spinning irresolutely in the air, and therefore could go neither forward or backward. Though I slept through the crisis, the visual situation of the car is such that there must have been a commotion of some duration.

INSPECTION
& JUDGMENT
Looking out at the lane from the terrace, I see Jean-Claude and Robaire walking carefully around Thierry's red car, smoking and shaking their heads.

I tiptoe to the terrace edge to hear what they're saying, without them knowing I'm hearing, to transcribe as carefully as possible their conversation as they look at the red car Thierry abandoned in the lane. It's as if they're considering a problem that might never be solved. It's presumed that Thierry had been drunk. How else could the car have gotten into this position? His drunkenness and the effect it had on the car was,

untenable: drunk, he'd high-centered the car, precisely, masterfully.

The car is *presently balanced as if on a needle.*

It will have to be expertly lifted, so as not to damage the undercarriage.

Furthermore,

High-centered, the car's vulnerable, one of its wheels can be spun without it touching anything; however, the question is not so much the position of the car, as much as the way Thierry might have extracted himself once the car was in its current position?

Had Thierry himself violently shifted his position the car itself might have toppled.

Any bodily shifting would have required great delicacy, a dexterity that Thierry never before demonstrated.

Jean-Claude and Robaire have propped Robaire's small wooden ladder against the rear of the red car to look inside. Having proof at this point that Thierry is not now in the car, they reason that he climbed into the rear and fell asleep; at dawn, more sober than he'd been, he exited the rear of the car and went inside his house to sleep.

As the exit is mysterious, unfathomable, they continue to talk.

There was proof enough that he wasn't in his car, enough proof to go knock on his door and ascertain his welfare.

Let him sleep.

He could be dead.
He might be elsewhere.

He has no friends.

Perhaps Teradact knows what had happened? He'd *gone for bread this morning, hadn't he?*

He must have seen Thierry's car, and seeing the situation of the car he must have been concerned.

Perhaps Thierry was in the car after all, asleep in the rear where all the his treasures were crammed.

THIERRY'S HISTORY WITH FIRE It's quiet now in the lane, no more discussion between Jean-Claude and Robaire about Thierry's car. They've each gone inside themselves.

I take my yellow notebook and go to the very edge of the terrace to note Thierry's car and its perilous situation.

The world is apparently based on the idea that there are followers and leaders, with the additional idea, now taken to be civilized, of the absolute necessity of an enemy. Jean-Claude and Robaire's entire discussion of Thierry's car is based on criticism of the way Thierry lives. Their words are exclusively negative, yet to this face I've only seen them kind, inclusive in fact, tolerant if slightly amused.

The car remains in peril for five days until the authorities devise a way to remove it safely from the village. No one sees Thierry for at least a month. Perhaps he's sleeping it off, upstairs in his big old house, amidst the little boxes, cast-off clothes, musical instruments, fireplace tools, gadgets, postcards, bric-a-brac, the paperback books he collected to sell at farmer's markets in the countryside...

...for not too long ago Simone thought she'd found Thierry dead.

SIMONE THE LIFE-SAVER Past midnight. Simone's reading in bed when she smells smoke. The poodles bark like maniacs so she knows something's wrong, walks to the window, looks out on the lane and sees smoke coming out from beneath the front door of Thierry's house. Jean-Claude is away at work on the graveyard shift at the factory in Clermont-Ferrand.

Simone runs to Thierry's and knocks on the door, grabbing, for a reason still unclear to her, the top slab of a stone bench Thierry kept beside the front door (the bench he kept for his friends to sit or to place their drinks on during warm summer evenings), bashing Thierry's big wooden door open with the rock.

She runs past flames in the kitchen, dashing up to the second floor to Thierry's bedroom. A small fire has started on the left side of the bed and is traveling toward the bed's bottom where Simone could see Thierry's feet protruding.

Simone finds a bucket near the bed and fills it with water from the bathroom—one bucket, two, three, four—putting the fire out in the bedroom, waking Thierry and walking him downstairs, past the smoke and outside into the lane.

Thierry's airlifted to a hospital in Lyon, his life spared.

AFTER THE AFTERMATH   There's a small story in the local paper, no names, just a few graphs about a man in the village of _____ who'd fallen asleep smoking and the neighbor who'd alerted the authorities, written in the French manner, like the story in the newspaper after Monique drowned herself in the river, just a few words.

Thierry's forbidden by the judge in Clermont-Ferrand to drink alcohol but drinks anyway with two little old ladies, one in the village and the other in Champeix. The judge has said he can't drive anymore so he depends on others, primarily the old lady who lives next door and with whom he drinks white wine and vermouth in the evenings, and Teradact whose charity towards Thierry continues to perplex us all of us who've never met a man less fit for living.

This morning the cab driver waiting in the lane below the petit maison waved his finger and shook his head at Thierry like he was scolding a little boy. He'd waited 15 minutes for Thierry so he could drive him to Issoire for counseling. Someone in the village made a complaint, had said Thierry was drunk, that the old lady in the village was still giving him wine and the judge ordered additional treatments.

Teradact stays out of the situation apparently. He's lying low, according to Jean-Claude. Teradact's ensconced in the villa, though he's still going for bread in the morning, hewing to his principles of long life—*avoid unnecessary activity and play dumb.*

When you are with some people you want to be somewhere else, without them, Jean-Claude says, meaning Thierry is one of those people. Neither Jean-Claude nor Robaire have had any contact with him for months.

Thierry's red car hasn't been seen since the accident.

THE STRANGE
RELATIONSHIP
BETWEEN TERADACT
& THIERRY

I now know the deal: Teradact's not to be engaged in conversation. I only glimpse him as he exists independently and only when he doesn't know he is being seen, carrying bread up the steps of the villa. I've never heard the sound of his voice. He must talk to his wife, and to Thierry. He must tell Thierry what to do.

No one in the village asks Teradact what he sees in Thierry or Thierry what he sees in Teradact. The relationship's off limits. Thierry trusts Teradact and Teradact trusts Thierry but the relationship is strange to everyone other than them. No one understands how the lowest meets the highest and the highest meets the lowest, or why they get along. Teradact is held in such esteem that some measure of regard is conferred on Thierry, who is otherwise thought little of. Simone thinks it odd that Thierry, her neighbor whose life she saved, now avoids her for the most part, and that his relationship with Jean-Claude is so strained.

Helena, knowing I'm intrigued, keeps urging me to make contact with Teradact. She thinks I'm shy and that my lack of French inhibits me. She still doesn't understand that any strength I have is in the silence I maintain in the face of things I don't understand.

She pushes me to a breaking point at dinner, insisting that I meet Teradact. *You have every right to, considering your curiosity,* she says. *I don't understand you. You have a need to see him and you don't. What's he going to do, hurt you? He's an old man. He can hardly walk up the stairs.*

I say, as calmly as I can, *Helena, imagine Blaise Pascal being asked "what's your book about?" What could he say? What he could say is what he did not say. Those things that we cannot understand we must pass by in silence,* as another philosopher says.

Two nights before Thierry dry-docked the red car,
we'd been invited to his house for barbeque.

Jean-Claude and Antonio knocked on the door of the petit maison:

*Thierry asked us to ask you. Would you like to dine with Thierry...he's making
barbeque...hahaha...HAHA. He has wine, many bottles of wine. We are all
his neighbors, we all have to see. It will be a spectacle, an entertainment.*

You must come right now.

Accepting the invitation, Helena and I cross the lane. Thierry's door is as
open as a stone, strings of red beads from the top of the door to the bottom mark the entrance.

Thierry, Thierry, Helena calls, pushing the red beads aside like she's hungry to see him.

Thierry's squeezed into a space beside his house, a footstep or two away
from Jean-Claude's. He's fit a hibachi in there, lit the match, and grills

meat—boudin, chicken, hamburger—while
he drinks rose. The air tastes of cheap wine
and petrochemicals. He kisses Helena and
shakes my hand, walks inside. The meat
smells like metal burning.

Jean-Claude and Antonio stand by the
hibachi, nearer Thierry's front door than
either of their own, pointing to the meat,
laughing as it burns but doing nothing to
stop it. They shake their heads when Thierry comes out of the house with
a stack of paper plates, they put on masks, they show kindness, they only
laugh when Thierry disappears, making faces at the meat, sticking their
fingers down their throats and laughing. They won't eat any of the meat

"I'd like some barbeque," Helena says to Thierry, taking a sausage and some
hamburger, stepping through red beads into Thierry's home. I follow, he
gives me a glass of white wine and a piece of bread. I find a soft place on
Thierry's maroon velour divan, second-hand, acquired at the flea market
in Brassac des Mines, and watch Helena and Thierry talk and eat. I worry
we'll wake Teradact, as his villa is directly across the lane. He'd returned

just the other day; I'd seen Thierry helping him — lift something heavy, a dog kennel perhaps, from the car.

I excuse myself to have a thought—*excuse me*, I say—when

—men like Thierry and Teradact bond it is the lowest meeting the highest, the lowest having some sort of bond with the highest and the highest with the lowest, as the positive has with the negative, so the middle is excluded, the extreme or the opposite granting access only to the other, the lowest to the highest and the highest to the lowest; therefore Thierry's s the only one in the village allowed to assist Teradact.

(as observed in the yellow notebook which I now keep under the bed Helena sleeps in, in the room beside the terrace.)

We eat, drink, make little sentences together until we're ready to leave. Thierry gives Helena a small leather traveling case, one of the treasures he's acquired in the Auvergne, without acknowledging the right latch is broken. The red beads of the doorway sway as Thierry hands the case to Helena. She makes a big deal of it. Jean-Claude and Antonio stand outside in the lane, smoking, talking and smoking. Teradact's asleep.

AVOID UNNECESSARY ACTIVITY   Memorizing Teradact's **Manifesto for Long Life**— *avoid unnecessary activity, play dumb*—I vow I'll walk more, read more, eat well, more greens, less bread and cheese, far fewer chops, only drink red wine (only two glasses a night) while attempting to live the way I want to live, making conscious choices about what's necessary and what's not.

I'm more often living this way though there are breakdowns, a cigarette now and then from Jean-Claude who now smokes Caporal, inheriting Robaire's stash when Robaire quit smoking and moved to Brussels. Jean-Claude still likes to roll cigarettes for me.

EXTINGUISH CERTAINTY   Helena lives like she's sure she's doing the right thing every moment of her life; France does nothing to alter the habit. On big subjects she's clear: there's no doubt in her mind that she's living and no doubt she'll die. If she dies tomorrow, she will have had a good life; if she dies in fifty years, she will have had the same good life, only longer. It doesn't matter to her if there is or there isn't a god, her life's the same with or without god.

I aim to extinguish certainty, I think it's a guise, the idea seems like science fiction, like an alien. I can't make a place for it on the terrace where I continue to spend late summer days, failing to get to the hour designated as my goal.

Perhaps it's time to go on a new crusade.

I IS NOT ANOTHER   I begin a letter to Helena, writing to discover what I need to say to myself in the yellow notebook—Helena

I am thinking of that moment when I became who I am incontrovertibly, that moment when whatever I might have become was lost to what I was, a loss from which there is no possible recovery…for there must have been a time when I became I and there was no possible recourse of becoming another

And that not being who I am is who I am…

SHORT HISTORY OF SIMONE'S DEPRESSION   Simone's depressed, crying the other day out walking with Helena.

Helena wasn't prepared, Simone's tears came out of nowhere as Helena and she approached the graveyard where Simone's mother's buried. She must have been thinking about her mother—though she visits her grave every day—or some horrible scene from her youth that she'd never shared with Helena.

The village had been all dark once, Simone admitted, *and the house was half a grange and half a house.*

Simone's house she and Jean-Claude now occupy was on the main road in the old days, before the big road at the bottom of the hill was built. Her father turned the back part of the house into a bar to lure in travelers. There was dancing in the summer.

Who knows what happened to Simone in that house? Helena says.

Wisdom sends us to childhood, I say to Helena. *It's Pascal.*

Are you still reading Pascal? You've been reading Pascal forever.

Helena, you said I should bring a book if I went to France. (*If I go to France,* I could have said, for though I'm undeniably here in the village, living in the petit maison, there are just as many times that I live as if I'm not here, live as if I could be living back there, or anywhere as is the case when I am feeling this way.)

—should I define the difference between being in France and not being in France: that the need to make someone less than myself is much less in France than it is not being in France, that the tendency toward making someone less does not seem to be a necessity here, where no one knows me, as it is where I'm known.)

WHAT I DO IS OF NO CONCERN If I go to France again, no one will have to know what I do; they don't seem to need that there, nor do they need to know who I am. There's none of that in France. I've never been asked once, *what do you do?* Not by Jean-Claude or Robaire, not by Antonio the painter. They're curious about me, of course. *Who is this man? He doesn't seem to speak,*

—*he's tall,*

he's with a woman,

he has brown hair with some silver in it,

he walks…

…they note individual characteristics but they never ask *"what do you do,"* as if what I do defines me.

CHRISTIANA, THE MARXIST By now I've met the ones I'm destined to meet: the butcher Chevalier who owns the big house by the chateau and has left his wife for a much younger woman. The banker from Paris. Pepe the dairyman keeps cows outside the village but milks them inside the big stone grange on the other side of the square. Antonio the artist from Sevilla, Spain, married to Christiana, a Frenchwoman from Cluny, a Marxist.

Christiana's against everything, Simone says, against the new houses the council wants to build in between our village and St. Julian, against the nuclear waste disposal station the government proposes tucked into the hills near Ludesse, against fast food, against whatever government there is.

As I've always wanted to meet someone *against everything*, I ask for a meeting to be arranged with Christiana, knowing her husband Antoine somewhat, meeting him briefly at the party at which I'd met the blind man.

We had a whiskey or two as I looked at his paintings in his atelier. He too stopped smoking, as Christiana was against smoking and against the government telling people not to smoke. It was too much trouble to smoke at home with Christiana against it, so Antonio stopped though he'd sneak a cigarette in the ruin he was restoring from time to time. Christiana couldn't be against what she didn't know.

A lovely man, Antonio, and a very good artist, coming into his own, having progressed from watercolors of the village (the church and the chateau)— executed from a safe distance, prominently from the flatlands in which Antonio grounded his vision, images of which almost everyone in the village owned at least one, at least those who lived at the very top of the village, hanging one or another of Antoine's watercolors on their walls—to a more conceptual approach, painting articles of different clothing (shoes, pants, vests, shirts) in which he, the artist, was pictured.

There was a show in Paris of the new work and a book, though according to Antonio, his village patrons felt betrayed and would have none of it, not buying the new paintings. But neither had they made anything personal out of their refusal, and everyone remained friendly.

We met Christiana at last, a much younger
woman than Antoine's a man. She's quite pretty,
trim and energetic, with a smile that has something lost in it, showing a
slight gap in the upper row of her two front teeth. Her Marxism's worn
off or she's outgrown it and she talks mostly about Antoine's art, her son
studying architecture in Geneva, the health of her garden.

She asks if I can *recommend any books to read in English*. Before I answer
she says, *I've read Howard Zinn,* A People's History of the United States.

In English?, I ask.

*Yes, of course. What did you think? I marched, I picketed, I wrote letters, I
organized in Paris and here in the countryside, I believed that the world
wanted to be better than it was, that we could make it better.*

*Politics is a real fantasy. We believe in such stupid things, that the people
who govern us have our best interests in mind and so on. That delusion is so
powerful that for years it overwhelmed me.*

I've given up caring one way or another. Leave me alone is my policy now,
Christiana says, without smiling. I never see her really smile, like Simone
smiles at Helena.

The great privilege of the century is privacy but
you have to go out of the way for it and take no
hard positions. I'm going to an extreme, I have strong feelings that seem
less and less relevant, I'm questing,

to remain without restlessness in my room for one hour.

I go up to the terrace almost every morning and write in the yellow notebook, read Pascal, take walks in the countryside with and without Helena.
It's so much easier to be alone here, though when I'm alone I often long to
be with others and with others I'm always happiest when they leave, less
interested in others than I ever was.

I don't progress or regress, I live in a quest that's not yet become an
addiction. Addiction is thinking I need something I don't need and acting on the thinking. I wait and watch the dust settle, make up a plot for a
novel out of the things I've read, but all the books on my bookshelf have
come down to just one book that I found in an airport—*Pensees.*

I think of things I want to say to Helena to prove that I'm getting something out of France. She'd listen, I think. But they're not fully formed, only scribbles in the yellow notebook from Auchan,

> —*our loneliness*
> *lasts a long time*
> *and we can never*
> *outlive it.*

so I don't share them, not yet, I let them pile up like the leaves beginning to fall from the trees. What's the point in sweeping up the leaves? More will fall to the ground in just a moment or two.

TERADACT TAKES
ANOTHER TRIP AS I
WASTE MORE TIME

Teradact takes another trip, to Saumar and a little hotel and restaurant he likes there in the Loire Valley. Madame Teradact's been cleared by her doctor to drink the champagne of the region.

Teradact tells Thierry who tells Jean-Claude who tells Helena who tells me. He'll be away a week.

There's a rumor Teradact's buying one of Antonio's watercolors. Jean-Claude doesn't think there's any art on Teradact's walls except portraits of the spaniels, numbers one through eight, and dinner plates Madame Teradact's acquired from restaurants on her travels, as far as he knows,

never having been in Teradact's villa, having stood at the door more than once thinking he might be asked in but not being asked, having to rely on Thierry for information.

The good to be gotten from Teradact is what he keeps inside. Every bit of his life must be up there in his head. I also have another theory: that he doesn't want to be seen wasting his time.

Time seems happy to be wasted here, proud of itself, no one who's wasting their time ever minds being seen. Jean-Claude stands by the fountain or at the dutch-door of his home in the evenings, smoking cigarettes, talking with whoever passes by. I sit on the terrace and scribble into the yellow notebook. Others, several of whom are still unknown to me, gather and talk in the street or beside the fountain in the square every evening, sans Teradact, talking about less and less as the weather changes, until they're talking about practically nothing.

The sentiment among those who matter is that Teradact should acknowledge Jean-Claude's position in the village, the gravitas that accrues from Jean-Claude's real, not feigned, concern for the welfare of the people. Everybody knows Teradact's asked Jean-Claude for protection twice, once in the supermarket when he was observed purchasing gourmet food items far exceeding his budget, asking Jean-Claude to keep the amount from Madame Teradact, and once involving an innocent indiscretion and a furtive trip Teradact made alone years ago to the Jura. But Teradact stays inside, gives off no signs, his time less wasted.

GETTING AROUND THE GROUP IN ORDER TO BE ALONE I learn to skirt the group that gathers to talk in the square. I nod when I think a greeting's necessary and go on, walking out of the village in the evenings toward Gourdon and Olloix, or I walk the longer way, the way they can't see me, taking the footpath beside the church. I don't walk at all if I think I risk having to say something to them in French or of having to stop and try to make sense of what they're saying.

And I like them all, that's what's so sad—Jean-Claude and Simone, Robaire when he was there, Antonio, Peter the Dutchman—and I despise them too. It's easy for Robaire to say *ca ve'* as I walk past the group, but should I ask him the same, knowing he has difficulty saying anything more than *hi, how are you?* knowing the conversation would end there, it would make both of us uncomfortable. They're all nice people. They talk behind your back only if you're not listening, they don't make fun of anyone collectively other than Thierry. Their talk is mostly cheerful, as when Jean-Claude calls the local wine *weed killer*, pretending to pour it on the weeds that grow up through the stones, or notes a contradiction in what he calls, *the French system*.

Jean-Claude prefers the total evasion of humor, makes playthings of his face, gargoyle after gargoyle. He has his fun, not believing in much of anything. It's a joke in the village that Jean-Claude married Simone in the village church, the church to which Marionette keeps the keys, that he's not been inside since.

Simone remembers the church in better times, having been born and raised in the village, when there were services Sunday and every holy day and all the seats were taken. It's a nice little church, symmetrical and small, 13th century, with the story of Montaigut the crusader in frescoes on the wall. The only one in the village having the keys to the church, Marionette is granted additional powers and is allowed to keep at least one goat, sometimes two, behind her house, despite the law. Helena and I always wonder where the sound's coming from. Clearly a goat, perhaps two are being kept in the village and, as roosters are more commonly kept, the sound differentiated itself. Roosters keep to themselves until dawn, goats do not discriminate as to time, goats sound off whenever they wish, and mournfully too.

Walking out from the village is more difficult than walking in. It's easier when Helena is with me, she has grace here as I do not, she's the superior. She can thank Thierry for the carrying case with a quick grace and keep walking. Though the latch is broken, she says nothing of it.

I learned from the group, then I left. When I'm alone, I want company and with company I want to be alone. Perhaps I've already laughed too much, used my quota for laughter all up, at the all the wrong times, a nervous habit that makes me self-conscious. It's unfortunate, I want the world to be at least a little light-hearted and partly-filled by goodness, and find that it's neither.

WHEN I STOP THE TALK'S OF DEATH

When I stop to talk with them, death's often the subject.

Pepe has died, the big old farmer from whom I'd always meant to buy fresh milk. He'd set the milk outside his grange in big silver canisters four days a week.

I'm sorry now I never bought milk from Pepe. Helena always meant to, but we preferred water, coffee and wine. Simone says Pepe's son is taking over the dairy, though there are fewer and fewer farmers in France as no young women want to be farmer's wives, and Pepe's son is a rarity.

A FUNERAL AS DISASTER   Pepe's funeral is a disaster—a disgrace if Simone can be believed (and who wouldn't believe what comes out from behind her brown eyes, as sincere as unshelled almonds, or from her full French lips?)

The memorial's held in the church. Marionette opens the doors at 10:30 for an 11:00 a.m. service.

Mourners crowd into the small church. They would've waited forever if they had to, not made a sound. Pepe lived his whole life in the village, a cow herder and milk maker, had no known enemies, a plump farmer who wore the same blue pants, a yellow polo shirt, and green cardigan sweater day after day. It's sad when someone like this goes.

By 11 a.m., the church is full and Marionette's tempted to close the door, sealing the church against the heat and the flies. A half dozen people wait outside.

Big problem, Jean-Claude says, *no priest!* Jean-Claude wasn't there; he doesn't go to weddings or funerals, as there's *always something wrong with them*, but tells the story anyway.

The archdiocese in Clermont-Ferrand sends a young woman instead of a priest for the service. She can't find the village, driving around the coun-tryside from village to village, arriving an hour late, not knowing the words to the sermon and mispronouncing Pepe's family name.

Simone begins to cry.

What's Jean-Claude mean, *there's always something wrong with them?* Is he trying to tell a joke?

Simone's crying. She'd actually gone to the funeral, looking good in her black dress, sitting in the pew toward the front. Everyone who thought they knew her felt their eyeballs wobble around when she walked into the church, and not just the men. She's so tender, cries at anything, even at movies on tv. I wish I'd been there, I want to know what kind of heart she has. When a beautiful woman dresses in black and goes to church it's something righteous, it makes us all seem that we believe in God.

Perhaps once one's mother and father are dead, one's attitude to life changes, Antonio, who attended Pepe's memorial despite not drinking milk or knowing Pepe at all, says. Antonio lives in San Julian, one village over, comes up to the square every evening to talk and smoke.

It shouldn't be so hot, but the beginning of
autumn's a string of hot days. From the terrace I
can see the top of The Sancy in the far distance, newly covered in snow. I
see no one other than Helena, take more breaks from the terrace. I can't
get interested enough to read, one Pensee a day is about it, and lie on the
bed under a soft white sheet. I lift it up and down from time to time to
simulate a breeze. Sleep's unsatisfying.

It's impossible to read when it's hot, the words on the page are like flies.
There's nothing to be done but close my eyes.

Madame Rocet said nothing of flies in the petit maison yet plastic fly
swatters are provided, one to a room.

By 2p.m. I give up and go inside to sleep, blaming the flies. When I close
my eyes I don't know if I'm in France or somewhere else. All I know is
that when I wake, I've fallen asleep on Helena's bed with Pascal's book,
Pensees, open where I'd stopped reading, draped on my stomach, somewhere near the middle of the book, nearer the beginning than the end,
nearer the place where I believe it's time to begin again.

I wake up covered with doubt, doubt smells like broccoli after it's boiled.
The only place I can think of living is in the past, in the time the French
poet called the *Europe of antique masonry*. Which poet? There are so
many of them. Not a troubadour, the phrase has too much of the social
critic for a troubadour to have said it. Perhaps Baudelaire, or Felix Feneon
or Paul Celan, though it must have been Rimbaud as it sounds like something he might have said.

The day after Pepe's funeral, Johnny Cash dies. I feel like going somewhere far away, but by this time it's evening. The group is standing in the
square beside the fountain as I begin my evening walk.

Johnny Cash is very very good, Antonio says.

Jean-Claude says, *Who is this Johnny Cash, I have never heard of him. I
know Jacques Brel but who is this Johnny Cash?*

I stand just outside a loose circle
of the 2 ladies and 4 men who
stand in the square talking about Johnny Cash. I want to see how quickly
I can raise my hand and nod my head so that they see me making the

effort to say something about Johnny Cash, so that I can walk away from them toward the road to Gourdon and Olloix without saying anything.

I wonder if they think I walk like the way I'm feeling, like I'm walking through a million small puddles filled with old rainwater. I think I'm walking like I'm made of water, and that I could take many forms. The heat uses me but the light lacks energy and has no inner life, no radiance.

There's a dog at the end of the road in Gourdon, I thought it would kill me the first time I walked up there. Its barking wakened other dogs, every house has at least one or two, so that means 20 or 30 dogs barking at once. Some were bearing fangs, and **None of Them** were small.

I'll never go to Gourdon again. It's too bad, there's a nice little park with a bench at the top of the hill, a good view of church and valley, and The Sancy.

WALKING BY
MYSELF AS MONSIEUR
AMBIVALENCE

I could go anywhere from here, I'm so loose by this time, so alone, but there's only so much that can be seen in the countryside.

The lambs are long gone and the joy I took in watching them play in the fields, their little bumpy steps along the grass, getting under their mother's bellies to suck tit. Every step the lambs took meant something real right in front of my eyes. Two days later they were almost running, by a week they ran so fast I couldn't see how they remembered their mothers. Then Marionette had them moved to pastures higher up and I lost touch.

Thinking about the lambs I think I must have missed something at the very beginning of coming here. I try to go back there, not to the very beginning or the very end, neither of which I understand, but to a place close to the beginning and not far from the end.

Now I walk for exercise. I don't even talk to myself anymore when I walk, I don't think about having fun. I don't want to think, I don't want to sit alone on the terrace thinking and putting thinking into the yellow notebook. I walk to free myself of the terrace and the little tyrant of the yellow notebook I can't get enough of. I'm Monsieur Ambivalence. I sit in the late mornings on the terrace where it is just cool enough to sit at the table under the Stella Artois umbrella to read Pascal and write in the yellow notebook. There really is no one in the world other than me. I live like this in France, day after day, I hold my ambivalence in both hands and bounce it like it's a rubber ball. The days carom away off cobblestones that can't be trusted to bring the ball right back to me.

NOTHING HAPPENS, SO I THINK ABOUT RELIGION

Most of the time nothing happens, I'm getting used to it. I wonder if the news of Pepe's funeral creates these stoppages in me. Simone said the funeral was *a disaster* because no priest showed up, and she cried when she said it.

It's possible the priest did not want to be a priest the day of Pepe's funeral. Things like this happen: the church in Clermont-Ferrand received the request for service but they were down to one priest and he was tired, overworked, refused to be a priest that day. The church sent a replacement who in the church's mind was a very capable substitute, in this case a woman. I wasn't there, I didn't hear her mispronounce Pepe's name as Simone claims she had. I'm on the side of the woman, the priest who isn't a priest, sent to officiate the service in the priest's place. It's not her fault. I wonder if it isn't the poor woman's clothes that are so distressing to Simone, that the woman, dressed in a black business suit and not a robe, as a priest would have dressed, upset Simone by not being in uniform, not wearing priestly clothes. And what does Simone mean by saying she read *the wrong passages*? How wrong could they have been, being from The Bible?

OUR MORNINGS TOGETHER

By the time I open my eyes Helena's already out the door. God she gets up early! Her routine begins when it's barely light—she makes coffee, reads her mystery or some Eastern philosophy, does what needs to be done in the house. And then she's gone, with me or without me.

She's left without making me anything to eat. There are eggs, there are always eggs and cheese, butter, bread, last night's Sancerre, over half the bottle, plus a little leftover coffee, enough to get going. I could cut an orange open.

She'll have reached the first mushroom field by now, the hidden one between Gourdon and Olloix. I think that's where she's headed. She took her little black pack. I heard the door close. She's quiet when I'm asleep or out on the terrace, tries not to make any noise. She knows I'm up there thinking even when I'm not.

MUSHROOMS   She started it, it was just a game when we
                started mushrooming, and once she started we
started doing it together and we couldn't stop..

The first time was in the field near Chazoux.

Helena and I were on an evening walk from the village toward Olloix.
We went around the group who gathered in the square, using her words,
passing the last house, the house from which we'd heard the strange
music behind the cypress trees, immersed in countryside in two minutes.

We walked separately, finding paces appropriate to our mood, one of the
ways we have of being honest with one another, a true expression of our
relationship. In France, Helena is always ahead of me, so she must have
seen the field first.

Do you want to do this, she asks?

Do what? I ask.

What those two old people are doing, she says.

ADAM AND EVE   I see the two people in the big green field beside
                    the road that runs toward Olloix.

From a distance they might be Eve and Adam.

The pair walk slowly through the muck, bending to the earth and unbending, a couple of French people. They look alike, she no more than he, at
least from a distance.

They're doing something, I say.

They're getting bogged down is what they're doing I thought to myself,
not saying anything to Helena who was advancing toward the field in
question, toward the old couple bending and unbending, stooped and
stooping.

I stand still and watch Helena advance.

She's taking the field in hand without storming it, I think. Her certainty
is admirable, she takes such possession! I can't come close to her finality,
the way she seems able to influence the surroundings with the force of
her mind.

Seeing Helena walk toward the field, I see the place making time for us. The green field opens up, beyond the barbed wire that keeps the cows safely away from infinity.

INSTRUCTIONS FROM THE ORIGINAL TWO The old couple carry white plastic sacks. Helena asks to see what's inside.

Mushrooms. Rose des pres. In fields like this all over France, the old lady says.

It's not like walking at all, the old lady says.

You have to look down, the old man Adam says, *you have to bend, you have to be tres flexible.* He carried a knife, hung in a leather pouch on his waist, his hand made a twisting motion as he spoke.

Get at the root if possible, at least below the surface to some of the stem, he says.

The old man speaks in some sort of patois, a man of soil. Helena nods at everything either one of them says. She's getting the gist. She thanks them, and Eve gives her a plastic bag in which to collect mushrooms.

It seems Eve's generosity shames Adam.

He walks toward his car, which he'd driven right into the field, empties his own white bag of mushrooms on the hood of the car and looks at me as if I understand what he's doing. I do and do not, not understanding French.

Adam wants me to have the plastic bag, and the mushrooms inside it as well. He spills the mushrooms, makes a nice warm pile of them on the hood of his car.

Thank you, I say, *thank you, thank you.*

Eve says there are *more mushrooms in that field. But be careful*, she warns, *they're not all rose des pres, some are toxique, mortelle.* Then they wave goodbye and drive away.

MUSHROOM SEX Well, Helena and I did fine that first day. Sometimes we stooped, sometimes we got down on our hands and knees just as Eve and Adam showed us. It was like being back in the old days when we were new to one another and couldn't keep our hands on anyone but each other.

Helena was better than I. I couldn't resist looking at her while she worked. I watched how she kept her eyes to the ground so she could tell good from bad, how she concentrated on something other than the self.

Helena's concentration! Even if you didn't know her as I know her you could tell there was no separation between who she was and what she was doing, that both were absolutely one.

There was a phase in our relationship when I liked to think about her making love to the boys and men who'd been in her life, either before me or after me. I'd imagine her naked and young, having sex with_____ and _____ and _____ and _____ , four I knew about for sure and _____ and _____ who she'd told me about years later. I'd think of her sexual passion as being a primitive form of concentration, of having nothing between herself and her partner other than herself and himself. For the longest time I liked thinking this as much as I liked acting this way with her myself. Her concentration was so charming, even when transferred to an object other than myself, that I began to think something was wrong with me and stopped thinking of her with other men.

I stayed close to Helena in the field, I saw how quickly her bag was being filled; she was natural, a good hunter of berries and nuts. The speed in which she gathered was dazzling. Several times I stopped stooping to watch her. She was completely involved in feeling for the earth, taking the mushrooms by her right hand as far down the stem as she might, shaking the severed stem free of any dirt, stuffing the fruit in her white plastic bag, one after another. I couldn't get into it at first. I loitered in the French sun, finding the one dry piece of earth in the damp field and laying on my back so that I could see the sky, watch the swampy clouds cross the border between Chazoux and Olloix. At some point I closed my eyes and slept.

When I watch Helena work it's like I'm already way behind, as late as September is to August, and I have to catch up. Rising, I pick every mushroom I see, I frenzy my picking, white ones, pink, brown ones, little golden haired mushrooms that grew in clumps, the demon mushrooms blossoming from the cow shit. I let myself believe I'm doing something biblical and gain energy from the belief. I look so long at what is being looked at, I look at looking that is, see the same thing or things, the same looking things, things looking the same that is, I see one mushroom becoming another and another becoming another and so on until I am not seeing mushrooms at all.

At last the temperature falls, the clouds themselves walk around in the sky in dark blue business suits, and my white plastic bag is full.

When I look across the field for Helena, I see that I have drifted far away and that she is a bent speck in a far field. If Helena looked at me the way I am looking at her she would see my body both beginning and ending. She'd see that life should test the limits of disintegration, and then disintergrate.

Mushrooms must have been the manna in the bible, Helena says at dinner.

A MINOR HALLUCINATION   The morning after mushrooming, I look at my writing in the yellow notebook. It's just after dawn. I'm sure that my looking changes what I've written, but it's early. I was happy, I was sad, I remembered, I forgot, I need someone else and I need to be alone, I must begin what's ended and end what's beginning.

I write the words I'm looking at, to make sure I've seen them correctly:

> *If I wrote about myself, would I recognize what I'd written?*
>
> *How patient things are with me, in direct contradiction to my old impatience.*
>
> *Patience uses so much of me it's as if I'm not here.*

Someone's awake in the house. I hear stones creak, I hear whoever's awake awakening. My friend Pascal says that I must sit in a room by myself, in the Dover Edition of *Pensees*, page 39, #139: "*I have discovered that all the unhappiness of men arises from one single fact, that they cannot stay quietly in their own chamber.*" I must, before too much time goes by, stay on the terrace alone for at least one hour, and then two, three hours if only to see what happens.

Helena's down below, her creaking comes up through the stones. She's chopping mushrooms, shaking the dirt from them and from the plastic bags. *One Russian roulette omelet coming up*, she says, standing at the foot of the stairs. I pretend not to hear as I am outside on the terrace and it is plausible not to.

Helena hasn't taken the mushrooms to the pharmacy in Champeix, not had the druggist judge their toxicity. She's sure she's sautéing only the safe rose des pres for the omelet, having had Marionette sift the bag last night and pronounce most of them *non-toxique*. She met Marionette by chance, in conference with Simone, the older huddled with the younger beside the fountain. I was on the terrace with a glass of Chateau Tiregrand, drinking from what I think's the next to last bottle. I'd heard them talking.

I HEAR PEOPLE SING WHO AREN'T SINGING   I move more and more outside, sitting on the terrace until my ears turn cold, sometimes dressed in wool socks, mittens, the wool cap I bought in Mount Dore, sometimes almost naked as the weather continues both hot and cold.

Helena often calls up from the kitchen, her voice is so strong, *how you doing up there?*

Fine, I say, *just fine*, when I hear her voice.

She cooks stews, makes elaborate omelets from the large eggs she buys from Pepe's son, and truffades, cassoulets, visits farmer's markets almost every day in Champeix or Issoire or Murol up the road. She's Helena, she buys lentils and cheese and mustard from an old man who wears suspenders, she drives into Clermont-Ferrand for harissa or down toward Millau for white asparagus, she likes to see the countryside.

When I go with her I find a church and sit alone, almost every village has one, in Blesle, in Montaigut le blanc, in Montpeyroux, Chalus, Ludesse, Olloix, in St. Nectaire and in Ronzieres...I sit alone and meditate, breathing like there's an ivory ring in my nose. I have faith. The church fills up with people while I'm sitting there, they rise up in me and start singing hymns, we rise up with each other, we're one. I see myself as believing in Jesus and all the stories in the Bible. Imagine, I imagine, what it sounded like when the churches were new and everyone was singing? It's such a miracle!

The sound of their voices is so beautiful I want to cry, but I can't.

BOOK FIVE

Men are so necessarily mad, that not to be mad would amount to another form of madness.

Pascal, *Pensees*

4 I 4

SECRET PACT   *Promise you'll tell no one*, Jean-Claude says, taking
me by the arm.

I'm on my way downhill for bread, half awake before coffee. I like to break
the fresh bread into little pieces and eat it with my coffee now.

Jean-Claude stands by the fountain, smoking, one foot up on the marble
step fronting the fountain. He's in pose, civilian clothes, blue workpants,
and a jean shirt with pearl buttons. He's never touched me before.

You must tell no one, he says, *I've chosen you to see my cave.*

**You must promise not to tell another person that you have been
invited, nor to reveal what you see there.**

You will be the only person to see my cave during my lifetime , and

Do you agree

To the conditions above?

We make a specific time in the indefinite future to visit the cave late at
night when the women are asleep. I promise to bring a bottle of Ricard.

A COMFORTABLE   I've hauled a small divan I found in the cave all
NEW SOLITUDE   the way up three flights of stairs for the purpose
of being alone in greater comfort, without clearing it first with Madame
Rocet, and placed it in Helena's bedroom beside the terrace. I lie on the
divan and close my eyes, keeping the yellow notebook open in case I have
a thought.

Meantime, Marionette causes problems. She's decreed that the church
bells chime only at noon and not in the morning and evening as they
chimed when Helena and I first arrived. She's the only one in the village
who has the church keys, the one who set the bells to chime three times a
day in the first place. And now she's shutting them down! It's presumed
to be a protest against the church for botching Pepe's funeral.

They're like lights, I argue, *leave them on, keep them on at morning, noon and night. Hearing the bells makes me think of time fondly, and of my mother and father for some reason. We can't let go of these things!* And why does Marionette have this power? What does Marionette think of climate change? Can she prove anything or does she just sense the weather changing? There are either more mushrooms or there are not. *What do the newspapers say?* That we mustn't let go of the way we see the world!

DISMANTLING THE COMFORT

It's weird the cravings I get, it's like I'm pregnant.

Suddenly I want to see a movie but the closest movie theatre's in Clermont-Ferrand. There's an American film playing there—a VO—an animation. But at least it's something. I tell Helena the movie starts in the late afternoon, that it would be good for both of us to hear some English. We can get something to eat in the city.

I tell Helena that I've come to a real standstill on the terrace. All sorts of intrusions keep me from my purpose—the attempt to close my eyes and to keep them closed for one hour to achieve the calm solitude Pascal advised. It's impossible for instance not to notice the dirt under my fingernails from the mushrooming the day before and reconstruct the time Helena and I had to ourselves in the fields. Rather than being still, I think how difficult it's been finding my way in the world, to muster the energy to get things to eat, a place to live. Sometimes I know myself and love what I know, knowing also that what I don't know about myself is also valuable...

...that the pleasure of pushing against something is not something to be overlooked... and how happy we all could be if we all loved one another.

But I just might get away with watching clouds or sitting in the backseat of Francoise's Citroen on the road to Blesle. Or to sit in the café with Helena and eat olives and bread and look at the wine list together.

To never really be comfortable unless eating or drinking, and then only provisionally so, wondering if I've eaten too much or too little, if more wine was wise or unwise, and so not enjoying the consumption as much as I might.

Still I think.

I break everything I touch. Not literally, perhaps, but everything I touch breaks down in me. Just standing up feels difficult. My head's top-heavy,

especially on the terrace. I live in the space and time where I've either just taken a drug or the drug is wearing off, is down to its dregs at the place where it begins to drag me down. Closing my eyes does no good. When I close them I see spots.

I should start, I should start again, I should start all over. Start with saying that I have a problem with telling the truth—and by not knowing where I am.

All I can think of at the moment is the memory of a fight I had with Helena that might have been avoided had I been thinking correctly and been more committed to my solitude, and not sung "Born Under A Bad Sign," a blues classic, on the way to Clermont-Ferrand.

A BLUES SONG IN FRANCE   I persist in singing *"Born Under a Bad Sign,"* the Albert King version, not calculating the song's possible effect on Helena, as we drove from the village to a Clermont-Ferrand.

Born under a bad sign/Been down since I began to crawl/If I didn't have bad luck/I wouldn't have no luck at all were as much of the lyrics as I could remember. Other parts of the song asserted themselves as I sang, and I sang as I drove, sensing Helena's displeasure by the time we reached Pluzat, a dim little village with the stone lion fountain in the center.

Helena stares straight ahead, won't look at me as I sing, saying nothing. It's as if her silence is helping create the condition in which the words would reveal themselves, the words now coming to me one after the other, *Bad luck and trouble/My only friend/I've been down/Ever since I was ten*. Even Albert King's guitar is in the car with us.

Instead of the movies, I decide to drive to Auchan. By the time I find a parking place, all the air between Helena and I is dry and hot and we can't wait to be away from one another. I watch as she walks into the great store, alone, wander in after her but without her seeing me, let her have herself to herself.

When I see her again, she's in produce, picking up bunches of romaine lettuce and shaking water from them to find the right bunch. There's a plastic tray down by her feet, almost full of food—cheeses, coffee, apples, a bottle or two of wine.

I walk up to her and stand by her side. She stares straight ahead, as I thought she would.

TEMPORARY INSANITY   Back at the petit maison, Helena asks if I want lunch, the first words she'd said since we'd left Auchan in Clermont-Ferrand.

I'm making lunch, she says, *would you like some?* It is, however, the way in which she asks, as if she is making lunch for herself and not for me. In point of fact she says as much, saying, *I'm making lunch, and I can as easily make lunch for two as for one* are her exact words.

I don't answer at first. Then I say that I'll make my own lunch, not liking to accept things from a person whose spirit is not in the giving. I reason: she didn't like my singing, not expressing overt hostility but something worse, questioning my choice of songs by staring out the window, and by a self-absorbed and thereby self-satisfied silence, without saying that she did not like the song or asking me to sing something else; then offering to make my lunch when she was in fact making her own, as if nothing had happened between us at all, thereby compounding the offense by doing something nice for me, the one who had committed the crime.

Standing in the kitchen, watching her shred greens for a salad, slice bread for her butter and cheese sandwich, not now in fact making a sandwich for me at all, I feel so misunderstood that I cannot think in the least. I pick up a bag full of unshelled, unsalted pistachio nuts and say out loud, *I'll have these for lunch.*

And then I say, according to Helena, *at least pistachio nuts understand me.*

Who are you? How could you think like this? Do you know how insane it is to say, "pistachio nuts understand you"... ? Helena says.

There are times when you are a microscopic man. Not only can I not see you, I can't hear you. If you meant to tell me something by singing that horrible song, tell it to me like a real man, in a way I can understand, not a little boy singing a blues song he never could have written in the first place.

The next day I ask Helena to dismiss what I'd said about the pistachio nuts at lunch. I'd felt misunderstood, my work from this point on is to understand myself, that there were in fact no enemies other than the self.

This is no way to live, Helena says. She's found a pool in St. Nectaire *where we can swim*. We'll walk there, *maybe tomorrow.*

BLACK SPEEDOS   I nod to Corinne, the young blonde behind the counter at the swimming pool who says *You have to wear black Speedo swimming trunks*, holding them up by a string and twirling them in one hand while her other hand opens for the ten Euros she says I owe her. What a little bitch!

Corinne says I *cannot swim in anything other than Speedos*, available in black or white bikini, if I want to swim. *It's French law*, she says. I choose the black Speedos, though the white might make less of an impact.

Now you know how a woman feels, Helena says. I nod, which means yes, looking up and down at myself as I stand in the shower in my shiny new black Speedos, washing myself as all swimmers must before entering the pool. It's possible I guess to feel how a woman might feel being looked at in a skimpy swim suit, knowing how her body looks to her and knowing others are looking at her body, and it's a long walk from the shower to the pool.

I wrap a white towel around my waist, my waist a little distended from the red wine, bread, and cheese of the region, slip the towel off poolside and slide into the water before anyone sees me.

Is something wrong?, Helena asks as we walk back to the village from the pool, through the hills behind St. Nectaire.

Nothing, other than nothing's ever what it seems to be here in France, I say, as much as I've said for several days.

Wanting me to say more, she says, *how did you feel about wearing the Speedos?*

I don't know what to say so I don't say anything.

What do you feel like having for dinner?, Helena says after some time.

I don't know, I say

DISLIKING A QUESTION The question Helena asks is adroit, food's something I'm really avid about these days. She knows how much I like to eat, that I'm only myself when eating or thinking of eating, it's when I'm happiest. She's asked a good question, it's something like a circle. The answer is: I don't know what I want, I only know that I want to be surprised by you. Therefore I don't like the question. We're both impatient, I'm impatient with being impatient with you, for thinking you asked the wrong question, a question that needed an answer too quickly or no answer at all, and you're impatient with me for not answering. You call it ambivalence, like I don't care. I care, I want you to care!

How could I not have been ambivalent about wearing the Speedos, which barely covered me, were made of a shiny metallic fabric that emphasized what I believed to be unflattering aspects of my body? And how could you have not understood my ambivalence, the Speedos were something I'd rather not have worn or talked about?

THE TRICK IS TO ACT LIKE A PUPPET When Helena suggests I *widen my search*, using the words without weighing them as I would have had I said them to her, I was tempted to comment on the way she's living, the decisions she makes—her adamant certainty, the long walks she takes now without me, her insistence on speaking French in the petit maison, knowing I only understand one word of ten she's spoken. Instead I nod my head, say nothing, my head's good at nodding now.

DEFINING THE DYSFUNCTIONAL COUPLE Helena's walking ahead of me when we'd vowed to walk together; for instance, she's three trees ahead of me when we walk in the forest. It's her idea that only dysfunctional people walk apart, couples mostly, and those who had healthy, loving relationships walked together.

She got the idea in Clermont-Ferrand, where we sat at a sidewalk café near the cathedral and watched people walking the boulevard. She pointed out women walking ahead of men more often the men ahead of women. In almost every case, the couple walking weren't walking together but apart, the woman walking ahead of the man by four or five steps. I'm impatient when I'm listening to her, I drink my coffee, I tap my foot. Helena walks in front of me half the time, I think. The other half we walk together. Should I put my hand on her shoulders, slow her down... if I walk in front of her will she do the same? I'm disturbed by my impatience—what's the difference whether Helena walks in front of me or behind me? Or that she's hurt or sad when I walk ahead of her? Maybe she has a point, that in the city we should walk together. But we should be happy to be walking home through a forest in the middle of France whether we're walking together or not.

So long as Helena's in sight we can be said to be together. There's no one other than me to judge our possible dysfunction, and we're alone in the woods near Grandyrolles.

DYSFUNCTION — A TEST-CASE   It's raining, Helena waits up ahead. She won't turn around, turning around would send the wrong signal, but she's stopped walking which allows me the time to catch up to her.

I want you to stay dry, she says without turning toward me, having opened the small umbrella she'd bought in Aurillac, a town famous for umbrellas.

I'm fine, I say. *Let's go. We can be home in a few minutes if we walk fast.*

Take the umbrella, please.

There's only room for one, I say.

This is real rain, she says. You'll be soaked. You could catch cold.

I'm fine. Let's just go. The sooner we go the drier we'll be.

But the faster we go the wetter we'll become, she says, stating this with such certainty it sounds scientific.

Helena stands her ground, holding the small pink umbrella and pointing it at me like it's some sort of weapon, meaning for me to take it. All I can think to do is to walk ahead of her, thinking that she'll follow if I do. And she does follow, finally, keeping a solid distance between us, holding the umbrella high above her head as if it is a lamp, as if she, not I, is leading us home.

When the village is in sight I think I should say something out loud, if over my shoulder, something like, *the first thing I'm going to do when I reach the petit maison is to pour a big glass of Sancerre.*

What should I say?

Helena, the unresolved is my paradise.

That I need no help in being alone, being alone is what I've come to France for. To be alone with you, of course. I know you like things settled, but that is not my way.

I know you are in France, I saw the tickets and the letter from Madame Rocet though I couldn't read a word. If I had to say today where I was, I'd say I feel like I am already here in France with you, that we are inseparable here in ways we are not there.

However, my withdrawal must go on, here or there. I must learn to be alone in a room for more than one hour. And not just alone but happy about it, not stirring, not standing on the terrace on my tip-toes looking to see if there's snow on The Sancy, if the sheep have moved from the fields near Reignant etc. etc. Every trace of the desire to walk, play, drink wine with Jean-Claude, read his old Tin-Tins, listen to Simone talk about growing up in the village, must be met and countered for the time being:

As usual though, I can't think of the things I want to say when I want to say them.

Once we reach the petit maison, walking into the village through its backside, I pour the rest of the Sancerre into a wineglass, walk upstairs to the divan, and fetch the yellow notebook to write:

The Difference Between Us

> *Peace is not in our nature. At some point, the point I desire*
> *by holding to my withdrawal, I must cease from being critical*
> *of others. I must celebrate. I must say I've done the best I*
> *might have done and let things go at that.*

> *Most of us cannot stand peace, as it means something is not right.*

THE TROUBLESOME DIVAN, OTHER ISSUES, AND A PLAN — I share the problems I'm having about the divan with Helena. The thing smells for one, having spent many years stored in the cave, a poor example of its type, mushy, not firm, well under the length I need in regard to the length of my legs. She buys a brown corduroy down-lined jacket for me in Issoire, acknowledging her commitment to my withdrawal, so I can better withstand the weather on the terrace, which changes day by day.

I insist we work out a plan for our time in France, saying *it's for the rest of our time here*, whatever duration that might be, not to be applied to time we might spend together elsewhere. She views this as my commitment to the place, agrees to stop referring to me as *Monsieur Ambivalence*, and indicates a willingness to give up swimming in the pool in St. Nectaire so that I will not have to wear the black Speedos. *You can leave them in a drawer in the bedroom or give them to Madame Rocet's son*, she says.

We work late into the night. I drink white wine and Helena drinks red, switching to tea after her first glass, drinking three cups of herbal tea to my three glasses of wine. I rip pages from the yellow notebook and hand them to Helena who writes down every idea that seems good to her in her clear, disciplined hand.

I want to go to Verdun, I say; *too depressing*, she says.

She wants to visit the Cevannes, follow the route Robert Louis Stevenson rode on his donkey, and the Gorge du Tarn. *We can do the gorge in a day*, she says, *and eat dinner in the inn in Millau, the place you liked so much, remember?*

Yes, Helena, I remember, I ate and drank so much I bounced off the walls walking upstairs from the restaurant to my room. That was a fine meal, but the bread, butter, cheese, the heavy sauce over the tenderloin, the wine, a Cote Rotie if I remember, woke me late at night. I never did get back to sleep. The bed was unstructured too, more than a little wobbly, and very small as is the custom in France.

She's a thorough negotiator, definite in her wants and needs, florid in specificities, naming precise places, dates, actions she wishes to take in the time remaining to her. But time remaining to her *is also time remaining with me*, I remind her, arguing for a more elastic framework that will allow me the time I need to withdraw and complete the task I've set myself of sitting by myself in a room for one hour, a task to which there needs clear direction of thought.

At approximately 2 a. m. Helena and I come to this agreement, as written in the yellow notebook:

1) Rise no later than 10 am.
2) Orange juice from the carton, Volvic water, coffee and croissants.

3) Choose one item of interest: a walk, a trip to Valle Chadefour, a
   meditation, a museum such as the Musee de Cochon in Tourzel.

4) Lunch

5) Nap

6) Dinner

A WHIRLIGIG OF UNPLEASANT FRICTIONS

Every morning after orange juice and coffee, I walk up to the terrace, sitting under the Stella Artois umbrella alone and un-restlessly for something more than fifteen minutes and less than twenty, to think and write. One notebook is almost filled, I'll need a new one pretty soon.

I write about Robaire and his art, whether he's a real artist or not. The painting he gave me is right in front of me. He's so proud of using only primary colors and making only crude abstract shapes, like he'd made a real breakthrough. He paints like he'd never seen another painting, like every painting he makes is the first painting he—or anyone for that matter—has ever made. The love he has for art is so sincere it leads him to believe he's a real artist, and so he makes paintings based on his belief.

But that's gone now, Robaire's given up on painting, is giving his paintings away. Ever since I found out he threw his paintings into poubelle I haven't liked the painting he gave me, and have come to dislike Robaire.

The yellow notebook fills up with these kinds of things.

Today, two or three minutes into my time alone on the terrace, a terrible sound interrupts me. As there is nothing to be done, I close the yellow notebook and walk to the edge of the terrace. The sound has become a loud whine, a whirr, a whirligig of unpleasant frictions...

...the sound may be traced to Robaire's house across the lane. God knows what Robaire's drilling, but he goes on into the late afternoon, a madman intending to close up the house and leave for Brussels in the morning.

WATCHING ROBAIRE, IT'S LIKE GOD HAS CANCER

Jean-Claude, witness to Robaire' madness, watches from his dutch-door in the evenings as Robaire walks back and forth in the lane, hands behind his back, talking to himself.

Robaire's stopped smoking, doesn't talk anymore with Jean-Claude, doesn't stop by the fountain in the evenings to gossip, doesn't walk to poubelle with Simone, doesn't take a drink at the little bar on the main road below. It's like he's become disenchanted overnight with the Auvergne and wants to put a For Sale sign on the entire countryside and leave France as soon as he can.

God, I say to Jean-Claude, *think what it must feel like to be Robaire. It's as if god has cancer*, for Robaire, for all his faults, and whether he is or is not or was or was not the artist he thinks or thought himself to be, once had a presence in which he dwelled, not unlike a god, almost completely within himself as an artist and a man. *This is a different creature we're seeing now*, I say, *and not the Robaire we've known, and so is not Robaire at all.*

Jean-Claude only shakes his head at what I say, almost imperceptibly, so that I might interpret the movement as either his agreement with what I say or his continuing mystification and sadness.

The problem with Robaire is that he's not French, I say to Jean-Claude. *He suffers from his not being what he thinks he is or what he thinks he wants to be.*

Jean-Claude isn't listening, perfectly within his rights, rolling a cigarette instead. I watch him sprinkle the tobacco into the paper with one hand in one unwasted motion, then roll the white paper in the fingers of his other hand until a kind of perfection's achieved and he feels it's right to bring the paper to his lips for a quick lick of the gummed edge of the paper and the completion of the cigarette.

You can't imagine, can you, what is feels like to be without cigarettes, Jean-Claude says. *Being without cigarettes' is the worst feeling in the world. And since you can't imagine you have no concept of what it feels like to be Robaire, living without something he loves. He's a very lonely man.*

I will take this cigarette to Robaire, Jean-Claude says, holding the cigarette like it's some kind of prize.

THE VILLAGE   The whole village is affected, even those who
IS INFECTED   don't know Robaire and Monica.

Every morning Robaire drills deeper into the old stones, dissembling fix-
tures, built-ins, the wood stove he attached to the fireplace in the living
room. *Mr. Bricolage* as Monica called him in better days when he was so
happy fixing up the old place, smoking cigarette after cigarette, putting
in hours of work, new kitchen, new bath with a shower, new stairs to the
upper bedroom chamber, now dismantles everything he's made in the
house. The place is almost down to the nubbins, it exists only to be sold.
Robaire's cut down all the ivy that grew over the stones, closed the shutters, sealed off all possible entries and exits.

Monica wears a white scarf around her head when she appears outdoors
as some sort of demarcation, a sign of her difference from others. She
invites Simone and Helena for drinks, but they decline, not knowing what
to say to her about Robaire. She's down to Thierry, with whom she drinks
the champagne of Saumar, punctually at noon.

It's very weird when Helena finds Monica stealing flowers from the window boxes of the petit maison. Geraniums, bachelor buttons, daisies. Not
that Helena wouldn't have given Monica the flowers, which belonged
by law to the owner of the petit maison, Madame Rocet, but it seemed
odd. Beautiful, gracious Monica standing on her tiptoes in her white
espridelles, picking the flowers in the window box of the petit maison,
making a bouquet with one hand and tucking her lovely silver hair behind
her left ear with the other.

Monica's to blame for Robaire's situation, Simone says to Helena, *taking
cigarettes away from him*. It's her opinion that Robaire became a cipher
as soon as his cigarettes disappeared. He had a cough, Monica insisted
he see a doctor. One thing led to another. Robaire's *change* came in the
course of a week when he began walking alone in the lane, talking to himself; in two weeks he disliked his stone home, then the village; by week
three he offered the house for sale.

Stopping smoking's not something to be talked about in the village, a
subject that shouldn't be discussed, a taboo even at the highest levels
of friendship. When I bring it up one night at dinner with Simone and
Jean-Claude, thinking it might be good if Jean-Claude stopped smoking,
Simone, a non-smoker, admits she buys tobacco for Jean-Claude when he

asks her to, then shifts the conversation.

I ask Jean-Claude if he gave the cigarette he rolled the other day to Robaire, as he said he would.

I thought about it, he says. *Every time I see Robaire walking by himself in the lane at night or hear him with his electric drill in the afternoon I'm tempted to roll a fresh cigarette for him and a fresh one for me and walk toward him with the cigarette and light his cigarette for him and take a nice drag and then hand it to him so things could once more be the same.*

But you did see—don't you—the way Robaire held his cigarette? Between his middle finger and ring finger, Jean-Claude says. *That's wrong. You must hold a cigarette between your thumb and index finger in either hand, either hand is ok.*

When I saw Robaire hold his cigarette the way he held it, I didn't like him anymore, Jean-Claude says.

LOSING FRIENDS   It's now public knowledge that Monica and Robaire are leaving the village. Helena overheard them being discussed at the boulangerie—they're referred to as *the Belgians*,

It's a shame they're leaving, they're such beautiful people, as much a part of the place as I was or Teradact or even Jean-Claude.

I met them on my first walk down to the river, strolling arm in arm just beyond the old milkman Pepe's grange. Monica leaned on Robaire as they walked, the taller of the two, a great beauty in the classic manner, her profile in greek or roman as might be seen on the head of a coin, the kind of woman men thought beyond them. It could still be imagined they made love, as it could still be imagined of Simone and Jean-Claude, though differently.

Bonsoir I said.

Bonsoir, both of them said, smiling. I understood them to say they were on their nightly *promenade*, walking a small white plastic bag to the poubelle.

Everyone in the village is of a different opinion. Robaire has inoperable cancer of the brain, Monique misses her son and daughter in Brussels, Robaire is on trial for mis-appropriation of gymnasium funds in Belgium,

Monica has a lover in Bruges. They're out of money and must return to work; no, they're moving to South Africa for the sun.

MONICA, THE
MEEK SAINT
Monica knocks on the door of the petite maison and gives Helena a bouquet of the flowers she picked from the window box plus a dried sunflower from her own garden as if nothing's out of the ordinary.

She tells Helena their house was full of *holes*. Robaire's drilling was half purposeful and half random, he drilled into many of the stones simply for the sake of the drilling. She'd bribed him with a cigarette to stop.

Monica and Robaire are taking the direct flight from Clermont-Ferrand to Brussels. Their son, a school teacher like Robaire, will come for their things.

THE GOSSIP
OF SILENCE
It's been a week since Monica and Robaire left. No one talks about them anymore, in fact, no one's talking. The little village takes a vow of silence on this and other matters. All households live behind their stones.

It's better for me that they're gone. It was such a distraction, the dysfunction of Robaire's walking in the lane and the cloud it cast on the village, the loudness of his drill. I'd had to think about the unhappiness in their house as Robaire made it ready for sale without knowing what their unhappiness was.

All I hear when I'm on the terrace the week following their departure are doors opening and closing, and only one or two of them a day. Then for reasons never known, we slowly come out of our houses and meet one another again by chance, each of us who knew Monica and Robaire, all people of some consequence in the village, beginning with Jean-Claude and up to and including Simone, Helena and myself, to take turns at explaining what might have happened.

It doesn't matter who talks first, or who said what, though I clearly remember what I said and I said this:

> Robaire's issue was one of power. He felt out of control, felt he had to reassert himself and his reassertion took a neurotic form. He felt he was having too good a time in France, felt repentance was in order, and so he had to think—hence the walking in the lane with his hands behind his back—and the thinking caused him to lose interest in France.

It's so sad, Simone says. *He didn't talk to me for at least three months. If he saw me walking in the village, he'd cross to the other side of the lane, keep his head down. I could have said something but it was so clear that he didn't want anything said.*

Jean-Claude frowns. *When Robaire walked in the lane by himself, he talked all the time. But he mumbled, or else what he was talking was nonsense, and I couldn't make out what he was saying.*

I tried, I even stopped him once. He held his hands behind his back when he walked, like a real philosopher might, like your friend Pascal once walked, like he was working out some problem. The sounds he made were unintelligible, complete nonsense as far as I could hear. He looked like he was thinking but if he was thinking the sounds he was making were not the sounds of good sense. It's possible that even he couldn't understand what he was thinking.

By this time, I did not know this man Robaire nor did he seem to know me.

Helena says Robaire should look for a psychiatrist, then take whatever medication the doctor proscribes. Her view is that Robaire is trapped in a depression without knowing he's depressed, the worst kind. *He's deluded*, Helena says, *and how do I know he's deluded? That I've never seen anyone change more quickly from someone healthy to someone sick.*

(I note how everyone—Simone and Jean-Claude—nod their heads. Once again, because she says what she says so forcefully, what Helena says is believed because of the force with which she says it.)

Robaire should never have stopped smoking, I say. *The moment he stopped was the moment that began his downfall.*

No, says Jean-Claude. *The problem with Robaire is that he's not as French as he wanted to be. And he realized he never would be French, no matter how hard he tried. He realized he was living a pretend life.*

Simone speaks what become the last words on the subject. Her voice comes out of nowhere since she'd just a moment ago been sobbing as she stood in the square with the rest of us.

About Robaire, you are all right and you are all wrong. In the end, Robaire simply became the kind of man who could see no future and became sick because of it.

Whatever the case, their big stone house is all wrapped up, a large **For-Sale** sign posted over the big window beside the front door. And who's going to see it? No one. Visitors to the village are rare—a handful of walkers a year at the most. Someone says that neither Monique or Robaire really care if the house sells or doesn't sell.

POSTSCRIPT FROM BRUSSELS   Most everyone in the village has forgotten them when Monica calls Simone from the hospital in Brussels where Robaire's taking *treatment for his heart*.

She tells Simone that she walked into Robaire's hospital room yesterday. He wasn't in his bed. His doctor couldn't say where he was. *Robaire was just* here, his nurse said, *he'd eaten all his lunch, a very healthy appetite he has*, doctor said, his hunger's *increased since he started smoking cigarettes again*.

Monica thought he was a goner, had the hospital turned upside down, fearing he was either dead or misplaced, wandering as he had in the village, talking to himself while he walked with his hands behind his back. She'd called the police, believing Robaire kidnapped, the victim of organ pirates.

They found him upstairs in the surgeon's lounge, sitting in a leather chair in his hospital gown, looking out the window at the city of Brussels, smoking a cigarette.

I'd rather die in France than be in this crappy little hospital room, Robaire supposedly said.

Monica's making plans for them to move back to the village, or so Simone says.

BOOK SIX

For what in animals is nature we call in man wretchedness;
by which we recognize that, his nature being now like that
of animals, he has fallen from a better nature which once
was his.

Pascal, *Pensees*
409

I keep reading *Pensees*, and wonder while I read
why I'm reading it. I'm probably the only person
in France reading Pascal. It's not like I understand what I'm reading, I
understand only a little here and there. The passages I understand I write
down by hand in the yellow notebook. Reading and writing still feel like
the right thing to do with my time—and time's a matter of doing what's
right—but I'd feel better if I was having my own thoughts, such as the
thought I had this morning.

Rousted awake by the rooster I attribute to Marionette, who keeps chick-
ens and a goat at the rear of her house, the major theme of Pascal's book
is revealed to me. On every page, in every entry, I see the same thing—the
distinction my friend continually makes between the self and the world.

Furthermore—by itself,

the self's good, that is, what comes from the heart and mind, if it be both,
is the true and the good, the whole of the individual, of a man such as
me. The world is what the self believes it needs to be whole, that which it
believes it is without, but is carried along by vanity, pride, desire, curiosity and so on. This is the world; that which lives without heart and mind
and needs something other than itself to be whole.

It's possible that the time spent on the terrace in pursuit of the one hour
Pascal mandated is beginning to bear fruit, that I'm on the verge of a
breakthrough. Helena however thinks the pursuit has intensified my
ambivalence, that I'm trying to think too much and that I'm thinking other's thoughts.

SHEDDING A
FALSE IMAGE I've asked Helena to stop calling me *Monsieur
Ambivalence*, I don't trust her with the name any-
more, she uses it too much and not as a doppelganger but as a familiar,
the *tu* not the *vous*. She doesn't understand that a name can become a
body, or that my name and my body belong to me.

It's the perfect name for you, she said when she heard me call myself

Monsieur Ambivalence as we biked the Loire Valley. It's my name for myself, meant to be private. She's taken it to an extreme, as if *Monsieur Ambivalence* is a fictional character to be consulted on matters that don't mean much, like choosing cheese in the outdoor market. Just yesterday she called out from the petit maison, *Monsieur Ambivalence, it's time for lunch*, without thinking that Teradact or Jean-Claude might hear here and would be amused and certainly share the name with others.

She says *Monsieur Ambivalence* is like good chocolate that stays in her mouth for a long time, or like red wine. She doesn't want to get rid of it or spit it out, it's not that easy. *Pretend I'm introducing myself to Blaise Pascal*, I say. *I can't call myself Monsieur Ambivalence.*

I tell her the name was created as a reaction to her certainty, that it's only in contrast to her, who's so sure of things, that I appear ambivalent. I say I'd prefer not hearing the name out loud any longer, that it's between her and me from now on in the privacy of our own home.

Time will tell if this impasse takes the pleasure out of being in France—the name seems to have caused a strain between us and the petit maison seems a little colder, a little more quiet than it did the day before I made my demand.

I can't speak for Helena, but I don't mind that I go to bed earlier and sleep in a separate bed.

LOVE OF A MAN DRIVING HIMSELF TO DRINK

Jean-Claude's drinking again, Peter the Dutchman says, having found empty bottles of Ricard in the ruin beside his house and attributing them to Jean-Claude. Peter takes pleasure in telling me this and says that he too would be drinking if he *were married to Simone, who now seems so sad she's crying all the time.*

Jean-Claude's at the door each time I look out from the terrace. It's like he lives in the door or just behind it, with the bottom half of the door closed and the top half open so that he can see outside. It looks like he leans over the bottom half of the door in order for the smoke from his cigarette to go outside to see for him what's happening in the village.

Not seeing one another, we don't speak, I don't wave down at him nor does he look up at me. We're aware of one another's presence, I more of him than he of me, for I have the advantage of knowing I am looking at him and he is at the disadvantage of being beneath me and looking straight out from his door which is only slightly above street level. His disadvantage causes me to love him even more and respect him for the care he lavishes on the village.

Just as Jean-Claude's not a man to shake hands with, not requiring that kind of gesture, neither is he a man interested in my pursuit on the terrace, nor would he recognize Blaise Pascal as being anything other than dead. I've never told him about the business I conduct on the terrace, which I have now defined as *the attempt to stay one hour by myself without squirming.* He wouldn't want to know this about me, unable to conceive of such a goal himself. I couldn't tell him I loved him, that would ruin the love between us, for I could only imagine he loved me, as our bond was so mystical and instantaneous it caused me to believe there was no other real concept to explain it.

It's not physical love I feel for Jean-Claude, it's the love of knowing there's another person in the world not unlike me, a love intensified by having no common language between us and communicated by something unknown to either lover. I celebrate his disinterest, cannot imagine telling him that I've come to France to learn to be alone with myself, to sit at a metal table on the hidden terrace and write in the yellow notebook.

IMAGINARY DIALOG AND THOUGHTS ABOUT JEAN-CLAUDE *I wonder what you're really doing up there?* Jean-Claude could say to me.

And I could say to him, *and I wonder what you're thinking while you stand behind the door, smoking and looking out at the village when it is, after all, only a little bit of the lane you can see, and three or four houses?* I could say to him.

Everything I need to see is right in front of me, it's all I need to see, he could say.

I could say, *But you don't seem happy. Peter tells me you're drinking in secret and leaving the empty bottles behind his house. That Ricard is nasty stuff, Jean-Claude. Are you looking out for Robaire, in the hope that he'll return?*

Peter thinks he knows many things, but like all people who think they know he's highly misinformed, which intensifies his having to know whether he knows or not, he could say.

Are you happy, Jean-Claude?

As happy as you are, my friend. I see that you've been keeping yourself mostly out of sight. So much so that Teradact asked about you the other day, who hasn't ever asked after a soul as far as I know. He asked through Thierry, who told me that Teradact asked, 'what happened to the American?'

Thanks for telling me, Jean-Claude. It's good to know that I'm missed by a man I've never met.

And what are you up to up there, my American friend? I know you're on the terrace, I can see you without seeing. And I know you see me standing at the door, which I'm getting very good at and can do for hours and hours.

If love can be said to contain facts, the facts of the love I have for Jean-Claude are these:

> That we're always interested in one another.
>
> That we're always happy to see one another.
>
> If not seeing one another, the contemplation of the other causes the contemplator to smile.
>
> That there's no other person in France who is like Jean-Claude to me and no other person in America who is like me to Jean-Claude.

I worry about Jean-Claude and his circumstance, it takes me away from my work which is to sit alone for at least one hour without distraction.

RUMOR & INNUENDO   The rumor, passed me from Helena who met Thierry in the boulangerie at the bottom of the hill, is that Simone's moving into a convent in the hills above Royat. A retreat of some sort.

It's caca the moment I hear it, though the news makes me wonder about Jean-Claude's stance at the dutch door, that he might not be looking for the village at large or for Robaire to return, but for Simone who's he lost :: :: That Jean-Claude, contrary to what he says, is looking for the past itself, which he hopes he may regain by looking outward long enough.

Simone's going to a convent?, I say to Helena after she tells me the news at dinner.

It's possible, she says as we eat dinner, a salad Lyonnais she's made. *Simone will spend some time at a retreat nearby, an old abbey that's been recently improved.* She's clearly on Simone's side, and knows more than she tells me, keeping what she knows as a point of power and perhaps from fear that if she tells me I'll tell Jean-Claude, who knows nothing of the plan.

Jean-Claude's said nothing to me, I say. *I don't believe he knows of Simone's intention to enter a convent. A convent! Jesus Christ, that's a radical move that seems beyond either one of their propensities.*

That's his way, isn't it, to keep things inside, Helena says. *There could not be two unhappier people than Simone and Jean-Claude in France at this moment.*

Helena and I sit at the table, silently. I think about how happy I am and think that she is thinking how happy she is, whether she's thinking this or not, since we are each happier than our friends. I am happier than Jean-Claude and Helena is happier than Simone and therefore we're happier than we might have been had they been happy. But are we happy, or is our own unhappiness lessened by their acute unhappiness, and transformed into a happiness only through comparison?

I clear the table and pour more wine, Les Close des Monts Cotes d'Auvergne, a Gamay I found on sale at Ecomarche. Helena allows me to pour her a second glass, watching carefully as I pour and saying, *that's enough* at a level she thinks approaches danger.

This is really nice wine, and from the region, she says, *which directly contradicts what Jean-Claude said of wines from the Auvergne...do you remember how he would pretend to spit out the local wine and call it 'weed killer?'*

Those were happy days. We were new to the village and just beginning to know one another. But things change, c'est normal I want to say but don't, smart enough now to let the silence soak through the space between us, no longer afraid of the silence between us.

I drink my wine and I drink my wine and watch as Helena drinks hers. She has the kind of mind you can see thinking.

I think it's time we do something, Helena says. *What if you gave Jean-Claude and Simone your copy of Pensees.*

MAYBE IS A GOOD IDEA Well, it's a good idea, perhaps, there's so much in my friend's book that might help them, but one reads and one doesn't and the one who doesn't read is the one who most needs my friend's book. Neither Jean-Claude or Simone read English and so the book I have, a translation into the English, could not be given to the one who reads, Simone, who needs the book less than Jean-Claude, who does not read books in either English or French.

You could easily enough get a copy of Pensees in the original French, Helena says. *There's a bookstore in Issoire, and if not there's certainly one in Clermont-Ferrand.*

Jean-Claude has Teradact's copy of Pensees I tell her, having been told by Peter the Dutchman the book was in Jean-Claude's cave, who was told by Thierry who was told by Teradact himself some years ago in the infancy of the relationship. Teradact's the one who requested Jean-Claude preserve the old book for him, that he wanted access to it from time to time to take up its reading again. Jean-Claude said to me of the book that it was *too full of Jesus*, which is what he also said of the village church, making light of what he'd seen in both places. He must have opened the book at some point, well into its second half, and found the references to Christ, to Christians and Jews, and lost interest, though it was clear that he revered the book *Pensees* as a physical object, held it in his hands as a treasure, felt privileged by Teradact's trust, saying so more than once.

Helena's gone upstairs to bed. I've poured more wine, broken off a chunk of bread and spread some St. Nectaire. I sit in front of the stone fireplace that has no fire. Staring into a fire that isn't there, I think this is as close as Jean-Claude and I will ever get, that this is as close as Helena and I will ever come to actually being together; seeing Jean-Claude standing behind the dutch door of his old house and looking out at the lane, and then collaborating with Helena to find a possible solution for Jean-Claude and Simone's situation, is as near love as I'll ever come. I have no real proof of course, it's the kind of time where nothing's actually happening, when my feelings may be catching up with my thoughts, both realizing that they're equals.

COMING TO NOTHING The idea to give Jean-Claude and Simone a copy of *Pensees* comes to nothing, so often the case with a good idea. The book's already in their possession—in its original French—and it's presumptuous to think they're in need of Pascal's counsel or would heed it even if they acknowledged a need. When Helena revisits her idea, which she does two days after its origination, it's with far less passion. Neither of us are at a point where we wish to appear to be forcing thoughts or feelings on others, so the matter drops and Simone and Jean-Claude are free to live with or without Pascal.

IN THE ARMS OF GOOD LIFE... We've taken to lying low in the petit maison, inside the stones, within the brilliance of the architecture, itself inside the genius of the town-planners of the early 13th century who arranged the village to be so brilliantly dense and private without arranging it at all. Often it's as if no one is living here, then a door is pushed open or a neighbor calls out in the lane to another neighbor and they talk for a few moments, then it is silent again.

The effect is that I start to say things I can't believe I'm saying once I start saying them.

For instance:

I'm not saying I'll come back to France…but I might, I say to Helena not long after I decide not to give Pascal's *Pensees* to Jean-Claude and Simone.

You are in France for God's sake, she says. *Even if you were in Paris, you couldn't be more in France than you are here in the village.*

Helena's taken to making fires. She gathers kindling on her walks now, dry sticks and small branches, and brings them into the petit maison, making little piles of wood here and there. I'm able to read only for an hour or so, choosing only to read *Pensees* and often reading the same passage over and over, deriving no sense at all from it, and closing my eyes. Writing in the yellow notebook takes strange turns, with passages like this:

> I've almost concluded that it's impossible to be myself,
> and so choose to live without personality, defining myself
> only in opposition to Helena, who's full of personality, so
> that my emptiness defines itself against her fullness and I have
> something of my own to share with she who's so full.

> However, not to know who I am or what I have in the way
> of a personality is also having something, as is being part
> of the community, the little village where I seem to be living,
> permitting Jean-Claude and Simone to live their lives without
> me, not saying a word to him for instance about the worry I
> have over his smoking and drinking, or of Simone's weight,
> which she admits, to Helena, is getting away from her since she
> stopped working, and to which Helena responds singularly,
> walking with Simone, encouraging her to take yoga classes in
> Champeix, without thinking something is wrong with her as
> I so often think, or that she enter the convent under any
> circumstances…

…but at the beginning of some sort of breakdown

TELEVISION AS DESIRE Now everything I say exposes the fundamental difficulty of my situation. I tell Helena that I'd like to have a tv, that images derived from a book such as *Pensees* are too ponderous, take too much out of me to understand. I'd like to sit back in a chair and receive images without having to think about their meaning, without having to make the shift from sight to thought as reading Pascal requires.

Helena stays clear by staying busy. She's found an iron pot in the cave and brought it upstairs. She'll make a stew tonight on an open fire, and the next night a cassoulet. There's plenty of wood in the cave and kindling stacked in neat piles in the petit maison . She's saved some mushrooms, bought a whole chicken at the market in Champeix, celery, leeks, carrots, cabbage. Why not throw it all in the pot, let it boil? It'll *warm up the stone house* she says.

Smelling food, all thoughts of leaving France, (of acquiring a television, of forsaking Pascal and *Pensees)* leave me. I go down and get a good bottle of wine from the cave. The wine once seemed endless, as if it replenished itself without me having to buy more, it's now clearly disappearing. There's one, maybe two bottles left of the Chateau de Tiregrand, the good red. Jean-Claude just bought a case of Chateau Lagrezette, a Cahors. I saw him lug it up the steps the other day.

Helena and I agree that it's a nice life but that some end is being come to, though it may be a different end than either of us had foreseen

AUTUMN IN THE HEART OF FRANCE   Autumn's coming, a future of eating and drinking, and almost all that's thought of is bread, cheese as well as red wine. All there is to think of is the next meal, once we've eaten, which foods might be brought together for lunch or dinner. I live as if I've already arrived and as if I'm waiting to leave at the same time, living as if there is time for everything, as I'm meant to live, though Helena lives presently, as she always has.

QUESTIONS AS APPARITIONS   Smoke's seen coming from both Teradact's and Jean-Claude's chimneys. Teradact's said to be in the Maritime Alps, if Thierry's to be believed. If Teradact is away, presumably with Madame Teradact, how can smoke issue from Teradact's chimney? Asked the question, Thierry smiles and goes inside his own home. Now he's a philosopher? Impossible! I'll knock on his damn door. First Robaire walking in the lane with his hands behind his back, pacing back and forth, and now Thierry acts inscrutably, not answering a simple question, knowing more than I know and mimicking a philosopher, walking with his hands behind his back as if he is considering great problems. I know the judge in Issoire has ordered his red car be taken away from him, that he'll never drive again.

Teradact's in his villa but it's a secret being kept from rest of us. Only Theirry knows and brings him bread, fetches it for him daily, a baguette and a caronne brought to Teradact's door every morning without anyone else knowing. I swear myself to secrecy, out of respect to Teradact, in the belief that no one other than Thierry and I are aware of Teradact's condition.

There are presently no distractions, whether outside on the terrace or inside on the divan. I say this for my own sake, as there's no one else to say it to who might listen.

For example, Jean-Claude's a whiff of tobacco smoke, an apparition I glimpse occasionally on his way to work, his bony little arms sticking out of the short sleeves of his white dress shirt, the blue tie (with company logo) he's forced to wear, wound so tightly around his neck his eyes bulge.

We passed one another in the lane yesterday. He wasn't himself. He looked down at his tie like it was the source of his sadness and shook his head, never looked me in the eye. He expected me to know what he was feeling and feel honored by the expectation, he felt the diminishment one might feel who did not have a job worthy of one's intelligence or one's time. He smoked and I might have asked him for a cigarette had I wanted one, asking would have brought him to a stop, but I didn't have a desire for tobacco nor the presence of mind to ask.

Jean-Claude, I said in passing, *I miss you. Let's have a glass of wine soon*, knowing he had good stuff, the Cahors. He'd drive to the vineyard himself, saving a few Euro's per bottle that way, a false economy as gas prices were not inconsiderable but a good reason to spend an off day, walking the vineyard with the proprietor, tasting the wines. Jean-Claude has one of the best cellars in the village, one thousand two hundred and twelve bottles, better than the banker from Paris who summers here. The cellar's in the cave, the cave full of fantastic things, the cave Peter the Dutchman called *legendary* without ever seeing it, and that Jean-Claude had promised to show me.

I think Jean-Claude smiled when I said I missed him and became a gargoyle again for a moment or two just before he said goodbye.

JEAN-CLAUDE DIAGNOSIS Jean-Claude's shrinking, which increases his self consciousness. His shrinkage isn't at all imperceptible; as he stands at the dutch door it's clear that either the door is becoming longer or Jean-Claude smaller, as the top half of his body declines in relationship to the bottom half of the door so that there's less of him, just enough to be able to see over the door into the deep workings of the village. Seeing Jean-Claude at the door, as he looks out on the lane, permits me to believe I too am seeing deeply into the village.

THE PHYSICS OF NASAL COMBUSTION CAUSE A CHAIN REACTION And then Thierry's sneezing ruins everything. I'm on the terrace, wrapped up in my *Pensee Swaddling Clothes*, as designed by Blaise Pascal, trying not to think of a thing, so close to not thinking I began to feel I am coming too close to myself, nearing at least half of the one hour by myself in a room as instructed by Pascal, when I hear the wooden door open, a footstep in the lane, and then a tremendous sudden sound.

Thierry sneezes not once, not twice, but three times and with extreme willfulness.

The sound echoes off the stones, as sound does in the lane between houses, a metallic tone that makes me think something's wrong over and over.

Thierry diverts me. He hasn't meant to but he has, and I have to start over. Starting over gets me nowhere and so I come inside.

Just when I thought I was getting somewhere, I bellow into the hollow of the petit maison without thinking that Helena's somewhere in here as well. *Thierry sneezed. The son of a bitch sneezed and sneezed and broke all the concentration I had focused on achieving Pascal's one hour. Why do people like this exist? Of what use is he?*

Helena's unresponsiveness at such moments is not her best quality, she often puts my feelings in a tomb. The day's just begun, perhaps she's down doing yoga in the cave where it's dry and just warm enough for her to take off all her clothes.

Helena, I call as I walk down the stairs.

What is it Monsieur Ambivalence?, she says, without looking up as I enter the room. She's stretched out on the sofa bed where I sleep, reading a mystery and eating cherries. *Are you having a difficult day?*

She might as well say nothing, since what she says is in a tone that isn't interested, since my time on the terrace is my time and has no relation to hers. As great as my need is of being understood, hers is to oppose whatever is understood with such certainty that a new understanding may be reached, one that more nearly corresponds to her point of view. She's never comprehended the quest, never set foot on the terrace, not even on a nice day, to take the sun, to lie naked within the privacy of its walls. The notion of sitting quietly in a room by oneself for one hour is so strange to her as to be unnecessary. She's as sure of this as I'm unsure of everything else. Perhaps it's impossible to do what I hope to do, there's no money in it as she points out, and no product other than the writing in the yellow notebook which she's never asked to see. These are only my thoughts about the situation, I could be wrong.

AN INTERLUDE   Hungry, I take the cast iron pot out of the refrigerator. *I'm going to heat up the lentils you made last night*, I say, *would you like a bowl?* She would.

Have you noticed how Simone has turned almost white since we've come to the village?, I say. *Not only her hair, but the rest of her. White may not be quite right, more like silver, which isn't a bad thing. She's vivid, glossy, and she's lost weight lately. She must be doing better, the yoga you helped her with, the walking and so forth.*

At the same time there's something very disturbing about Jean-Claude, Helena says. *I've noticed that he stands at the door less and less and that he seems smaller every time I see him.* [See how we've each come to similar conclusions about the other's concern— Helena about Jean-Claude and I about Simone! This small exchange with Helena gives me hope! After lunch, I'll go up to the terrace and try again.]

INSTEAD OF   What would I say to Helena if I could talk to her
TALKING, WRITING   without her seeing me as Monsieur Ambivalence and without me seeing her as already being so sure of everything, not talk to her as someone trying to talk her into something, to convince her for instance that the quest on the terrace is a noble one and worth her support or that it might be time to be thinking about packing up and going home, but talk to her directly, express my feelings as clearly as possible, that I am destined to stay in France until I complete my quest?

Alone on the terrace, I open the yellow notebook, and write to Helena in the slowest, most legible hand I can manage—

> *I've seen no one for 3 days, I'm doing what I always wanted to do,*
> *withdrawing, to see if I can sit alone in a room contentedly for*
> *at least one hour. I've not done so yet, either outside on the terrace*
> *or inside on the divan, in large part because...because...*

> *...I'm now able to wait as if I'm not waiting, not waiting for*
> *something better to come along, to occur, but to sit, relatively still,*
> *in the waiting itself, not for an hour perhaps but for a longer period*
> *than when I first started the project.*

> *It's like I'm leaving my own life when I'm up here on the terrace,*
> *doing what I'm trying to do, which is trying to become the person*
> *I believe myself to be...*

Should I tell her how my own writing gets in the way? It's probably a good idea to disclose whatever comes to mind.

in the yellow notebook, Helena, I find many strange things:

Shutters

humble servant of small arches
and places possessive of their owners
when nothing's heard
and it's all
hibernation
in the house of the village
show the visitor the shadow
made of stone
The hibernation
where the shutters are now blue
and open only to wake
the one staring into
the dark

stands watch
over the yellow tulip
in spring
to see how dreams
are used

Is that the river we hear?

To live inside
is to keep track
of time

CHANGING MY MIND Helena, I'm not sure whether to go forward or pull the plug. My soul's flying a white flag. Say something please! I need your certainty, even in the form of condemnation.

I come up to the terrace for the one hour, searching for one hour of self-denial, come the next day and the day after that. Sometimes I rise from the table and dance I'm so happy, or peek over the top of the wall and look down at the lane and think how blessed I am to be interrupted from my search by all the beauty! The soft hills folding one after another in the distance, the little villages that sit on top of the folds, the sight of Jean-Claude standing at the dutch-door like he's guarding the secret of the entire village of Montaigut-le-Blanc. I'm happy just to stare, why tamper with it? Why sit at attention for the time arbitrarily chosen by Pascal five centuries ago as if it's a contest in the Olympic Games? And if I ever do reach one hour, if I come to the place where I can be alone and not be restless, not want to be somewhere, anywhere, else, what then?

Writing to Helena is one thing, giving my writing to her is another, so I decide not to give her writing but to talk to her honestly. I'll talk to her when *when* is now. Better to have her ear than her eye, though mistakes may be made verbally. It's an impasse I've come to, nothing that she can solve, but she should be informed of the severity of the situation—that all I've come to France to accomplish is threatened. I'll talk to her tonight at dinner, perhaps.

I TALK TO HELENA Dinner's everything I hoped for—lamb ragout with harissa, a salad of fresh greens from Christiana in St. Julian, the last of the romaine lettuce she grew in the community garden, and potatoes, sliced and fried in olive oil. I light two large candles, set the table, try to find music on the little radio Madame Rocet's left in the petit maison. But there's no music, only farm reports, news from the BBC .

I hope to convey to Helena the differences between laughing and crying and how the differences may apply to our situation.

If I laugh it's because it's preferable to crying as a way of going through my life, as a response to what challenges me, though there are times when crying is appropriate. Overall, a laugh is more helpful, laughers live longer, perhaps not as profoundly. Let us then look at this problem as laughers.

As a cryer, I might say I was forced to come to France and that you forced me, that it was your idea, not mine, that led me here. I gave in to small roads, rich sauces, red wines, empty churches, of living in a country in which I could not speak the language. Simone is an extreme cryer, crying is the method through which she manages her life. Jean-Claude is more a laugher, to whom crying might be funny. Who would you rather know, a laugher or a cryer?

Helena seems interested, so I continue:

There is also the question of sexual relations. We have often wondered about Simone and Jean-Claude—are they having sex?—and concluded that they are having sex, that the physical part of their relationship is still alive. The question then is, 'what is private and what is not?' That we often watch other lives more intently than we watch our own.

But our lives are being watched here, make no mistake.

I'm especially uncomfortable on the terrace and don't think, under the conditions, I can fulfill the obligation I've made, however self-imposed, of sitting alone there for one hour with total tranquility and without anxiety...as Blaise Pascal indicated.

Helena, never one in danger of going too far inward, doesn't know what to say to what I've just said. She neither laughs or cries, but abandons her food and wine and stares at me. The silence in the petit maison is as profound as one of the little churches we sit in to meditate, a quiet space in which what is human is both diminished and dignified.

I continue:

I want to go back to America and watch tv. If I stay in France, I want to have tv here where I am.

I pause here, drink a little water instead of wine, then continue.

I have, by the way, been invited to Jean-Claude's cave where, I'm led to believe, there are a multitude of tv's.

I look at her and she looks at me as I say,

I wasn't supposed to tell anyone...please don't mention it to Simone, as no one in the village has ever seen the cave it's quite an honor. I don't know why I've been chosen. One night, Jean-Claude asked me and I said 'yes.' I believe  *this might be the new question to which I devote myself in whatever time remains to me in France: why was I asked to see Jean-Claude's cave?*

Helena, having set aside her wine, thinks as she responds. I see it in her eyes:

You are the exact opposite of Pascal, she says. *You are kinetic and fight your kineticism with a physical deprivation you believe to be spiritual. Your attraction to Pascal and the attempt to sit alone in a room without restlessness for one hour, is a direct challenge to your being. And no one, short of a saint, is capable of such a thing, of denying their own being, of who they are.*

By now I've re-filled my glass. Helena's invited it, leaving the bottle on the table, knowing I like wine more than she does, that it keeps me happy.

You always have a something intelligent to say, a comeback, I say. *And you may be right about most all of what you say. But the big problem with having to have a comeback is that it proves that you live thinking you have to be right. And I don't know that I want to live like that.*

We stand at rue Impasse, facing each other. Her one blue eye and her one green eye look at me, my blue eyes look at her, we wonder what we are seeing, if we're seeing the nothingness in each other and whether or not we must be together.

It might be true that you don't have to be right, she says, *but you always have to win. And what is the difference between being right and winning?*

WE WALK AMONG
SECOND THOUGHTS
Helena decides to walk to Ludesse for the apple festival, a long walk to a little village crammed between two small hills and often bypassed. Somewhere between Thierry's sneeze and my withdrawal from the terrace I'd missed a lacuna— that time when I was ripe for things to come to me—and was at such loose ends that I agreed to walk with her.

Ludesse isn't here or there as far as a village. Inside the village itself, which I'd visited a handful of times, I feel as a man might feel between the breasts of a smallish woman in not unpleasantly plump country. I under- stand there are apples in Ludesse but have never seen any. The apples being celebrated must be in orchards out of town, I mused, as Helena and I started walking, the cold cracking our jeans.

Walking, we must pass through San Julian. I suggest we stop at Antonio and Christiana's to see how they're progressing on the restoration of their recently acquired villa. I was positive that Antonio would offer whisky, since Christiana permitted him a whisky or two when I was in the house, and show us new paintings. I'd remarked of my admiration for his art and asked the price of several paintings, seeing his evolution as an artist as remarkable; he no longer painted landscapes of our village, the church, the chateau etc. etc. but self-portraits in which he assigned himself his- torical roles, adorned in costumes of the ancient and contemporary world, up to the space-age helmet of a Russian cosmosnaut.

We decide against stopping and walk on toward Ludesse, hearing, as we walk through San Julian, live music booming from the equally small vil- lage of Ludesse, a rock & roll band, no doubt a part of the apple festival proceedings.

The band is finishing a song, "Hotel California," the homemade display stands are being dissembled and the traveling carnival rides for the chil- dren being loaded into idling semis when we finally arrive in Ludesse. The effect on us is of walking into a lively party and having the conversa- tion stop.

We should have come earlier, Helena says, *but I'm always so afraid of dis- turbing you. There are times when I don't know what to do. I see you out there on the terrace or on the divan, I try to be as quiet as possible, to make myself as invisible as I can. I don't want to be a distraction.*

TRUDGING HOME   Helena and I continue to share a desire of never wishing to walk the same path twice and so take a different path back towards the petit maison, walking along a dirt road and through the beet field toward home, seeing our village within minutes of departing Ludesse, the outlines of the church and chateau rising steadfastly on the pointy little puy.

I'm walk-heavy, trying to trudge forthrightly, feeling around for my next breath as if I'm walking in the mountains. The cold's a big frozen breath, inhaling and exhaling over the plain. Helena walks faster on the other side of the path, her hands in the pockets of her coat. I think of the whisky I might have had with Antonio—how one whisky might have changed everything for the better, made the disappointment of the apple fair less keen. Walking, I'm filled with images of things I haven't done or didn't do when the time was right. What I might have said the other night had I wished to be understood. While I've been faithful, making time for the terrace every morning after orange juice and coffee, resisting invitations from Helena to explore more of the Auvergne, reading nothing but Pascal, often saying *no* in the morning to the pre-agreed *one item of interest* that Helena and I typically determine the night before, results do not seem commensurate with the commitment.

Helena slows, stops and turns toward me. Her impatience is palpable, demonstrated by her walking ahead of me purposely and turning around suddenly as if she'd just remembered I was there, putting her hand on her hip as a sign of intolerance, standing in the middle of the beet field, sighing ever so slightly so that if I hear her sigh she can deny she is sighing. The situation's so potentially poisonous I feel as if my feet might spoil the beets.

What are you really doing up there on the terrace? she asks out of the blue.

I'm doing philosophy I say, my voice not sounding quite right.

Helena hums. When she says *up there* she means the terrace or the divan, the time I practice withdrawal, the pursuit of Pascal's one hour alone.

It's not just the time spent, I say, *but how the time's spent, restlessly or contentedly.*

Well, they're worried about you, she says.

Who?

Thierry, for one, she explains. Helena says Thierry came to the door yesterday, bringing her another little treasure, a porcelain doll he'd found in the flea market in Paris. It was small, and fit in the suitcase he'd given her with the two bottles of Vosnee Romanee she'd bought from the winemaking Grivot family in Beaune and meant to take back to America.

He's brought something over every day, Helena continues. *A parasol, an antique cheese grater, a hand-sewn peasant vest, walking sticks from Salers, one for you and one for me he specified, cologne with a spritzer, hand-knitted doilies from Quimper…don't you hear the knocks on the door?*

Helena, we need to keep walking, I say. *It's very cold …perhaps we should stop in St. Julian and visit Christiana and Antonio*, thinking how nice a whisky would taste now and of the pleasures of talking with people who keep up with the arts.

We resume walking.

You must hear when Thierry knocks on the door, Helena says, *the sound goes right up the stairs and up to the bedroom. If you're on the divan, you must hear him knock. I suppose I can understand not hearing if you're outside on the terrace. Your ears must be numb out there…*

While she talks I feel like I'm walking downward right into the center of the earth, as if I may be doing damage to the countryside, each footstep boring a hole into delicate tissue.

JUST PAST THE BEET FIELD, I GET EVEN   We reach the far end of the beet field before the field becomes the village of San Julian, agreeing not to stop for a visit with Christiana and Antonio but to continue on toward our village and the petit maison.

I've not said a word to Helena, not knowing what to say for some time, nor has she said anything since her last outburst.

Wanting to say something right out of the air, so as to disturb Helena's walk in the manner in which she'd disturbed mine, I finally say, *Helena, what about the dinner at Simone and Jean-Claude's? That didn't turn out so well. You said yourself you wished you hadn't gone.*

The flowers were a mistake. You meant well, but the flowers were wrong, wrong, wrong. No one had died! The flowers made Simone cry! I saw her put the flowers on her mother's grave the next morning. We'd wanted them to think well of us, hence flowers and the two bottles of wine, both reds when we should have brought a red and a white, something for them to put in Jean-Claude's cave.

It was far more fun when we weren't concerned about how they thought of us. We had more fun looking at Jean-Claude's "Tin-Tin's," playing his old harmonica, making the gargoyle jokes, laughing about politicians, the French system.

And what was that oil Simone soaked the white asparagus in? Was it of walnut? Inedible. And the bread was old. Jean-Claude didn't eat a thing, smoked cigarette after cigarette...

THE LAST DINNER PARTY   We ate with them last night.

At midnight the snow takes us by surprise. Jean-Claude and Helena and I stood by the dutch door and watched the big bright spots of snow falling in the lane while Simone washed the dishes and listened to a symphony on the radio.

Jean-Claude opened the top half of the door, reaching his hand out to catch snowflakes. I thought he was playing again, but he was seriously bringing the snow inside to prove to Simone it's winter.

Suddenly, Jean-Claude disappeared, returning with a bottle of champagne. *Watch*, he said, holding the bottle in one hand and a knife in the other, pulling the cork while simultaneously sticking the knife down the bottle's throat so as to stifle eruption. *Voila*, he said, holding the bottle above his head and titling his head back, pouring the first of the good champagne into his open mouth, making a clean pour, leaving a good two to three inch space between his mouth and bottle so that we could see the champagne travel from the bottle to his mouth.

Simone was washing champagne flutes when the phone rang. She answered as if the phone always rang at 1 a.m., then handed the phone to Jean-Claude, shaking her head as if she was sorry for him.

It's Madame Charnes, Simone said to us, *she's crazy. After she calls the mayor, she always calls Jean-Claude. She's lost her mind and Jean-Claude's a fool to talk to her. He gets nothing for it, he just listens until she stops talking.*

She's rich, she made a fortune singing in Paris. That's her house near the square, the one with the porcelain chicken on the mansard above the front door. You've never seen her, I'm sure. She never goes out.

She's been drinking with Thierry again. Thierry goes to her; she buys the wine, and they drink together. I took her soup once, that was enough. I had to leave it at the door. She never returned the bowl or the ladle....

We watch as Jean-Claude, holding the phone to his ear as he rolls a cigarette, says *oui, oui* every so often. Otherwise he nods at the phone, smokes and his sips champagne. He doesn't notice that we're leaving.

Helena and I kiss Simone goodnight, open the dutch door and walk down the lane to the petit maison, counting footsteps to seventy-nine.

It feels to both of us that we'll never have another dinner with Simone and Jean-Claude, never again spend the time we've spent with them, eating, drinking wine, laughing, looking through Jean-Claude's trinkets, listening to him play harmonica, listening to her crying.

HELENA'S CERTAIN UNCERTAINTY   Helena says days after our dinner with Simone and Jean-Claude, *we must accept no more invitations.*

She asks me to start keeping a record of my time in France, as if by observing things moment to moment and noting them in the yellow notebook certain goals might be accomplished. She seems devoted to my withdrawal, whereas in the past it caused unspoken tension between us, the worst sort of tension between two people.

She's in favor of the terrace as well, not that she ever said she was against it—she hasn't—but she'd made several comments about its remoteness, that a door could be closed between us, whereas the divan posed no such problem, on the divan I was inside the petit maison, as devoted to my withdrawal as ever, yet without physical separation from her.

Now she urges the terrace, noting however the cold weather, advising me to wrap up, wear wool socks, the knit cap, long pants, at least two shirts and a jacket, gloves if necessary.

Gloves? I said, affronted. *Gloves!* repeating the word! Knowing she'd seen me writing on the terrace, sometimes at great speed, having filled almost three of the yellow notebooks, how could she think I could wear gloves while writing? Wearing the knit cap was a concession, as thinking seemed less accessible when something such as a hat or a cap sat on my head, but necessary as a great deal of a body's warmth escapes from the head. Gloves, however, were out of the question unless gloves could be found that let me grip my pen convincingly yet with some tenderness, as necessary when writing.

Helena's demands constitute a crisis, as they're unexpected and come at a time when I expect the other Helena, whom I've known for some time and with whom I have shared the greatest intimacies, to be opposed to my further withdrawal and hence the one farthest from my best interest. By asking me to keep an even more diligent record of my time here, I could see she was encouraging, however unconsciously, what I myself was hopeful of encouraging: a more thorough knowledge of myself, of my situation in the world.

Yet would this be living in the spirit in which we'd agreed to live in the village?

True, she'd not eaten a steak and no meat other than the sausage she'd eaten at Thierry's barbeque—only eating half of it. She'd kept her word for the most part. Money hadn't been the issue here as it was there, no one had asked Helena or I how much money we had or what we did for a living. Our circle of friendships is as wide an arc as possible in such a small space and includes the employed and unemployed, the old and young, rich and poor, those who valued thinking and those who did not, the active and the indolent...

...and to keep a strict record, as Helena urged, seemed not to be living as we agreed to live and therefore not real life, which is to let time go by without thinking of time as we had once thought of it.

IN JUST A MOMENT
JEAN-CLAUDE KNOCKS
ON THE DOOR
The earlier I rise the more ideas I have (or think I have) the ideas themselves often waking me at night when I wish to be asleep. And though I'm committed to my pursuit, thoughts come to me on the terrace as opposed to ideas which are much different.

Every morning I begin on the terrace by imagining a place with no men or women in it—no Jean-Claude, Thierry, no Simone or even Teradact, who's all but vanished anyway, allowing my imagination to have an actual starting place, as none of the aforementioned correspond to my current state, my being on the terrace or the divan, which is now smaller and more circumscribed. I yield to France by seeing this way, by seeing how much withdrawal I can bear.

Increasingly it's important I close my eyes and stay here in the village, follow that path which is no path—exactly its point—where it leads, although the path is fraught with wanderings, diversions, circularities, and has no discernible destination.

Time and time again, my eyes closed, Helena comes to me, though it's not like she's here on the terrace with me. She's out somewhere with Simone or Christiana, doing yoga, or walking, or below in the kitchen making lentil stew. Sometimes I can hear her down in the kitchen with her pots and pans, having turned Madame Rocet's little radio on to the BBC. With my eyes closed I make her just the way I want her, her dimple intact, widening her smile which is her acceptance of me and is therefore a token of my acceptance of myself, changing other small things about her, not in her body, which suits me, but in her mind, in the way she sees me.

In just a moment, Jean-Claude will knock on the door.

TERADACT'S   Jean-Claude says Teradact's bought another dog!
NEW DOG   The ninth spaniel. No wonder I haven't seen him,
though I really haven't been looking. Teradact's slipped from my grasp. There will probably be no encounter, I'm pretty sure he's going his way as I'm going mine.

His habits have changed. I followed them for a time, tracing his descent every morning to the boulangerie and his ascent to the villa, discerning the patterns with rigorous patience. I was pleased by my devotion, but now it seems as if I've learned from the great man as much as I am meant to learn.

Teradact teaches circuitously, leading me one morning as I followed him, at a discrete enough distance so that he didn't know I was there, down the steep hill to the boulangerie where he bought his bread each morning. It was there that I met the blonde who owned the boulangerie, the woman who'd taken a younger lover, and learned that she was the mother of the young man who'd made the music Helena and I had heard on our first walk into the countryside. The instrument was a sitar and the young man was besotted with it, hoping he could make a living by playing music rather than working as a lawyer.

I assured her that her son made beautiful music, describing the sensation I'd had when hearing him play that day beyond the cypress trees, as *like hearing the music of gods. This is the world I've always wanted to live in!*, I thought when I first heard the music. Lately he'd been playing Bob Dylan songs on his sitar.

She smiled and said that his father, her former husband, wanted the son to study law and this had caused conflict between them. The husband lived in Paris, pursuing a divorce, while mother and son lived in the big white house lined by cypress trees on the road to Olloix just outside of the village, where she'd taken her young lover.

TERADACT CORONATION — Teradact's here, there's evidence of his presence though he's not to be seen.

Knowing Teradact's here, having forensic evidence, I am, however, shy about seeing him. The worry is that if I see him, he will not see me. And if I am to see him, I in turn need to be seen by him. Of this there's no guarantee. I'm told Teradact isn't seeing well, has had trouble with his eyes for some time, curtailing excursions to the boulangerie. Were I to solicit him—that is, to approach his door and knock, seeking recognition—it's possible he won't respond or, responding, neither recognize my need of seeing him by seeing me. Not that I expect him to say my name, my name might come later to him, once the formalities of an introduction are made. A simple nod, a hand put forward, an invitation to enter his home would be enough.

King Teradact: the designation is the smallest component into which he may be reduced. So powerful, he says nothing nor feels compulsion to reveal himself, and stays inside, hidden, so that a subject is the one put into the position of having to approach him. Furthermore, The King is unapproachable, other than to a subject such as Thierry, willing to take humility to a new degree, with little status in the village other than that of a misfit prone to alcoholism. That so humble a man has such exclusive access to The King is humbling. I am tempted to make a friendship with Thierry—a friendship I would otherwise not be tempted to make—to gain access to Teradact, but my better nature prevails however, thinking the thing through and seeing that such access would compromise the promise such a meeting might hold for me.

TERADACT VOID   Without Teradact what am I to do?

The question rephrased: how am I to live in France knowing he's not to show up in my life at some point, having made the decision earlier not to go to him, not to walk up the stone steps of the villa, slippery when wet, and knock on his door, but rather waiting for him to come to me?

Teradact will not be seen for some reason, nor do I force the issue by taking the unilateral step of walking up the stairs of his villa and announcing myself.

TERADACT DECISION   It's late evening when I decide to ascend the steps of Teradact's villa for the purpose of meeting him face-to-face. It's my hope that it's neither too early or too late and that he's had his dinner but is not yet asleep, and that Madame Teradact should not answer the door.

There are thirteen steps from the lane to the front door of Teradact's villa. Counting them the first time, I descend to count them again, counting them on the descent and on the re-ascension in order to confirm the original count.

Facing the front door, my hand shakes as I raise it to knock. I test my voice, in case I knock and Teradact answers. I have no voice and when I do manage a sound it does not sound like me. To knock on Teradact's door is one of those things that can't be done, that if done will have consequences far from the one I desire. So I don't knock. I walk away from the door and down the stairs, to prepare myself for the possibility of never meeting Teradact.

I'll quietly seek a replacement—candidates must be older than me and live in the village, with basic language skills in French and English and rudimentary knowledge of the local wine and cheese.

BOOK SEVEN

We do not trouble ourselves about being esteemed in the towns through which we pass. But if we are to remain a little while there, we are so concerned. How long is necessary? A time commensurate with our vain and paltry life.

Pascal, *Pensees*
149

TRUE OR FALSE?　　It's mostly to appear like I'm doing something that I continue my retreat to the terrace, in increasingly vile weather, in order to further the attempt to stay for one hour alone in my own chamber as stipulated by Blaise Pascal?

True or false?

—I've extended my ability to sit alone without anxiety, day by day, to thirty minutes, thirty -three minutes, thirty-nine, and onward through the mid-forties?

—The project's held together by monofiliment .40 lb. fishing tackle pasted to particle board and is questioned daily by Helena, who either refuses to be interested or makes time to do what she wants to do without me, based on the belief that I'll be out on the terrace or on the divan, unable to join her for what she's planned for the day?

STATUS REPORT　　My intention on the terrace faces all standard stoppages. Helena never asks '*what are you doing up there*'? as she did when I first began, doesn't care to read what I write in the yellow notebook, doesn't inquire as to the progress I am or am not making. She doesn't see the space I occupy on the terrace or the divan. When I invite her to either place, asking if she'd like to see *art being made*, she says that it's *too small a space for two of us*.

Yes, it's a cube I say. *It's small and what I'm doing is small.*

She looks at me like she might actually love me, whatever love means to her, and says,

I think of it more as a box.

It's a question in a box, I say.

I'm confused. First she's for it, then against, then for and once again against. She stands against it presently but might change. It must be good to be as French as Helena.

RESOLVE   When the weather turns wild and much colder, I get up and walk off the terrace and come just inside the petit maison and lay on the divan.

I'm determined to achieve Sixty minutes—(and it will be attained, perhaps out on the terrace where the air is clearer, though I'm forced to bundle up there, as Helena insists, inhibiting prolonged concentration. Hat, coat, wool socks, gloves. It's the only time she actually looks at me, making sure I'm dressed for the terrace. *That's real snow*, she says, pointing to the Sancy. *French people are skiing up at Super-Besse*. She watches as I dress in the mornings, makes a thermos of hot coffee like she's sending me out on some great expedition. *You need to love yourself more, love yourself enough to take care of yourself and not get sick)*—

I don't mistake her words of solicitation for love or for any real interest in my project.

Perversely also, new projects present themselves, in no apparent order, that interfere with my purpose:

     1. To find, i.e. identify Teradact's replacement before his demise.

     2. To obtain a television.

     3. A visit to Jean-Claude's cave, promised long ago but never activated.

     4. The proposal of a trip to Verdun to see the World War I landmarks there.

HAVING LOST WHAT WAS ONCE   Once, some comfort was to be gained on the terrace when I hear familiar voices, voices I know the sounds of, knowing who'd gathered beside the square. Now no one's there, I hear nothing, I no longer hear Teradact's car humming in the early morning or Robaire's drill bit or the heavy wooden door closing on Thierry's house. No one comes knocking on the door of the petit maison. Silence has most of the life there is.

LIGHTING A CIGARETTE CHANGES EVERYTHING   My back, everything I can't see about myself, hurts me most the very moment I begin to place my eyes inside myself and look around. I suppose it's only a strain, feeling for it and feeling only some fine hairs down there where my back is fashioned to get to the bottom of its self, its backness, where it could wave goodbye to me if I was to get up from the terrace or the divan and abandon the project of being alone there for at least one hour.

In retrospect, there's no indication I could ever sit still—no precedence or propensity. From the moment I was born I was born restless, wherever I am is the place I least want to be. I live in a state of constant change, and if not change then the desire for it, the desire creating a cupboard full of diversions to which I've become addicted at one time or another.

Everything changes when I light a cigarette.

Not long ago I'd stop every evening and ask Jean-Claude for a smoke on my walk down the hill to the river, seeing him leaning out the top half of the dutch door, smoking and watching his poodles play in the little lane. He'd roll up a cigarette in a hurry and off I'd go. Happy at the time of anticipation and miserable the moment after I lit the thing, I'd smoke by the river, standing on the little bridge in the dark above the water, watching everything become something else, something they weren't, the moment I inhaled the first smoke.

THE MOMENT MY EYE HITS THE RIVER   I always walk myself to the river, always a different path down the hill, a different lane, there being infinite way to descend, where the river waits all alone for me. The river's my only exercise. The walk down the hill walks off the wine I drink, the bread and butter I've eaten, the cheeses of the Auvergne, cheeses so important that the world can't be conceived without them, the walk up hill works off all other excess.

The moment my eye hits the river I'm taken, but where I've yet to know. Perhaps somewhere far more important. Sometimes seeing the river is all I need, as I'm much better at seeing than hearing, the dark sound of the water like a secret being shared between people I love who won't tell me what they're talking about.

I stand by the river more than one minute and less than five, then meander by The Marie and the main road. Passing Monique's restaurant, shuttered now, I look toward the river, wondering where she drowned. The Marie's dark, the recycling bins locked up, the other little shops closed up tight.

From the bridge, above the river, facing the direction of the water running right at me, I see I have everything that is possible: Helena in the stone house at the top of the hill, making something of the fallen pears she's found on her own walk, stirring red wine and sugar in a saucepan; Jean-Claude either at work or standing at the dutch door or watching tv; Simone either happy or sad, not entering the convent as previously believed.

The neon yellow and red lights of the sign atop the bar and tobacco shop sparkle through the darkness of the river. That the tobacconist is a man I'll never know makes me sad. I've heard his laughter several times, walking past his shop in the evening, concluding from the sound that he's a man worth knowing. A man's laughter is his signature, the sound defines him as much as what he laughs at, and from the sound of the tobacconist laughing I hear a good man, not a great man perhaps, but a man able to stay for hours in one place, his little shop on the main road beside the boulangerie to which he's affixed a patio in the rear and where he serves drinks in the spring and summer.

I walk every night, though the small but sometimes excruciating pain on the left side of my mid-to-upper back, a knot of a strained muscle or a pinched nerve perhaps, contracted, most probably, on one of the many vigorous walks Helena and I have made across the countryside (perhaps on the walk from Boudes, after lunch and the bottle of Sancerre at the inn in Boudes, to the Vallee of Saints in the heat of late summer, climbing the red dusty rocks without water, becoming dehydrated and disappointed in the scenery, one of the few treks which were ill-planned and not repeated), increasingly keeps me from my walking.

SMOKING AND NOT SMOKING   Smoking prompts thinking but kills ideas, but when I'm thinking or trying to think I want to smoke one cigarette after another.

Smoking, I am standing beside a small river in the middle of France; smoking, a veil of sameness drapes itself over all things and the river becomes every river I've ever seen, the sound of it the same as every other river in the world, nothing special, just water.

Not smoking, all the change I want is in the water, in watching the river for a minute or two, alone in the dark, feeling, as I come closer and closer to myself, that it's possible that I'm getting rid of parts of my life that aren't like myself at all, but without hope of finding new ones.

Not smoking, each night is different by the river; smoking, each night is the same.

Smoking or not smoking, the time comes to leave the river.

ALWAYS WALK BACK A DIFFERENT WAY THAN YOU CAME   I walk a different way up one of the steep, narrow paths toward the petit maison, my heart taking as many footsteps as my feet, knowing I am closer the end than the beginning, not able to walk much longer down and up, the capricious pain in the small of my back acting up more often than not.

Soon I reach the places I've named—*the avenue of discouragement, death's oven, the path with failed lilacs, botched glass-block villa, place of the beautiful teenager*—and I stop to rest, only walk again when I feel rested. I keep walking and resting, walking and resting, away from the river, uphill, disappointed by the blue light I see made by the televisions inside the stone homes, the light like a fish tank of squiggly eels being passed out one-by-one through the windows and onto the cobbled little lanes...the thought of all those who are watching, watching when they could be reading, praying, thinking, *why do they sit night after night, some of them my friends, and hear and see one lie after another, lies and entertainments presented in great unnatural light, giving their time on earth to such ghostly meaningless words and pictures?*

It's one thing to see smoke coming out of a chimney and another to see the light of a television set flickering behind a lace curtain; there's life in one and death in the other. The smallness of the village overwhelms me.

GOOD WINE, BAD WALK FROM BOUDES   It's during the walk from Boudes to The Vallee of Saints that I first feel the pinch in my back, feeling poorly about walking, not wishing to put much into living the way I'd been living—heavy lunches with at least a half-bottle of wine—or hoping to change. Drinking the majority of the wine is always left to me, Helena always drinks only half a glass and I am left to drink the rest of hers, not liking to see good wine go unfinished.

Helena talks me into the walk after lunch at the inn at Boudes—chicken in heavy cream for Helena, lamb shank gateau for me; bread and butter; a Sancerre from the Loire and not cotes d'auvergne which the restaurant pushed. She'd brought her little map of the region and stretched it out on the table, pointing out that The Vallee of Saints was nearby and that we could walk there. Interesting red clay rock formations there, she said, a spiritual place, uninhabited.

I knew I shouldn't have gone, and that The Vallee of Saints would be hugely disappointing. If you're in the region I can recommend the restaurant in Boudes, La Vigne, or a walk through the villages ending in the village of Collanges with its tiny unlocked church and its treasure of frescoes, but don't advise a big lunch and a walk the same day or making a special trip to the valley.

For dehydration sets in not long after we enter the borderlands of the Vallee of Saints, the scenery itself taking on aspects of our thirst—scraggly trees and disfigured remnants of brush greeted us, red dust of our own making that got into our eyes. The first mistake is walking without water, as the day was unseasonably warm and we'd had wine for lunch; a second mistake always follows a first and I continued walking behind Helena. It's like my pain is leading me now, showing me the sights—tight corridors of strange orange and red eruptions that emanated from the crust of the earth to a height of no more than six of seven feet—when I might have stopped and followed my own instinct and turned around with or without Helena and walked back toward Boudes and water. Instead I stayed faithful to the leader, though the pinch at the small of my back began to ache and the need for water became drastic.

Of the Vallee of Saints too little can be said, other than it's a place where landscape meets mood, outer and inner, a place you might go only if you are following another and their will is stronger than yours, as there's very little to see there and no water at all.

A POEM WAITS FOR ME   The poem waits for me to walk back from the Vallee of Saints, tired, thirsty, my lower back inflamed.

The words come into the open one-by-one, like the poem is seeing the pain I'm in, and forms itself as I walk behind Helena who is walking away from the valley toward a small village she sees at the top of the hill. I think she's walking toward water, thinking she's as thirsty as I am or thirstier and suffering from the burden of being a leader.

> ...little hilltop towns in France
> with their graveyards unlocked
> and the stones not going anywhere, the flowers not going
> anywhere,
> the people not going anywhere either, the husbands and wives,
> the children who stopped living, the bachelor, he must have
> lived alone all those years
> so he could live here,
> and the new people coming up the hill, all by themselves
> after lunch,
> to this tiny village in the middle of France.
> The iron gates sound
> like they are smiling.

Helena stops near the top of the hill we've climbed, the village she saw in the distance now obscured by a tall grove of trees. So often the case in France, the closer we come to where we think we're going, the more hidden the place becomes.

She opens the gates to a small graveyard, turns to see if I'm still following, and walks into the graveyard all by herself.

I wait without her, think up a title for the poem—*Wine at Lunch*. I'd prefer the title be **revealed** to me rather than **thought about**. *Wine at Lunch* isn't quite right, something's wrong with it, tells only part of the story. Whose crazy god-dammed idea was it to walk after lunch, full of food and white wine, into the Vallee of Saints? Helena's, that's who! I didn't want to, I could have said something, she could have gone alone as I could have not gone at all. She's become this other who's always right, with whom I'm at odds or cannot please, make happy, am sure to disappoint, not being equal in her mind to the rightness I should be equal to.

Yet it's a privilege to be asked, *what should you do with your life?*, as Helena asked me while we walked in the Vallee of Saints, the question that brings me to the dead center of France, near enough to the birthplace of Pascal for there to be a plaque in Clermont-Ferrand.

The answer to Helena's question comes long after she asks. Why hadn't it come to me until now:

Some people love their lives.

With some effort, I'm finally able to like my life

for nearly an hour at a time.

THE MAN WITH
THE HUGE NOSE,
ET. AL

I begin interviews for Teradact's replacement.

A somewhat older man than Teradact who showed up in the village the other day as if from nowhere, saying he'd given Mitterand the former president a tour of Lac Chambron, is a possibility. It's possible he's telling the truth, it's possible he's a liar. He's blind but looks so strong. I know he can't see me as he speaks, that's a problem, a count against him. I want to tell him that *I'm blind too, that this always wanting to be somewhere else is a form of blindness, that we all live like we're living with our eyes closed*, but I couldn't, not knowing the language. He'd have to dress differently, the green suspenders don't work, and lose some weight.

Then there's the man with the huge nose. He has the qualities of a leader, a plumber from Egliseneuve, he's run a business. But the nose! It's as if every man in the Auvergne has put their own nose on his nose so that his nose is a veritable collection of noses. I can't help staring at it, while trying not to.

I tell Helena that a picture *must be taken*. She agreed to come to the interview but backed out at the last minute. We agreed it would be cruel to photograph his nose, whether he knew it or not. He drives a white van with the name of his plumbing company and the picture of a drainpipe, an entrepreneur. He's qualified. I make my own jokes—would his nose get in the way?—would he stick his nose into other people's business? I think I smell cognac on his breath, but it could be cheese. The nose might be a distraction, I could see how the villager's might not get around it. There's something disturbing in his eyes as well, when he looks at me it's like he's looking down the barrel of a shotgun.

My interest in Teradact wanes in direct proportion to the number of interviews for his replacement I conduct. There've been no sightings for at least a week—but I wonder how he and the wife are getting along, the only signs of life in the villa is the smoke in the chimney and the opening and closing of the one shutter over the big window.

The village smells of milk now that Pepe's son has taken over the grange, milking the cows in the grange itself rather than in the fields where Pepe milked them. A number of people have complained. There's a meeting to discuss the problem, to force the son of Pepe to return the cows to the field, tonight in The Marie at 8 p.m. but I'm not invited.

THE THOUGHTS OF A DEALMAKER Every night after dinner I wash the dishes—it's the deal I've made with Helena—scrub the pots and pans or leave them to soak in the small ceramic sink, and walk to the river. I walk with my hands behind my back, like a philosopher.

Tonight, walking back to the petite maison from the river, a swarm of tiny bats descend from the dark and brush my head like black pebbles dropped from the moon. It's different and I'm glad it happened, for I've grown tired of walking and of thinking like this every night in France, slipping into the routine of both so blithely that it is only the pinch in my back that alerts me to the danger of my habit.

I keep a list of thoughts:

1. Jean-Claude watches television as if it's the truth.

2. It's no different here than it is there, where I too was discontented, that I too am missing my life deeply, differently perhaps than the way in which Jean-Claude and the others are missing theirs, in a manner unique to me, taking so much time on the terrace and the divan, that all I'd come here to accomplish is to change, to live differently from the way I was living, to eat the cheese and bread and drink the wine, but that I was failing, vaguely and as inexactly as they were failing by watching tv night after night in conditions otherwise ideal.

3. ...there's no number 3

4. I'm floundering around in my solitude as much as they flounder around their televisions, trying to get up to one hour on the terrace alone, without distraction, without deviation from self...

...and so, I must in the time left me nurture my solitude as if it is something other than me, like it is a god, if only to honor my friend Blaise Pascal, but it might not be...

5. ...and that it's possible that not having a god is a god as well...

Breathless near the top of the village, in sight of the petit maison, alone, determined to write down the new thoughts that come to me on my walk to the river once I reach home, I see Helena's asleep, not seeing any light in the room she calls her own.

Sometimes she waits for me, making something of a dessert from what she's gathered during the day, the fruits and nuts that have fallen along the road, or stays awake by stirring lentils in the big black pot, or reads in bed, detective fiction written by Swedes or English women.

It's difficult not to disturb her, the wooden door of the petit maison makes such definite sound, like a person moaning at the scene of a terrible accident, the sounds made louder by the silence, the shock of the accident itself. So I open the door slowly, decreasing its moan, and prepare my bed, the couch that rolls open in the big room beside the kitchen. *Pensees* is on the little table I've placed next to the sofa bed, to which I add a glass of water and a yellow Kleenex should I blow my nose.

Now that we sleep separately—in recognition of the problems I'm having with my back, the bed upstairs in the bedroom where Helena sleeps unable to support me properly, and Helena's problem with the smell of the room downstairs in which I'm sleeping—I'm free to read in bed, whereas in the past I wasn't.

I open Pensees randomly, allowing my eyes to go where they want, and make a note in the yellow notebook of the entry, #229:

> *This is what I see and what troubles me. I look on*
> *all sides and I see only darkness everywhere. Nature*
> *presents to me nothing which is not matter of doubt*
> *and concern…*

Helena's the better sleeper, gets more out of her sleep. She trusts her world and sleeps almost anywhere, in cars, on trains, strange hotel rooms, in unfamiliar beds amongst unfamiliar people. I heard Helena tell Simone of the time in Paris she fell asleep at the dinner table at the restaurant Chez Mamy, sitting beside Isabelle, a Parisian who'd brought her dog to the table and who told Helena one story after another of her troubles, in French and in a voice to be pitied, leaving Helena no choice but sleep. Isabelle hadn't noticed and went on talking for another fifteen minutes, finally waking Helena by stroking the back of her head.

I'm the archaeologist, I dig into sleep well before it's really sleep, feel myself sink into its possibilities, pressing the bed from my head to my feet, testing all the exits before I enter. Prone, my head propped on the thinnest possible pillow, I think or stare, staring preferable to thinking, get ready for my sleeplessness.

Once that's settled, I set another place out for sleep itself to be beside me. *Goodnight Helena*, I call, though she's already asleep or if awake can't hear me from my level to hers. (I've come to expect no reply from her, though at first the silence hurt and I told her so. *If there's no light up here that means I'm asleep*, she says, *and if there's light up here and no reply that means I didn't hear.*)

I need less sleep now that we sleep in separate beds, particularly good sleep, good sleep measured by my waking, when waking is as good as going to sleep had been. Sometimes I want her to come to me, but all on her own, but this isn't happening; I guess she too must wish to be alone. And though I feel that she's trying as hard to have the feelings I have as I am trying to have hers, we sometimes try too hard to feel what the other is feeling.

SAYING "I LOVE YOU" OUT LOUD As the relationship between us shifts to the degree that no leader or follower can be identified, sleeping separately makes us equals. We're trying to say we love one another at least once a day, and must be sincere when saying it or it can't be said. We say the words out loud, *I LOVE YOU*, it makes us feel both worthwhile, I'm trying to have the feelings she has and she's trying to have mine. It's always odd to hear I'm loved, as odd as it is to hear the word *love* come out of my mouth, like hearing the song of a strange bird.

FORTUNATELY, INSOMNIA IS A TEMPORARY CONDITION Couldn't sleep last night, so I went upstairs and crawled into bed with Helena, who isn't sleeping either. The bed's very small and made smaller with me in it, so that Helena must place a leg over me or turn her back to me as I turn my front to her, which is bad for my back. Finally we sleep—it isn't easy—without a tension between us other than the tension of love, loving ourselves enough to leave each other alone, without knowing we were sleeping, the best part of it, and waking together, which is rare as I usually wake up alone in the sofa bed below..

HELENA, HAVING
SLEPT WELL,
LOOKS AT ME   In the morning, Helena looks at me as if I exist
only in the past.

I feel as if the past she's seeing is saying things about me, talking to her about what's wrong with me.

I preempt her, I say,

I'm paring myself down to just myself more and more.

She asks if I,

want bread, and if bread do I want butter, if butter, jam?

I think the things I once told her, I won't tell her anymore.

THE INVENTION
OF TV   Jean-Claude asks if I'd *like a television set*? He
has several in the cave, solid old color tv's, aging like wine. *Vintage tv's* he says in French. I can see the televisions he's stored there and can choose one I like, *the one that fits you*. He can't believe I live without television, the fact's beyond him. *Even Teradact watches tv*, he says.

Watching tv, Jean-Claude hand-rolls his cigarettes without taking his eyes off the screen. Watching him roll a cigarette while watching tv is much better than watching tv itself, for the cigarettes he rolls without looking are perfect, as if made by machine.

When we smoke together I think of sharing with Jean-Claude the purpose of my mission in France—to sit alone in a room for one hour without becoming restless. He might understand, telling him could explain my disinterest in television, it's possible he'd either understand or it would ruin any affection he feels toward me, change the dynamic that now exists between us the same way smoking a cigarette changes the nature of time once the cigarette's lit.

I say nothing about the interviews I'm conducting for Teradact's replacement, I keep them secret. I'm meeting a man from Paris tomorrow at the bar-tabac in Champeix, a crummy, dark little place but the only one I could think of close enough for me to walk while maintaining some distance from our village. Jean-Claude wants a man from the countryside, who knows the peace and quiet, and *the hunting*. It strikes me my quest is much more American than French. America believes in replacement, in filling voids; in France, the void is the void and a body when dead is bundled up and given a good burial in the cimiterie at the bottom of the hill.

The news about Teradact isn't good. *He's dying*, Jean-Claude says. *He's been dying for years, ever since I've known him.* Teradact's pursued slowness to the end of the earth and look where it's led him, to this tiny village in the Auvergne.

DESCENDING INTO THE CAVE As we're walking in the lane, halfway between his house and the petit maison, Jean-Claude asks me if I'd *like to take a drink before we see the cave.*

Right now? I ask.

He says nothing but turns from me as if it's understood I'm to follow.

Jean-Claude leads, tells me to watch my step and my head as we descend into his cave. It is like stepping into a small black rectangular piece of space, as if entering the painting of an abstract expressionist popular after the Second World War—Josef Albers and Ad Reinhardt possibly—in which the color black is portrayed as a primary reality. I can only see what is right in front of me—only see my hand if I put it to my face.

I've already lost Jean-Claude, can't even hear him breathing, he's somewhere. Only the stone steps, ancient and narrow, give some feedback in the dark. I place my feet on them as if I'm wading across a trout stream, tapping my left leading foot twice on the stone surface to make sure it's secure and then following with the right. Three steps down I find a wall on which to place my right hand. It too is made of stone.

Jean-Claude...Jean-Claude...are you there, I say. It's only right to whisper, anything louder than a whisper will be will be destroyed, swallowed up in the incredible throat of the cave.

I stop my descent, having walked into a total wall of silence. *Jean-Claude*, I whisper, but he's nowhere to be heard or seen. He's playing a trick? Has he fallen, banged his head on the stone and passed out? Am I being led to some forlorn place where something unfortunate cannot help but happen? What kind of friend is this who does not answer in the dark?

I can't go forward, which is to descend. The idea of turning around and walking back up the stone steps is no more than an idea, physically impossible at the moment. There's no space in front or in back of me, no space

I can feel at the present in which I might be able to re-orient my body, point it in the opposite direction and walk back up into the light. As no other action is available other than to keep descending, which is untenable, I stay still. It's not unpleasant, I'm braced by the cold stone wall, lean against it with my feet on the solid steps, knowing there are x or y number of steps leading back up to the cave's entrance and z number of steps leading to the floor of the cave itself should I have the courage to continue. The air's pure and quite cool, though not cold. Given some light, a little food and drink, this could be a good place to live. While my eyes don't adjust to the degree where I can see much of anything, it's nice to be free from the visual, like the freedom I feel when I'm not wearing my glasses.

The *predicament* I'm in is as good as an analogy as could be hoped for to describe the quest I've undertaken on the terrace, that the few moments I am spending now stranded in the darkness of Jean-Claude's cave are the most un-restless moments, the moments closest to the spirit of how I've interpreted Pascal's message, that I've yet experienced in France: that all the time spent alone on the terrace of the petit maison, writing in the yellow notebook, trying to stay still for at least for one hour and failing, has come to this.—nothing other than darkness, one foot and then another suspended upon a step, going nowhere.

You know, nobody's ever been down here before, Jean-Claude finally says, out of nowhere.

REALITY TV   The television's are pathetic, valuable only for their antique possibilities, old Zenith's and Philco's and RCA's, hanging from meat hooks from the ceiling of the cave like sides of beef. Jean-Claude sweeps a big flashlight back and forth over them, while I take stock of the cave.

It's Smaller than I imagined. No pre-war Volkswagen, as rumored by Peter the Dutchman. A row of dolls, each doll propped up and sitting in a baby's high-chair. A rock ledge on which are balanced old metal irons, medieval weapons, wine bottles whose labels had badly faded, and other bric-a-brac of unknown constitution and provenance.

I present the past to you, Jean-Claude says, pointing the flashlight at me and then at the things I'm seeing so that I can see them more clearly. He insists I take a television.

I really don't want a television Jean-Claude, I say. *I'd rather see the copy of Pensees by Blaise Pascal you're keeping for Teradact.*

WE TOAST
MY TV
Jean-Claude hops off the small cane chair he's been standing on, taking the light with him. He's turned the light off.

You must take a television, Jean-Claude says from the dark.

You really don't want a book.

A television is the present and a book is the past.

Your problem my friend is that you're living in the present as if it's the past. The only way to free yourself is to have a television, a fine vintage television.

He's standing now beside one of the tv's, on a small wooden ladder, on his tiptoes, taking the tv off the grappling hook on which it's hung for so many years. The tv's primal—a tiny screen, a tube, a mass of wires—one could look at it as if it were a piece of art.

This is a most amazing tv, Jean-Claude says, carrying it carefully over to where I am standing. *This tv will reveal the present to you in a way a book, even a book as well respected as Pensees, could never possibly begin to reveal.*

He hands the tv to me. It weighs little more than a book.

Now let's take a drink, he says. *The wine's a Burgundy from the Domaine Grivot near Autun*, tapping into the wooden cask that sits in the exact middle of the cave, tilting a wineglass so as to catch the dark red wine. He's forgotten my promise to bring Ricard.

BOOK EIGHT

For the present is generally painful to us.

Pascal, *Pensees*
149

WINE TO WATER RATIO Provisions run low. Helena makes me inventory the cave—more and more she's asking me to do things like this.

7 bottles of lesser wine and 2 bottles of the Vosnee-Romanee, a bag of lentils from le-Puy-en-Velay, 3 tins of sardines—and what's in the refrigerator, as small as it is—a bag of mushrooms, bleu cheese, pistachio nuts, coffee, two bottles of Belgium beer Robaire left on our doorstep the morning he departed, a dozen or so of the mustards Helena's collected, a bottle of Salers, a gift from Simone and Jean-Claude, a liquer made of noxious weeds...

...I lie, tell Helena we're down *to 2 bottles of wine and a dozen bottles of St. Diery water*, my wine-to-water calculation out of whack since I seem to be drinking more wine than water. I infer by my lie that we need more wine. (Antonio the artist tells me of a place to buy wine in bulk from a man in San Julian, Mr. Goujon, and I plan to buy as much red and white from Goujon as I can).

Eggs are almost all we eat now, big lustrous brown eggs of the village with golden yolks that look too big for the shells, purchased from Pepe's son. One egg's a meal, with a little butter, a spoonful of Dijon mustard stirred in, a dash of real cream. One egg keeps us going, provides the energy needed to walk down to the boulangerie for bread and a few greens now and then, butter lettuce or spinach when Chevalier has them, and walk back up. Helena's weaning me from cheese—the eggs and cream are enough dairy—though I've saved a little Pavin in its orange and blue wrapper and wrapped the last of a round of unpastuerized St. Nectaire in an old flannel shirt I've quit wearing.

I don't ask the whereabouts of Marionette's goat, but the animal's evaporated. I'd hoped to taste the cheese Marionette makes of the goat's milk—Jean-Claude calls it *"superb,"*—but it doesn't appear that will happen.

It's difficult not to want to drink more than my share of wine, wanting to make something happen, to effect change in these colder and increasingly darker days, so I pray and drink, pray and drink, thinking I've found the best of both worlds.

THE MIGHT OF
EMPIRICISM

Helena's eager to re-examine the stone hut where the leek man lived, first shown us by Madame Rocet months ago, to measure the place, stand up, sit down, stretch, assume a yoga position to see if it's possible a man of her height and weight lived there for over twenty years as it's claimed.

She hops the stone wall enclosing the garden and walks to the Hut, a structure placed in the exact middle of the garden as exactly as Notre Dame was once placed in the middle of Paris, all the roads of France hypothetically measured from it. Helena pushes on the wooden door of the hut. It won't open, so she walks the length of the structure, finding it 7 strides x 5 strides, approximately 20 ft. long and 15. ft. wide, each of her strides approximately one yard in length. A metal pipe protrudes from the southernmost side of the roof, presumably for a stove. I watch as she peers in a window of wavy old-world glass, surveying the leek man's living quarters, wonder what she's seeing.

In regard to the garden there's nothing to know, only to surmise. She can't find leeks but the garden's still a garden, remnants of tomatoes, squash, swiss chard, all gone to seed. It's clear the garden's still in the possession of an individual, is someone's garden, someone's taken great care with the furrows, harvested the vegetables, propped garden tools up against the stone hut.

She thinks it's possible a man once lived in the Hut, there's just enough space for one to imagine a bed, a table, a chair, the necessities. The garden itself has a hose attached to a hand-driven pump, which Helena pumps to prove there's water, the place seems sustainable, the man Madame Rocet calls *the leek man* may have lived here. How he lived is another matter. For he smoked a pipe, according to Madame Rocet, *you could smell his pipe all over the village* she says. Madame Rocet makes it clear that you knew when the leek man was coming, that he reeked of tobacco, garlic and leeks, confirmed by Simone, a girl at the time and as poor as the leek man if Jean-Claude's to be believed, and of the same society.

How could he have smoked in the Hut? Perhaps in summer with the door open, he'd step outside to smoke in the garden, getting the leeks ready to take to Clermont-Ferrand. How were the leeks transported, for he had no car or truck and no one in the village was ever seen assisting him?

And where'd he bathe, as being un-bathed was his undoing in the end?

AND A IMPROBABLE
ENDING TO THE SAGA
OF THE LEEK MAN

This much is known...

...an old man, no longer able to raise leeks, having lost his contacts among the markets and restaurants of Clermont-Ferrand, hoped for only one thing, to visit the South Seas, Samoa, Tahiti, Bora Bora, and purchased a plane ticket from Clermont-Ferrand to Orly, from Orly to Los Angeles, and from Los Angeles to Papette, but denied entrance to the plane in Paris, more than one fellow passenger complaining of his smell, died in the hospital closest to the airport the next day, the stone hut empty ever since.

SOME COLD
CONSIDERATIONS

I've stashed the yellow notebooks under Helena's bed upstairs for the time being.

I think the plan through while sitting on the terrace, having regressed, from upwards of forty minutes to less than twenty, unable to stay still, going backward to the state of my former distraction so that anything written in the yellow notebook is not what might have been written had I kept still. The struggle to be with myself, content for at least one hour alone, becomes a distraction, disguising itself as the object of my effort. To live up to my friend Pascal's maxim, once desired by my whole being, appears unattainable at the present though there's still time.

It's good coming to the end of something without knowing where the end is, walking into the petit maison from the terrace, clapping my hands together to shake the cold from them, taking off the woolen mittens Helena insists I wear, peeling off the wool cap, warming myself by the fire downstairs. Helena's unhappy I sit in the cold, exposed on the terrace, rather than lie inside on the divan. I see her logic. The snow swirls around me, falling on the Stella Artois umbrella and melting there almost imme-diately. Finished for the day with my work on the terrace, I feel like I've done something good and the day's young still, relatively, there's still time and light, though the light's less, there's much less of it now than when I first arrived here.

If I ever leave France, I'll leave the yellow notebooks right where they are, under her bed.

I haven't told her about the tv.

INCIDENT WITH TV Helena's out walking this morning, so I carry the television up from the cave of the petit maison where I've been keeping it ever since accepting Jean-Claude's gift. I haven't told Helena, keeping the tv a secret and intending to watch it only when she's away.

I prop the thing atop the stone lintel, close to a electrical outlet, at eye-level. The set is elemental—a small convex screen, made more convex by the absence of a box, a holder, a frame—and all exposed, which makes it more interesting.

I notice there's no dial.

If there is no dial, there is no choice, if there is no choice it is not worth watching, if it is not worth watching it is not tv. This logic's pretty good but doesn't quite hold, though the tv is a beautiful sculptural element when looked at without knowing its purpose, which is that it's fun to watch tv. The phrase 'I'd rather stare than think', presents tv's situation adequately. Tv's arguably as powerful as the bomb. The possible destruction of the world=atomic energy: the other possible destruction of the world=tv.

There is no dial and there is no antennae, therefore it's likely there is no reception, though an antennae can easily be made from a wire coat hanger.

I walk to the closet for a coat hanger and untwist it.

After months spent sitting on the terrace, I'm so hungry for television that my innate fear of mechanical and electrical contrivances, especially electrical—having suffered from shock several times when changing a light bulb or painting a wall near an electrical socket, feeling the charge come through the hairs of a wet paintbrush—leaves me and I plunge into the experiment with my whole being.

I plug the thing in to the wall and watch as a small silvery light travels along a set of wires, twined together, from the back of the tv toward the front, finally igniting the screen into a consolidated image consisting of… of…of…of…

...it's impossible to say what the image is of, since it's neither of nothing or of something, it's an image of both light and of dark, a mixed image of each dancing wildly across the screen, an image left up to me. I must make it mean something, so I take the wire that was once the coat hanger and touch it to the back of the tv, leaning the wire against the other wires, the wires already part of the tv, the wires that seem to be conducting the image that's ending up on the screen.

A small fire ensues, five poppings and a flash. The tv burns right down to its cord. All lights go off in the petit maison, the house is submerged into the dark of mid-morning light of a small French village in the month of November. The whole house smells like an old cast-iron frying pan in which onions have been badly burned.

APPARITION THE
NIGHT BEFORE
I flee the petit maison like it's on fire, half to find Helena and half to escape the mistake I've made, gambling that she's walked out the back road toward Olloix, rather than the road downhill toward the main road and the river. For hadn't I come across Jean-Claude last night, half by chance and half on purpose, wanting to ask him about the tv, to learn more about its operation, to ask him if he wouldn't mind coming over to the petit maison to give me instruction on its use, not that one thing has to do with another.

I'd seen him in the street last night, from a distance. How thin, how small, how fine, how exquisite he appeared. Even from far away, from having not seen him for several years, I never get past how small Jean-Claude is, how thin, especially when he's dressed in the clothes of the night watchman, white shirt, grey pants, red tie with tie-clasp, black shoes, his professional outfit. He must eat practically nothing! Simone now outweighs him. She's told Helena that she's eating too much cheese, pate, and bread but *it's either eat or cry* she says.

Jean-Claude hadn't seen me seeing him, I'm quite sure. He turned sideways and so almost disappeared. He stood in the middle of the lane, practically facing me, with a dark sky behind him and soft evening light in front so that only I could see him. It was like he was on a stage. He looked like a man who is falling and does not know how to get out of his fall. It was clear how important it is to him to appear to be someone who doesn't take life seriously, and how serious his life is to him.

Jean-Claude, is that you? I said when I thought saw him, though I could see he neither saw or heard me.

Then whoever it was lit a cigarette.

I smelled the cigarette smoke, it came toward me like a friend. I walked toward where I thought Jean-Claude was standing and he wasn't there.

ONCE AGAIN IN THE PRESENT, I SEEK HELENA TO INFORM HER OF A SMALL FIRE

When I step out onto the street it's like I'm stepping on silence itself.

I walk towards the fields where the lambs once were, looking for Helena, out the back road of the village toward Gourdon and Olloix, the one of two ways out of the village, along the winding but level "D" road. I walk myself out of the village this way, having thought carefully about walking the other way, past the farmhouses and sheds that gather at the backside of the village, brimming with canisters of milk and broken-down farm equipment, reaching the large linden tree on the right in less than two minutes, step-by-step stepping forward, more freely than before, able to see my breathing so clearly in the morning light that my breath is leading me more than my feet.

It's possible Helena's walked the other way, down the hill towards the main road and the river. I wish I could walk the way she walks! Like someone who actually likes to walk, walking as if there's no other way of being in the world, walking toward something rather than away from. It's possible she's walked the way I used to walk every night before I was released from the need of seeing the river, released from the ghost of Monique and her sad, abandoned restaurant, from the need of finding a different path to walk from the petit maison to the river and back each night.

I GIVE UP ON THE RIVER

Yesterday, after many days of sitting by myself on the terrace trying to attain one-hour in the name of Blaise Pascal, nothing came to me and I gave up, fetching the yellow notebook from beneath the bed to write

the moment my eye hits the river, I'm taken

Writing, I no longer felt the need to walk to the river every night after dinner and have abandoned that practice. I might have applied the same process to Jean-Claude's cave, writing about the experience before having the experience, which would have alleviated the drama with the television. For my instinct told me to avoid Jean-Claude's cave, the first ever tour offered to an outsider. *Not even Simone has seen it* etc.etc. When he said he'd *open it Sunday for me*, I should have resisted.

The night of the news I'd been invited to his cave I couldn't sleep, knowing there's something in me that shouldn't see Jean-Claude's cave, that we'll both be disappointed—I in what I see and he in my disappointment—so that it's better for both of us not to see it. I couldn't tell him the truth, not understanding the truth myself, that we'll both be disappointed if I go. I hadn't come to France for Jean-Claude's cave, I'd met him by chance. I know his heart now, we're brothers but we'll only stay connected by keeping something from each other. It's just a bunch of junk in there I'm sure, car parts, pump handles, bric-a-brac gleaned from Thierry, who does have an eye, and old wine... and all described as a miracle by all those who've not seen it!

There's no other way out of it besides writing him a letter of explanation, or taking a vow of silence. So I say nothing for eighteen days, not a word, I pass by the matter in silence, a philosopher, in hopes of not offending Jean-Claude, not offering a plausible reason for not seeing the cave as there is none. Jean-Claude will understand, if I ever tell him.

And now the possible crisis with Helena! A burned television, the inescapable proof of my increasing avoidance of the terrace and consequently the work to which I've come to France to perform—being with myself without disturbance for at least one hour...

In the meantime I walk on, continuing my search for Helena on the road to Olloix.

AFTER THE MEANTIME Surely she's somewhere up ahead or behind or to my side, unless she's taken the deep path through the woods or the stone trail that runs along the butte on the other side of the village of Olloix, the path along which the cherry trees give forth nice little fruit filled with tiny worms.

Often, there's nothing to be done but to keep walking. When walking, it's good to be slightly ahead, not so far ahead that you can't be seen or heard by the other, but Helena's walking by herself without knowing I am looking for her and can't be blamed.

I can always turn back to the terrace, I suppose. Conditions have improved philosophically. I have all the silence I need now that there's nothing to be heard down below in the lane, not even the opening and closing of Thierry's door. The belled goat's been silenced. Marionette's shushed the chimes in the church—they only ring once in the evening, seven bells, one-at-a-time, at 7p.m.

Remarkably, Marionette increases her visibility as everyone else decreases theirs, wearing an additional sweater and a bright orange wrap around her neck, walking the hill twice a day now, once by herself and once with her granddaughter, a strange girl who shows up in the village out of nowhere, dressed in jeans, a blue parka and white tennis shoes she wears day after day.

The granddaughter's very pretty in a weird way. It's said Marionette's encouraging her to leave the village, take a college degree, get a job in Lyon or Paris. But she won't—anyone can see this way ahead of time just by

looking at her—she'll stay in the village the rest of her life, leaving only to go into Issoire for two or three days at a time like she's trying to disappear.

Marionette trusts Helena and I with the keys to the church now, as long as we leave them at the secret, pre-agreed hook beside the fountain and tell no one else in the village about our advantage. I meditate in the church two or three times a day, cold but happy; the flies are gone. Helena takes pictures of the frescoes in the church, a saint slaying a dragon and other legends of the Crusades that once had some relevance to their age, making notes in a small red leather-bound book she bought at Ecomarche.

Meditating in the village church, I try to imagine other people in church with me. Every seat is taken, each occupied by a believer, each believer listening and hoping and singing as they must have once years ago. As I always cry when I hear people singing in church, I cry now, hearing such hope and faith in their voices, singing to a god they'll never seen.

NOW WHAT   Walking comes down to two decision points working as one. Walking toward Olloix and seeing the sign for Gourdon, a small village where Helena's been known to walk in the past, I'm confused, neither not knowing what to do or having so many possible courses of action I can't act on any one of them.

The problem's this: from morning to night Helena acts as if she needs something to do. I don't find fault, it's hard on her when I'm not talking much and not particularly listening either, sitting out on the terrace for longer and longer periods of time while she's inside the stone walls of the petit maison, talking so I can't hear what she's saying, supportive I suppose, of the attempt I'm still making to stay alone for one hour without restiveness or discontent, though I can't be sure, having not spoken to her, or her to me, for days.

On the terrace, I hear her voice inside the petit maison but can't know what she's saying as her voice must pass through a stone wall and a pane of glass. She talks as if I can hear the meaning of her words and keeps talking, not knowing I can hear sounds but not the words themselves, keeps talking, stops, waiting for a response, talks again, then finally, hearing no response, stops talking, leaving me to start over in my attempt to reach one hour alone.

INSCRUTABLE HELENA I never find Helena, on the road to Olloix or elsewhere in the countryside. She's back at the petit maison when I return, doing yoga in white panties, sitting on the stone floor of the main level, topless. I don't say a word to her, knowing she likes to do yoga in silence. She never says anything about the tv which I've taken to the cave before I walked out to look for her, she never says anything about the smell of the fire.

There's nowhere else for me to go but to the terrace.

Thus begins the era when very little is said, one to the other.

BOOK NINE

The greatness of man is great in that he knows himself
to be miserable.

Pascal, *Pensees*

397

THE
TEMPERATURE
OF US

Helena's not cold, and not warm.

When I speak she often doesn't respond or asks me to repeat what I've said, at least twice, sometimes three times, so I have to say things over and over which changes the meaning of what I'm saying and which, to my thinking, has the effect of her speaking for me. She thinks my ears may be damaged from the cold of the terrace and rummages through her bag of clothes for a knit cap she believes she purchased in Vannes, suggesting also that I use one of her heavy wool scarves to wrap my whole head, from the neck up.

IN RELATIONSHIP,
ONE MUST
ACCEPT WHAT
THE OTHER CAN'T

I should shave but don't. Helena can take another day of stubble. We've held our faces close this way before, her smooth face to my rough one; she's never said she minded. When we first arrived in France she touched my face when I was unshaven as if she was pleased that I have stopped doing what I do, that to stop doing what I'd always done was why I'd come to France in the first place. But all that's changed, so much that I often stop in the midst of what I'm doing—reading Pascal, drinking wine, writing in the yellow notebook—being myself in whatever action I've begun to withdraw, rethink, do something else or do nothing, as I want to be doing.

If she won't touch me as I am I see no reason to shave.

It doesn't help that you have that haircut either, she says of my head, shaved now next to nothing, a full tonsure, taking the Bic every third day to my scalp. At first she'd loved the feel, tiptoeing out to the terrace to rub my head at odd moments, often catching me unawares, once interrupting a solitudinal flow that seemed destined to reach the hoped-for 60-minute mark. I'd had to collect myself, taking my head in my hands to begin again. Helena believes it's a pose, at least the hair if not the entire quest on the terrace, though she doesn't say so directly. She evinces less interest, never inquires of the time I've spent out there thinking, as she did when the weather was warm and my progress detectable. She's far more capable of going inward than I, for whom going inward continues to be the primary struggle, my time alone on the terrace lengthening in actual time but decreasing in results hoped for in some sort of perverse propor-

tion. It seems even to me that I'm getting nowhere, even less so on the divan, which has become a place purely for sleeping and reading, but not for the sort of original thinking I'd envisioned.

About the following I'm clear, writing it down in the yellow notebook:

I never want possibilities between Helena and I, between myself and the person I might become if I am fortunate to attain the quietness, the calm, the certainty of God's love for me that Blaise Pascal says is my destiny, to diminish. I only wish the possibilities to expand.

If possibilities must be narrowed let the possibility that I may have been born in France and hence am French; that the endearments I have made for Helena—nicknames such *as red wing, Vermont maid, jiminy cricket, Missy Capana,* are inexhaustible; that I'm in a place where no one other than me has even been. Therefore, I cannot know what is happening.

SHE SHOULD COME FIRST, THEN I SHOULD COME

Sleeping separately now night after night, wanting Helena to come to me all on her own, holding out hope that I wouldn't have to call her, for I wouldn't, but that she would come alone late at night, not wanting to be alone herself, and we would be joined by her desire first and then mine.

QUESTION AND ANSWER

You know Helena, I say at dinner, the one time in the day we come together to eat fresh eggs and drink Goujon's wine (which is a little rough) *it's possible that your disinterest in my attempt to achieve one hour of sitting by myself without distraction only serves the purpose of my persistence?*

She shakes her head, not saying yes or no, not agreeing or disagreeing. She must know that the answer is the misfortune of the question, as

Maurice Blanchot once believed.

If what you're doing up there— up there being the terrace as I call it—*is thinking then I think I'm ok with it. But I worry about you, that it must be cold even on the daybed, or whatever you call it, that old ratty thing you've brought inside.*

Then she says,

Why don't you just write a novel?

I WALK AS A PHILOSOPHER WALKS   After my time in the morning on the terrace, I wander through the village alone, hands behind my back, neither going to the river, as was my habit, or walking out the back road towards Olloix. I walk the village, the inhabited and uninhabited districts, top to bottom, side to side, lane to lane. Thoughts come to me as I walk,

how different is a beginning from an end?

Are they not one and the same? Is one not the other?

If an end is being reached here as it was there, there is sure to be another beginning as well.

For the beginning is attached to the end, and the end to the beginning though the attachments have their own, singular nuances, as one is older and one younger.

A beginning deserves to exist equally with the end, and the end with the beginning......by giving up trying to change, I accept my nature; by accepting my nature I will change; real change is possible anywhere, on the terrace and elsewhere. The one hour alone, the striving for the stillness of a self etc. etc. is therefore superfluous...

Out walking in a time when leaves are falling from the trees, the village looks like a place where God's been once but isn't coming back.

A FASCINATING DIFFICULTY   And then come days when everything's more difficult, the thinking especially and the not-thinking, the striving toward the goal of sitting calmly on the terrace alone for one hour.

The weather's against me as is the smell of the French disinfectants Helena uses to scrub the petit maison, including a big blue lozenge strategically placed in the toilet which emits a noxious petrochemical smell and must, to achieve effect, remain in the bowl for at least seventy-two hours.

It's impossible to write, wrapped up as I am against the elements on the terrace, having to take my right glove off and maneuver my pen with a cold bluish hand, my handwriting and hence my words are sometimes unrecognizable. I've taken more and more to writing less, not writing unless I'm sure the idea deserves more than one word, and then writing in large block cursive letters that can be read later.

THE THINGS YOU HAVE TO DO TO BE HUMAN On the terrace, two minutes after noon I'm hungry, starved for thick bread, sausage. No, for white cheese, chevre, and two crackers. Yes crackers, and for jambon and baguette. An omelette, no, not an omelette, quiche, yes quiche. Baguette and butter. A salad of the Auvergne with blue auvergne cheese and endive. One espresso and one lemon tart, something to fill the time. There might be something, but where? No, there's nothing.

Helena's hoarding an apple. I know, I saw her wrap it up and place it in her black bag. A rather large apple. A Fuji if I'm not mistaken. She might split it if I ask, though she seems unhappy with me and consumed with her reading…

YOU HAVE TO WRITE THINGS DOWN *Getting to the end of anything*, I write in the yellow notebook, *really reaching toward the end and feeling the end closer and closer, is like running out of ink.*

Writing, I feel the tip of the pen giving me feedback, *I'm tired, I want to lie down and sleep, I'm getting old* and so on and so on.

WHAT'S A NOVEL? I ask Helena at breakfast, *what's a novel?*

It's the fully living, fully aware state of being, she says.

BOOK TEN

We run carelessly to the precipice, after we have put
something before us to prevent us seeing it.

Pascal, *Pensees*
183

HIBERNATION AND ITS DOWNSIDE Helena decides the petit maison must be cleaned for any number of reasons—Madame Rocet may stop by unexpectedly or Simone who we haven't seen for some time, or Christiana from San Julian.

She means to scrub every stone. I count them; the fireplace and hearth alone are composed of at least one hundred fifty-six stones, as far as I can count, then there are stones on the risers between stairs, stones around the four windows, lintel stones at each of the three doorways.

It's stuffy I agree, old stones keep matters inside for a long time and we haven't been opening the windows in consideration of the cold. On the other hand, a patina is being gained that makes me feel as if I'm a real part of the place, a small stone home in the middle of France. The fragrance is of wood smoke, soup made of fresh vegetables, slices of three-day old bread and half a glass of white wine, smells that have started to seep into my clothes so that I am able to more fully empathize with the others who have lived this way for years—Teradact, Jean-Claude et. al.—the hibernators of true France. Helena says I don't have to help with the cleaning, but how can't I? How can I sit on the terrace or inside on the divan reading Pascal, which I believe she believes is the same as doing nothing, while she's busy sweeping, dusting, polishing, wiping down the small mirror in the bathroom, disinfecting, relieving the plastic shower curtain of its mold etc etc. She wears a white towel on her head, which she's wrapped up as a turban, as if to emphasize her action, the moral rightness of her determination to make the house clean.

We're in France, Helena!, I say. *Let's have fun!*, trying not to raise my voice or become a salesman. *This is how the French live, they live within themselves, staying inside most if not all of the day when the weather turns cold.* I imagine the warmth of spring, how nice and warm it will be if we stay in France, that the windows might be opened, bed sheets, towels, blankets might be shaken in the lane, hung from the windows in the sunlight, however cold it is, to be purified... I could help with the cleaning then, clean the petit maison from top to bottom, take the top floor on all by myself, and the cave too, for the cave's dirty, has been so for hundreds of years.

Helena doesn't hear me, having borrowed a small voluble electric vacuum cleaner from Simone and sweeping the walls from top to bottom while standing on a chair. I watch from the landing just below the terrace as she works and she knows I'm watching, which makes her work harder, which in turn has the effect of making me want to help her do the work she's doing.

I'll do upstairs, I say, but she doesn't hear me or, hearing me, pretends not to. I don't want to clean but I need to be considered an expert in most things, including cleaning, to feel needed, though I'd rather not be needed to clean. I'd rather watch her clean than not watch her clean, but watching displeases her, so I don't watch and then I do, I watch when she's not looking and don't watch when she is.

FREE WILL   Helena climbs off the chair and snaps off the
                        vacuum with a deft balletic flourish.

Well, Helena says, *you're free to do philosophy up there on the terrace and I'm just as free down here to be on my hands and knees scrubbing the floors, if that's what I want to do…and it is!*

SAY   It's as if we're cleaning the time between us,
NOTHING   Helena and I, clearing away whatever's accumu-
lated, getting down to the silence that might mean something. I'm happy not to speak, not knowing what to say, thinking about saying what Teradact might say, and saying nothing.

DO   Helena doesn't think this way.
SOMETHING
                        *You could write a novel, or a practical book of sto-
ries for Americans who travel to France, she says.*

I could call it "Monsieur Ambivalence", I say

Call what "Monsieur Ambivalence?", Helena says.

The novel you say I should write!

Writing a novel would mean that you're doing something positive, she says. Trying to *sit alone in a room for one hour is not positive. With all the time*

you've had and with the conditions in France, which I think we both can agree have been excellent and conducive to the kind of creativity necessary to produce a novel, it seems a fair thing to expect that you might have writ-ten at least one, maybe two stories by this time. I'm just saying that the way you've used your time here has been specious, that the business of learning to stay in a room for one hour without becoming restless serves no purpose but your own and is not your destiny.

That's the point of, I say. *To be so at peace with myself that I'm not a con-tributor to the problems of the world. It's true I seem to get nowhere, but the closer I come to the sixty minutes Pascal set as my goal the further back I go, the reversion makes me start all over.*

Helena turns on the vacuum cleaner once again, beating the pillows of the sofa-bed with the head of the thing so that the dust in the pillows rises, turning her full attention to cleaning of the petit maison, stone by stone. This consumes her for seventeen straight days.

NOT KNOWING
WHAT TO DO, I DO
NOTHING
There's the right thing to do at such a time and the wrong, though neither the right or the wrong may be known to the one who should be doing something, who might be doing one or the other, either the right or the wrong, and time itself becomes the impasse in which the one who should be acting becomes stuck and so does nothing.

I can only watch as Helena picks up the tv, which has changed color since the fire from its original black and silver to a gelatinous orange object bearing no resemblance to the machine that Jean-Claude gave me, and puts it in the trashcan. She's not said a word about it, nor have I offered an explanation.

By the time I put my right arm around Helena, calling her down from a stool, on which she is on tip-toes to reach the top of a previously undusted doorframe, it's the right time gone wrong. She comes down willingly enough, smiling that wonderful dimpled smile to which nothing negative could ever be reported and I put my arms around her so that we are face-to-face, my face above hers as I am the taller one, but not threateningly so.

Helena, I say, *isn't it a miracle that we don't have to worry about money anymore? That we're in the fortunate position of having enough, if not to live like queens and kings, then at least to live well modestly, and where we want to live, in France for the moment at least.*

Not worry about money, she says, *not worry about money? That's impossible! That is money's purpose. Money is to be worried about!"*

She says this while my arms are wrapped around her and while I look her in the eye. I have to act larger than I am and I do, though I know she's caught in a contradiction of her own making, on record somewhere in this book saying that she didn't want to worry about money anymore, furthermore that the village was a place meant for her to escape from the social conditions money placed on her previously. I tell her that I must return to the terrace and resume my work there.

I could have kissed her then but I didn't, I walked to the terrace instead.

HELEN'S INTENSE EXAMPLE   I've come to the point where I dedicate myself to a specific philosophical consideration during the time I spend on the terrace by myself, trying again and again to successfully achieve sixty minutes alone.

Helena's cleaning, now on its seventeenth day, progressing downwards to the cave of the petit maison, gives me the idea: the order in which she's scrubbed, the materials she's marshaled, discovering resources Madame Rocet or some previous tenant left behind, (mops and pails, solvent, a feather duster, a pre-war vacuum machine I assume Simone has leant her). The intensity of her purpose, wherein meaning has been found where none previously existed, encourages me to approach my situation in a similar fashion.

FOUR AGREEMENTS   The morning doesn't begin well, particularly in light of the previous evening when we'd agreed on the following:

1. We must kiss one another in the morning, instead of passing by in silence as we've become accustomed in these colder times.

2. Any and all problems we have with one another, or with our situation, must not be allowed to come between us and our kissing.

3. Post-kiss, I must disappear to the terrace and Helena to a lower level or go for a walk, do yoga etc.

4. From this point forward there must be no communication between us until evening.

Helena, I say, *I'm trying to do what a saint does, but I can't. My philosophy's derailed. You are as different from me as I am from you, as different as Teradact is from me and me from Teradact and Teradact's wife, who is now one with Teradact, as different as Jean-Claude is from Simone and Simone from Robaire and so on.*

LOSING THE YELLOW NOTEBOOKS, I MUST RECONSTRUCT WHAT I'VE WRITTEN

It's likely Helena's either tossed out or relocated the yellow notebooks in her zeal to clean the petit maison. I've just reached under her bed where I'd stored them, confirming the absence by lying on the floor face-down to see for myself. Not a bit of dust down there, no notebooks, nothing but stones. It's also possible she's put them someplace safe...

I'd rather not ask where the yellow notebooks are; I'd rather come upon them by accident. I'd rather not know if she's tossed them away. True, there were some ideas, well-phrased, that I'd grown fond of, that proved I was getting somewhere. I'll have to recall them one-by-one:

I want to live in a country where I can't see a flag wave

That's one thing in there, others will come, or they won't. If poetry is what remembers itself, as a poet once told me, philosophy must do the same. It's difficult to remember what's not written down. Paper's another problem now, having none, but not the essential problem having lost the yellow notebook where everything not remembered was written down.

As to paper, there's butcher paper in which the butcher Yves wrapped the chop we ate last night. Helena hasn't thrown it away, though I'll have to act quickly. The paper around the Pavin cheese is much too waxy, and orange. Such paper might suffice for art, for a person working in acrylics or oils, but it won't work for philosophy. Kleenex might work for a quick note or two, written delicately, as might toilet paper if it were the right kind.

It'd be nice to have tv, to sit back and watch tv as Jean-Claude does, as he is this moment, sitting in his blue canvas chair, smoking and watching tv. Such a serious man! I could tell by the first sight of his face that here was a man trying to understand his life! I could see by the aggressive lines on his forehead, forcing themselves down the sides of his face, that he was a thinker. There's not one ounce of Jean-Claude's face that's wasted, every part of it goes into his understanding (in this I'd like to become more like him), and his understanding believes all the meaning he finds there is funny. Jean-Claude's is a tragic face that has thought through tragedy and arrived at comedy. Helena thinks him a gargoyle, has linked us as such, as actual brothers once upon a time. We haven't said goodbye properly. I'd drifted off the night of the first snow as he was talking on the phone with the crazy lady, sipping champagne. I could knock on his door. It's been so long since we've had time together.

Nor is it the same now with Teradact, whom I've never actually met but who stays in my mind as the highest ideal!

 The last time I saw him I made a note of it in the yellow notebook. He was being helped along by Thierry, who was holding Teradact's right arm while carrying a sack of groceries in his left, Teradact's groceries I presumed, undoubtedly gourmet. Having Thierry with him diminished Teradact to the point where he was difficult to see, to the point he was not a man but a god. Step by step he disappeared, around the corner from the lane in front of the petit maison, which is where I last saw him, and up the steps to his villa.

This is how I remember the last time I saw Teradact. An account is written in one of the yellow notebooks that's now missing, so I've had to start over, as I'll someday have to start over on Jean-Claude and Simone, Monica and Robaire, Helena and myself to resolve this little travelogue satisfactorily, so that everyone's pleased with the outcome.

BOOK ELEVEN

The philosophers did not prescribe feelings suitable
to the two states.

They inspired feelings of pure greatness, and that is
not man's state.

The inspired feelings of pure littleness, and that is
not man's state.

There must be feelings of humility, not from nature, but from
penitence, not to rest in them, but to go on to greatness.
There must be feelings of greatness, not from merit, but from
grace, and after having passed through humiliation.

Pascal, *Pensees*
524

SLEEPING AWAY   All systems other than sleep are decomposing.

I nod off in the blink of an eye, walk in from a session on the terrace, remove my gloves, jacket, sweater and shoes, flop on the divan or on Helena's bed in full daylight without as much as pulling the curtain.

I fall asleep on my back.

I sleep for an hour or two. Often I wake, hearing Thierry's old wooden door creak open. Waking, I call out *Helena*, *Helena* though she's not there, she's out walking or running errands or someplace else. She never leaves a note.

MYSTERY OF
THE YELLOW   I haven't confronted Helena about the yellow
NOTEBOOKS   notebooks, it's not worth the time.

It's possible that when she was cleaning she moved them, meaning to put them back under her bed where she'd found them once she was satisfied with her cleaning. It's possible the yellow notebooks troubled her, that the time I spent on the terrace thinking and making sentences of my thoughts were threatening. She'd never mentioned anything of the sort, seemed supportive of my mission at the beginning, one of the reasons she advo-cated France, never asked to see the notebooks or for me to read from them as I had every evening when we first came to the petit maison.

ONCE MORE I   I start again, that's what a philosopher does, I
START AGAIN   start by remembering what I'd once thought,
it's much less trouble to start again, much less disappointing. Confron-tation only leads to disappointment, Helena would be disappointed that I asked if she had anything to do with the disappearance of the yellow notebooks and I'd be disappointed in her answer. The yellow notebooks are somewhere, their existence can't be elsewhere, they'll either turn up or they won't.

Hadn't philosophers dealt with this before? Wasn't it Epictetus, as invoked by the early Irish novelist who wrote (and I paraphrase now, remembering from an early entry into one of the first yellow note-books)????

????????????????????????????????? Yes, it's Epictetus

> *Men are not disturbed by things (pragmata) but by the*
> *opinions (dogmata) they have of things. Thus death is*
> *nothing terrible, else it would have appeared so to*
> *Socrates. But the terror consists in our opinion of*
> *death, that it is terrible.*

There's also the painter whose name I can't remember, who said that the *only thing valid in art is that which cannot be explained*, another fragment I remember writing in one of the yellow notebooks. He was a Frenchman, I'm sure, of an era in such awe of technology that he insisted on being formally dressed while talking on the telephone or riding in an automobile, wearing a suit and tie and white gloves.

HOUSE OF REST AND RELAXATION Helena starts to call the petit maison, *the sanitarium.*

I tell her she suffers *from a mild depression or a cold, that such a feeling is not uncommon in the climate in which we find ourselves.*

I get out of bed, get back in, sleeping alone on the sofa bed in the room beside the kitchen, making it difficult for Helena to get up at a regular time and make coffee, as I sleep no more than two steps from the kitchen. Though we sleep separately, I assure her this has nothing to do with sex, that I still find her attractive, that I have found and still find great delight in her body. I've taken more than my share of her beauty—her hair, neck, lips, eyes, breasts—making sure to mention the pleasing way her ears stay so close to her head, how perfectly they're shaped, like pink little roses.

Not having her beauty myself, I wonder how might I repay her? If not repay her then mollify concerns she has about my quest, either by encouraging her interest in it or by taking greater interest in her, which-ever might come first and be more natural. Helena's changing her mind about France, radically, from singing praise to finding fault. The fault lies mostly in the silence she casts upon everything she sees, things she is seeing for at least the second and often the third and fourth times and are no longer new and delightful.

Lately I feel like I could live here forever, though living here the way I do is taking more and more of my time.

HELENA BEGINS
TO WANT TO
LEAVE FRANCE
I can't leave now, I say, feeling the pressure of her silent opposition begin to come between us.

Things are unresolved. I'm only beginning to become a philosopher, learning to live where no one finds fault with me, no one judges or, if they judge, I'm no longer concerned with their judgment. Jean-Claude and Simone, Antonio the artist— though I don't see them much of them anymore. Yes, they may not like this or that about me, that I don't speak French for instance, but I'm granted some leeway as I'm a philosopher and accepted as such. Instead of thinking **'what should I do with my life' or thinking 'am I doing the right thing with my life,'** *I am doing my life, and they see that I am doing so.*

The truth is I'm as far away from France as I was when I first came here, when I wished to be far away from the United States. The village can't be blamed, having been all I could ever have hoped for. I couldn't have prayed for a better place to devote myself to the quest of trying to sit quietly in a room by myself for one hour—which I never could have imagined in that other country, opposed as it is to such projects, knowing at some archaic level that since Pascal was a Frenchman it might be easier to achieve what he advocated in the country of his birth.

And I'm so close, so close that the issue becomes the question of <u>can I do this without Helena, can I sit alone without restiveness for one hour</u> without her material and spiritual support which she so subtly withdraws day-by-day?

214

I TRY TO CREATE NEW ENERGY   I can't sit quietly on the terrace now for more than a few minutes, having regressed, by virtue of my concern for Helena, downward to as little as :30 seconds , a record low. I shouldn't keep track of the time here but I do, not being able to not keep it, keeping it then not keeping it, keeping it and not and so on, so that keeping it takes all the time I have. The dislocation between my quest and myself becomes so severe I begin to suspect it's similar to the problem Helena's having with France.

Still, the responsibility for re-orienting the energy so that I can continue the work begun on the terrace and Helena might enjoy France once again lies with me, and I am torn between the need to be alone and the need to have Helena happy so that I might continue the work.

COME WITH ME TO THE MOST BEAUTIFUL PLACE IN THE WORLD   I suggest a walk through Valle Chadefour, *Eden* I call it, one of *THE MOST BEAUTIFUL PLACES in France*, if not the world, and am surprised when she agrees.

So Helena and I set out in the car from the village, for the walk through Valle Chadefour is enough walking all by itself without having to walk to it from the village in the first place, a journey of more than twenty kilometers.

As we walk together down the long entry path cloaked with fallen leaves, close enough to hold hands without holding them, we meet a procession of school kids in the process of leaving the park. Their enthusiasm engages Helena and she stops to chat with several of them.

I walk ahead, I'll wait for her at the fountain where the water of the Chadefour can be tasted. Not that I fault her for stopping, the children are good for her, their joy's visible, out of the classroom, walking about Valle Chadefour in the shadow of the great snow-topped Sancy, the stream flowing, the Chadefour itself a little dour in its early winter clothes but vivid as Poussin is vivid, mostly verdant, meadowy, a landscape that looks like it's showing the earth the right way to be...

...I bend down to the water and fall on my knees, turn the spigot, let the water run into my cupped hands and splash it on my face, then take a long drink of the stuff—there's no better water anywhere, straight from the heart of the earth where creation is always happening.

(I'd meant to bring bottles and fill them, putting five empties in the car, thinking better of it when we arrived at valle Chadefour, seeing I hadn't brought anything to carry them in and would have to ask Helena for help).

It's not legal, Helena says, seeing the bottles in the backseat of the car and guessing what I'm up to. *There's a sign on the path, it says* NO *very specifically.*

No one's here this time of year, I say, *all we're talking about is a couple of St. Diery bottles, that's all. No one will know.*

Therefore the empty bottles I'd brought to tap the water of the Chadefour stay in the car, the one-to-one water-to-wine ratio I devised no longer operational, the scale tipped in wine's favor since I'd found Monsieur Goujon in San Julian.

I buy red and white wine in five-gallon plastic vats from Goujon, the only way he sells it. The wine's decent, the red a little rough perhaps, country wine of the Auvergne. Jean-Claude won't drink it, thinking there's no good wine in the region, and the white is far more drinkable with ice or a squeeze of lemon.

I drink them both, in what Helena classifies as *copious amounts.*

YVES RESTAURANT,
WHICH WE'D ONCE
LOVED

Let's go to Yves's for lunch, I say the next morning to Helena to cheer her up, thinking eating a little something in a nice restaurant we both love will change her present view of France.

Yves knows us by now, he'll make the Salad Auvergne we both like. We'll have a carafe of the white wine, watch the mothers wait for the school kids from Yves's window. If we get to Yves in Issoire by 2, we'll have the whole place to ourselves, I say.

But the time comes and we don't go to Yves's, we stay in the petit maison instead.

Helena makes something from whatever's in the refrigerator. Eggs, some lettuce, lentils, Goujon's wine, if in smaller quantity. Lunch is often our main meal, a late lunch taken almost silently, talking to one another only when there's something to be said, listening to the radio while we eat.

As the radio's fickle, working sometimes, other times not, we're in the dark as to world events, hearing of a possible war in the mideast only when we were out one rainy afternoon eating lunch at Yves's restaurant in Issoire, driving home quickly to the petit maison to hear more on Madame Rocet's old brown radio.

Now listening to the radio declare war on Iraq, I try very hard to eat slowly without Helena noticing that I'm trying, taking small bites and smaller sips of wine than usual, trying to enjoy the meal at a pace which might stimulate a dialog. It's hard for me to speak, having been defeated twice in attempts to improve her mood, once in Valle Chadefour and once with the idea of taking her to Yves's. I'm of two minds as to what to say should I speak, for Helena isn't someone who can be sold. So I say very little and what little I say comes to practically nothing.

DILEMMA I'm of two minds—one to continue my outreach to Helena by promoting walking and eating—and the other to do nothing in regard to her feelings and thoughts and concentrate solely on my quest.

I can't say, for instance, *what would you like to do today?*

Nothing, she says

Let's do something, I say. *Anything, I say, let's do anything*, I say, trying to amuse her, saying it like an Englishman could say it.

I say, it's a nice day, I say. *We could walk to Tourzel and the pig museum there. Have lunch at the restaurant in Clemensat, the one with the long tables and the pitchers of wine. Take a drive to the Sancy, to one of the mountain towns, Bourbole perhaps. Do you remember the spa there, the one with the Spittitorim*, hoping her memory of it would amuse her and that she'd consent to some change of mind, for she's been talking of leaving France for a few days now.

DIVERSION Day after day the terrace is inhospitable. I'm inca-
FROM DILEMMA pable of consecutive thinking, pulled between the two irreconcilable poles, feeling and thinking—wanting the best for both Helena and myself. There's nothing to be done but find diversion.

I take the car into Issoire for light bulbs at **Mr. Bricolage**. I ask Helena to compose a shopping list and go to the little Ecomarche in Champeix for groceries. Made brave by the trips I've made successfully all by myself,

I travel to Auchan in Clermont-Ferrand to buy more paper, buying more than I need. There's paper everywhere in the petite maison, stacks of white paper tucked away on kitchen shelves, stacked on the lintel above the fireplace, on the northeast corner of what is now Helena's bedroom. She doesn't seem to mind as long as things are neat. She thinks I'll use it soon for the book about France she thinks I should write.

But the paper just sits there like it's waiting for me to change, to use less rather than more when more might actually be better, to improve my own handwriting to the point where it might be read by others—as it cannot be read now by either Helena or myself unless it's written on a scrap of paper, whatever's lying around—and consist of no more than a dozen words or less.

I become satisfied with fragments.

A HAPPY OUTING FOR THE TIME BEING   She's happy to walk to Tourzel, it's a nice day and the pig museum there has little hand-made histories showing how the whole pig is used, from head to feet. We stop for Kir's at the Two Louise's, a restaurant run by pretty young girls from St. Etienne whose mother's were both named Louise.

Go ahead, read to me, Helena says out of nowhere, having tipped back the black-pink-and white floppy hat she wears in the sun, waiting for her Kir. She's seen the white paper sticking out from my back pocket—two sheets of 8 ½ x 11 paper placed together and folded into fourths to make a little book.

Read to me, Helena says when our Kir's arrive with a plate of salted peanuts. I clear my lungs of salt, sip the Kir (a cocktail of Chardonnay and cassis, served chilled) which unfolds in my mouth like a piece of white paper, and read:

A Painting in the Midst of France

A small oil painting of five lemons on a brown table, one of which has
rolled away from the others, and a ceramic bowl that appears to be empty,

purchased by Mme. Georgette Sirac (who since last summer shows a few
gray hairs on her blonde head) now hangs on a white stone wall in her
home near the chateau in Montaigut-le-Blanc. The painting has nothing to
do with the success or failure of art when the name Antonio Barcella is writ
ten by hand at the bottom right corner of the canvas.

HELENA SAYS
NOTHING VERY WELL
At the end of my very short reading the words come forward to meet their silences, one at a time. I can't tell if they like what they see. Helena says nothing for the longest time.

Mmmmmm, she says at last.

Is it the Kir or the words you like, I ask.

The Kir's good.

The Kir's good is all you can say?

The Kir's good.

She could thank me for sharing the writing, she knows both Georgette, the owner of the painting, and Antonio the painter. Yes, it's an experiment, an extended fragment, but I'd gone to great lengths to write about what I know. She'd asked me to read and it's never easy to read new writing

Both Kirs are consumed in silence, at a pace singular to each drinker.

I EXAMINE HELENA
FOR SIGNS OF LIFE
I check for signs when we're in bed together, which is rare, not that sex is something we don't have, we do, we have sex now to show that we can have sex, far more than because we have to have it. Checking, I find she's changing profoundly for the worst and rapidly. She's eating more and walking less. I know gaining weight concerns her, not that she's vain, though she doesn't complain per se. Not that she's denying herself anything, the refrigerator is full of cheeses and eggs and *the real milk* she buys every other morning from Pepe's son, plus the days are shorter and colder so she has more difficulty arranging her time.

She's changing day-by-day in France, France is changing her not for better or for worse, since what may be better for me may be worse for her and better for her the worse for me etc. I diagnose Helena as ambivalent to both person and place, perhaps slightly less the person than the place. The village has come to a crawl and it's an effort to get out of bed, much less to walk as she once walked.

I can't help but ask to help, though she doesn't ask for it. It's in my nature, yet I know better. The worries that my project of quietly staying in a room by myself for one hour, in perhaps its most critical phase, is being waylaid by my concern for Helena's welfare—her increasingly evident desire to leave the village—lessen as I begin to concentrate once again.

AND KEEP MY QUEST TO MYSELF   **Thus** I don't tell Helena I've decided to make one last attempt to fulfill Pascal's observation (*Entry #139*) by staying quietly by myself in my own chamber for at least one hour.

I'm taking my copy of *Pensees*, Dover edition, a paperback, with the preface by T.S. Eliot,

some scraps of paper if something occurs to me,

my wrist watch, a black-faced Seiko with a stopwatch feature,

breaking the mission into seven discrete sessions, to be used completely at my discretion, consecutively or otherwise.

THE END IS NEAR BUT VAGUE   Time's come to start thinking about the beginning of a resolution, and accept the possibility that the project of reaching the end is impossible, as the end is, at this point, indescribable.

WHEN DIVERSION IS PERMITTED   The only two diversions allowed:

    1. to look occasionally at my watch,

2. to write down thoughts as they occur to me and if they qualify as inspired.

I've considered a third diversion: to smoke a cigarette. But it no longer feels natural to light a cigarette. In the old days, lighting the cigarette was the most pleasant part of the deal but now it feels completely unnatural, wrong, even perverse.

I PUT MYSELF INSIDE PASCAL Strengthened, newly resolute, I act like a bookmark in Pascal's book, setting my whole being inside Entry #139, reading at least an hour each night.

> *The king is surrounded by persons whose only thought*
> *is to divert the king, and to prevent his thinking of self. For*
> *he is unhappy, king though he be, if he think of himself.*

I can't rest, can't be alone, can't think for myself, thinking of a self only brings problems. There's no quiet glory of an original self as I once thought, to sit quietly in a place alone is impossible, even if I was a king or queen.

I read and think like this while Helena reads upstairs. She amuses herself with mysteries before she sleeps.

Helena, I call, *do you mind if I read something to you?*

Silence.

Helena, I call again, *are you there? I'd like to read a passage or two from Pensees to you to hear what they sound like when they're read out loud.*

Rustling of bedcovers, reaching for bookmark, small sigh of having been interrupted.

Go ahead, she says.

When we imagine a king attended with every pleasure he can feel, if he be without diversion, and be left to consider and reflect on what he is, this feeble happiness will not sustain him...

Is that all?

He will necessarily fall into forebodings of dangers, of revolutions which may happen, and, finally, of death and inevitable disease...

Yes.

So that if he be without what is called diversion, he is unhappy, and more unhappy than the least of his subjects who plays and diverts himself.

Yes. Is that all?

Yes for now.

Then goodnight.

Goodnight.

**A CROWN FOR
TERADACT** I make a king of Teradact and order the crown.
It's gold, with little jewels that spell his name. It
better come quickly, before he leaves on another trip or buys another
dog. He's the genius, happy or unhappy. I could look at the way he walks
forever, the way he lets his feet fall to the ground without a trace of dis-
satisfaction. If I could only be that way sometime!

But no, no, no, no and no. It saddens me to think of the satisfying dis-
cussions I might have had with Teradact if I'd spoken to him. I had the
chance as a newcomer to the village, he might have been receptive had
I gone up to him and spoken! Something in me resisted, withdrew, went
upstairs to the terrace where I was alone to create my own Teradact in
the image and likeness I've made for him.

I need help! But who can help me? Helena's not interested. She slips away
day by day into the commonplace plots of murder mysteries, in whatever
salads and casseroles can be made out of lentils and will stay edible for
several days, sometimes weeks. She concentrates on the co-dependent
relationship with Simone, who herself is in a bad way, having been
advised to try and remember her childhood.

**SIMONE, BY VIRTUE
OF HER BEHAVIOR,
REJECTS SAINTHOOD** Simone comes to the door of the petit maison
like a sniper's bullet.

I hear the sharp knock from the terrace, it's a strange thing, something
hard hitting something soft. The sound falls upward, increasing its
urgency. I could hide like the poet who hid behind curtains in the man-
sion her father owned, watching from her study on the second story until
whoever it was at the door went away. But I don't, I go downstairs to see
who's there.

There's Simone crying, her tiny little shoulders moving in rhythm to her
sobs.

Having no language, I take Simone in my arms, I don't know what else to
do. I'll hold her until she stops crying, at least that's a plan. *It's ok*, I mur-
mur, *it's ok*. She's sharper than I thought, her shoulder blades move up
and down like a bird that has two beating hearts. I hold her until they
stop shaking.

She might have stayed in my arms a while longer if Helena hadn't
appeared at the top of the stairs. I'd no idea she was in the petit maison,

I'd presumed she'd gone walking or to the farmer's market. The house was so quiet I thought I'd had it to myself.

Helena takes Simone out of my arms so suddenly it makes Simone laugh. I watch as they walk the lane toward Simone's house, arms around one another, without saying a word to me. I ask myself what I just lost.

YOGA   Later, I ask Helena, *what's the matter with Simone, why'd she knock on the door crying.* Helena says it's nothing yoga can't cure. She's going to teach her yoga, she's found a studio in Champeix with mats and ropes and hardwood floors. Every morning they drive to Champeix to do their yoga, have lunch in the town, returning to the village in the early evening.

Helena seems happier, leaving little notes around the petit maison when she leaves for yoga, often before I wake, making things for me to eat, mostly involving lentils, filling the thermos with coffee for me to take to the terrace. One evening she brings home a hand-rolled cigarette, a gift from Jean-Claude she says, who she saw briefly. Jean-Claude's working double shifts at the tire factory in Clermont-Ferrand, so he can retire sooner, *The French system*. He sends word through Helena that he's sad he hasn't seen me but that all he has the energy for when he's home is television and sleep.

Helena and I eat dinner together from time to time and drink Goujon's wine, liking the red more, believing it keeps us warmer than the white. Sometimes I sleep in Helena's bed, however uncomfortable, just inside the terrace, though I always wake in the morning in the sofa bed down below beside the kitchen. Helena tiptoes around, making coffee, getting ready for yoga, and I pretend not to hear her—if she thought she was waking me she'd be sad—preferring to start the day silently. Alone, I drink a cup of coffee and head for the terrace, as cold as it is.

RE-DEDICATION TO WHAT'S IMPORTANT   Stepping onto the terrace these days is like removing a bandage—it must be done decisively and without worry about how much skin might be lost. Helena thinks it pointless to sit as I sit, under the Stella Artois umbrella, out on the terrace as long as I do. It's cold, yet the time's come to go forward with the task or quit. The conditions themselves—the solitude, silence, the conviction that no one wants to be where I am or to have what I have—couldn't be better than ideal.

Nothing can keep my from my quest, I repeat, *nothing*, not cigarettes or wine, not walking, not the lambs or lack thereof, not the failure of not yet speaking with Teradact (and now that he's dead never again having the chance) not Helena whose displeasure is either with the person or the place, not the silence, for no village on earth could be as quiet as this village, tucked up into its own hill, accessible only by two small narrow roads, the people hidden away in their stone homes as if they weren't here, a place equaled in its quietness only by the villages of Chazoux or Gourdon, slightly quieter villages perhaps, depending on the time of day.

Thus, I find myself more and more in the position I'd sought for months and months—to achieve one full hour alone, on the terrace or elsewhere, in which there's nothing other than myself. I told Helena just last night, *I musn't fight the seeking, I musn't let the end consume the beginning.*

On the terrace I lie in state.

BOOK TWELVE

Two errors: 1) To take everything literally.
2) To take everything spiritually.

Pascal, *Pensees*
647

Chapter 1

THE DEATH OF
TERADACT In any event, Teradact's dead.

There's no fanfare. Thierry saw a strange car in the car port of villa Teradact. A nephew from Angers, or was it Orleans? Thierry can't remember. The nephew inherited the villa and the field to the rear where Teradact once grew beets, unbeknownst to everyone in the village. They either never found a body or those who knew a body was found never said a word.

Hearing news of Teradact's demise, I seem to recall that I'd heard what sounded like a hole being made in the village, an explosion of silence, a sound signifying absence, like a bird flying away from a tree, something that might in retrospect have signaled his death, the day I was informed he'd died. In retrospect, not knowing, until the news reached me from Helena at least two, perhaps three days after its occurrence, this is what I remember, though there was no such explosion, rather its opposite, the almost complete silence that was a recognition of the absurdity of his absence and my failure to communicate with him before his death.

Thierry—who spreads the rumor that the nephew will use the villa as a country home or rent it in the summer to tourists—has been willed Teradact's car, the silver Renault, and already stuffed it with bric-a-brac. I learn this second-hand from Helena who learned from Simone, Simone from Jean-Claude and Jean-Claude from Thierry.

SILENCE
DESCENDS
AT FIRST The village changes profoundly now that Teradact's passed—it's like the place's been told to make peace with nothingness. Birds stay away, the sparrows and doves that visited the rooftops, tip-toeing along the stone top of the terrace morning and evening, have flown back into the big green trees of the countryside to live in exile. Snow made at night stays on the ground until well after noon, disappears altogether until the next morning.

No one's saying a thing. Marionette's glimpsed, out walking up the hill, dressed in the darkest colors imaginable. When she comes to the door of her house she looks right and left, right and left, then opens the old wooden door and enters quickly, careful not to make a sound.

There won't be a service, Teradact's to be buried in Paris, yet for several days the whole village, every man and woman in it can be seen, at one time or another, walking down the steep hill to the cimetierie to honor a man of consequence.

FRANCE LOSES INTEREST That things are like this in France may exist solely in my imagination as no more or less than what I want to have happened and not what happened at all. In any event, the project—staying alone in a room quietly for one hour—begins to feel like nothing more than an experiment. Perhaps there's not the time or the place for what I'd hoped for, perhaps I'm not the one to work out my own philosophy on the terrace or elsewhere.

Helena's tired of the village, hasn't asked about the terrace for weeks. She's practically stopped talking, starting to lose the weight she'd gained, no longer eating either bread or cheese, drinking only a thimble of red wine with dinner, becoming less French every day. At the moment, there's no more rigorous opposition to my project than her silence.

I bear down relentlessly and try to act like I know what stillness really is, I sit quietly. There's not much time. I can feel time feel around for me, but I must wait and wait and wait where nothing happens, out on the terrace, dressed warmly, for one hour.

THERE ARE NO WORDS FOR IT Everything's in the past to Helena while everything's coming toward me.

Religiously now, I bring *Pensees* to the terrace, along with some pages I've torn from the phone book Madame Rocet's left in the petit maison to use for paper and a thermos of strong coffee. I sit at the metal table, beneath the Stella Artois umbrella, alone and try to drum up a little business. I set my watch, the little hand moving more slowly than the larger. I roll the cigarette Jean-Claude's rolled for me back and forth on the metal tabletop, but don't smoke it.

Fourteen minutes pass. I write,

Everything that is

has to come to climax;

it has no choice.

Then,

Somewhere in the present is my adventure. Here, the earth spins
in favor of mountains
and there, the seas.

Then,

I'm committed to what can't be done, to go on from here…

…these scraps I've kept from the last several weeks on the terrace, the hour toward which I am progressing perhaps unattainable, having thrown many of the things I've written into the fire, taking pleasure in their death, having never found the yellow notebooks I thought I'd stored beneath Helena's bed, now writing in margins of a French phone book, beginning again the next morning, faithful always to the beginning, resigned more and more to the end.

AS AN ENDING
WON'T QUITE
COME, I BURN
WHITE PAPER

Thierry scrapes his front door across the small stones he uses to keep the dust down.

I rise from the table and pace the small terrace, hands behind my back, thinking, counting this as time spent in pursuit of my prize; but once agitated I subtract the counted time and start over, sit again quietly, compose myself, directed once more to the task that is perhaps unachievable, to stay still for one hour.

Everything depends on an ending, and I'm ready for one, staying here on the terrace, speechless, mostly mute as a button in the petit maison, knowing the end will come to me, though I've had to lie to Helena, telling her that I know how everything's going to end, sounding so conclusive that she's now thinking that she will flip to coin to see whether she would stay or go…

…the hard thing, I said to her, *is not being with you, it is being without you. I mean every word of what I say to you, but I still have to achieve what I set*

out to achieve, to sit alone in a room for at least one hour.

And therefore I simply cannot leave the village, unless of course you leave,
which will make this a different story, one we will both feel differently about.

I write in the margins of the phone book, page by page, in a clear legible
hand, and burn the notebook paper I'd bought at Auchan, watching the
neat little piles flame up and turn to ash.

A TERRIBLE
DEATH
It troubles me that I can't remember how
Teradact died. He slipped and fell to the point of
disappearance. That's the best I can do. And so Teradact dies without me.

There's no proof Teradact thought of me at all, having not made the effort
to know him face-to-face, having lacked the courage to knock on his door
when there was still time, having thought I suppose, however subcon-
sciously, that I might be rejected, not knowing the language, and feeling
poorly about my decision only when it was too late.

Of Teradact's death, this much can be said: the whole idea of civilization
is that we must be good to one another, wherever we live. When I consider the magnitude of the loss, I see that I have nothing and that I am no
one and that I'm at least 300 years behind the times.

TOWARD THE END
OF OUR DAYS
Somewhere near Moulins, on a short trip I took
with Helena toward the end of our days together
in France, should they come to an end, for it is as yet undetermined
whether we will stay or we will go, together or apart, or if indeed I was
ever in France, having more doubt now than I had then, when I supposedly committed to the trip, I was struck by a cluster of words which came
to me as the words of a poem might come to a poet, if I was a poet.

This happened at the train station in Moulins while I was separated from
Helena, believing her lost, having evidence that she'd boarded the train
from Clermont-Ferrand without me. As I was alone I began to think, having nothing else to do, sitting in the drab Moulins station, wondering if
indeed Helena had gone ahead to Clermont-Ferrand or had gone into the
town of Moulins by herself, purposely or by mistake.

Some time passed, and then some more time, and a little more until a
good hour had gone by in which I was alone in the train station, without

making anything of my solitude, without being aware of it necessarily, not reading or writing, not brooding, content, it seemed, to have no questions and therefore to desire no answers, having let Helena go, wherever she might be, when The Pledge at Moulins was revealed to me—

To be the person I wish to be I must first think of myself

as if I was another person and then ask myself if I would love

the person thinking about the person I wished to be

I TEAR MYSELF IN TWO   Near the end I told Helena that I'd go to France when I finished reading Pascal.

I confessed that the French of the village, par example Teradact, Jean-Claude, Simone, were *as close to getting it right as possible*, the village itself, small and hidden within its smallness, quiet enough to read and write and think, to hear and see myself do all of these things, to build up toward a home where I might consider God, where I might progress from

the ecstatic past of primitive and extreme Christianity and into the meditations of empty churches courtesy of the Catholic Church—the same church in which my friend Blaise Pascal believed so fervently—drinking in the bequeathment of the best thing the church has done with its time, that is to leave these old churches mostly free of people in rural France, to leave the majority of the churches unlocked and willing to give so freely their treasures of emptiness.

And as it's nearly all two's here—Simone and Jean-Claude, Christiana and Antonio, Monica and Robaire (absent now, living in Brussels)—and the significance of twos, the *twoness* of the village, in which a small population is so predominately comprised of pairs, of one female and one male, the notable exceptions Marionette and Thierry, is a problem I feel compelled to follow, should I have the time to do so.

For two may share tension more easily than one, may split an anxiety between them thus lessening its pressure, the anxiety of the fear of death, of not having enough food, of not being honored, and perhaps most supreme the fear of not having someone to talk to, which is the real fear of being alone.

So I'm torn between one and two, this and that, here and there, I'm torn between being alone and being together. Alone, I want another, with another I want to be alone. The contrast between where I was living in America and where I live now in France has far more attraction for me now than for Helena, whose idea it was to live in France from the beginning. And Helena is torn too, but says nothing.

Nor does it do any good to talk about such things. Talking only makes one of two feel better, either the talker or the listener, and then only by chance, so that the entire enterprise of the conversation consists of the wonderment of the two wondering if the one is capable of talking to the other or the other capable of talking to the one

Near the end Helena consoles me, while going her own way, by saying, *you know you have your own story, you have yours and I have mine. And what in the end is it that either of us want? Only to be listened to!*

Inasmuch as there is as much energy to an ending as to a beginning I am devoted to an end, my days in the village now directed toward the discovery of the proper words for it.

BOOK THIRTEEN

Silence is the greatest persecution; the saints were never silent.

Pascal, *Pensees*

9 1 9

METAPHORS FRACTURE By now, everything happens that's going to happen. The door that opened is closed and the closed door's about to be opened. My story about Helena and I, such as it is, is now ready to acquire the constitution of closure—that popular concept, as if any human other than a sociopath has the ability to ever move on beyond what's happened—which is the god-given right of any story, good, bad, or otherwise.

The tremendous loss of Teradact, followed by the break with Helena, has left me with so little of my own that I've realized, at long last and with a protracted struggle, that I really need very little to live on. And that it's my god-given right to do nothing. Now I don't think about what to do; that's all in the past. I do nothing, as I live in a place that's been through all this before. Finding myself doing something I stop and instead of being in the action I'm in, whether it be walking or drinking wine or thinking or writing, I withdraw, re-think, and do something else or do nothing.

By doing nothing, I seem to be losing everything. Almost everywhere I look in France something's falling apart.

AND HELENA LEAVES ME Yes, Helena's gone home. My heart for her is no longer the heart she has for me; it's a separate heart, and quite distant. Either she's taken the yellow notebooks or she hasn't, but I've not found them.

I watch her walk down the stairs of the petit maison slowly, careful not to slip as the stairs are steep and the tiles slick, and shut the door of the petit maison neither with deliberation or force but firmly so that she is completely on the other side. I hear her footsteps in the lane. She's taking the long way down, hoping Marionette might be walking up the hill, if she is walking, with her bread, hoping Marionette might be the last person in the village she sees, unbeknownst to me.

She walks out of the petit maison without me, with or without the yellow notebooks, for they're not under the bed, not under either bed I should say, as I have been sleeping downstairs in the pull-out sofa bed, keeping the now lost yellow notebooks submerged for safekeeping under Helena's bed during our time in France. This is not how I imagined her leaving, though I have imagined many times what it would be like to live without her, and she me, but never from so far away, never from the standpoint of her leaving the place where she knows the language and me staying in the place where I not cannot speak.

ONCE AGAIN, A QUESTION THAT WON'T BE ANSWERED

The question, as I phrase it in English to Helena moments before she walks out of the petit maison, *is not whether to go home, but where is home?*

She opposes me, saying, home *is where you know the language.*

I say to Helena , *you're a hero to me for knowing two languages. Besides, you're more at home in France than I am.*

She says nothing. I say:

Helena I can't leave now, I'm only beginning to become a philosopher. And things are unresolved amongst us, not to mention Jean-Claude and Simone, and Antonio the artist. Furthermore, I'm just learning to live in a way where no one can find fault with me. There are issues, it's true, they may not like this or that about me, that I can't speak French for instance, but I'm begin-ning to learn how to live correctly. **I'm thinking 'am I doing the right thing with my life, I'm living the way Teradact and Pascal might want me to live...?**

SHOULD A DOOR REMAIN OPEN OR CLOSED?

The last straw, the final disagreement, is the disagreement we have about leaving the door to the petit maison open or not leaving it open. I'm on one side and Helena's on the other.

A DOOR HAS TWO SIDES

(ME)

The door should be open. It shouldn't be a ques-tion, there should be no question at all that the door's meant to be open. If you were to ask the door, the door would say it preferred being open to being closed. Being open is what the door is made for the door would say, to let the light in, the air. Not completely open perhaps and not at night, at night the door's purpose changes, the door is to be closed. The door itself concedes that. At night the door's to be closed and locked, locked tight for the peace of mind only a locked door can provide. But open in the day, open enough for at least a little fresh air, unless it's winter. In winter of course it's closed, but open at least a little if it's warm enough. Ajar a crack perhaps. And open for others in the day and in the daylight, not locked, open a little even if it's cold, so that a neighbor could come in out of the cold.

(SHE)

The door is a door for one reason—to be closed—to be closed in the door's answer if the door could talk. Every door has this in common with every other door, it's what makes a door a door, that it should be closed for the most part. Why can't you see this? Is something wrong? If a door was made to be left open there would be no need for it! The door would be denying its doorness in the same way you would deny your humanity if you did not breathe! If a door is not closed it is not a door. Doesn't matter if it's made of wood or steel or plastic. A door with a window is another case, I admit, an entirely different problem. But let's stick to the old wooden doors of France! I don't deny that doors were meant to be open and closed, no doubt, hence the hinges. But the closing's the door's most salient attribute, whether it's hot or cold, the door's designed to be closed...

BOOK FOURTEEN

Might is the sovereign of the world, and not opinion.—But opinion makes use of might.—It is might that makes opinion. Gentleness is beautiful in our opinion.

Pascal, *Pensees*

303

MY LIFE CHANGES   Now that Helena's left France, the petite maison
WITHOUT HELENA   seems larger and smaller, a room or two is always
being added or taken away. I go down the hill at least once a day to get
bread from the blonde at the boulangerie, she's expanded her line, sells
some fruit—bananas, apples, once in a while oranges—and other little
things Her son's made a CD. I bought it but don't have anything to play it
on. The blonde thinks her son and I should meet, that he could put music
to my lyrics. I'm not sure how she decided I'm a poet, it could have been a
conversation we had, she misunderstood some words I'd said. I'd said her
son was *a poet*, not me, such a little misunderstanding.

Every day, nothing happens. I don't know what I'd do if I had to do something, it would be like being tied down with rubber bands and forced to
lie on a table with a strong light an inch or two from my eyes. It might
be good for me, though I doubt it. It's not like I just sit here. Sure, there
are times I just sit here as there are times I have to make myself sit here
There's a difference and the difference is a mystery. I watch the weather,
it's something to do, especially the sky, clouds running or standing still,
the wind itself in the trees like music being played from somewhere you
can't see, lightning and thunder, soprano and bass.

I'm grateful there are times I don't have to think. It's gratitude itself I
thank. It's so great to be in love with gratitude, gratitude is becoming the
greatest part of my life. I'm never lonely when I'm grateful, the possibility
of making a life here increases and decreases exponentially according to
the strength of my gratitude.

Now that the past has greater depth than the future, it's a good life, but
sometimes I miss Helena so much I don't know what to do. The old house
is cold and almost silent, other than the sounds I make or that come to
me, and I still don't know the language. Alone, I divide sound into what's
outside and what's inside: a sound outside is what happens when I can
hear; a sound inside is what happens when I'm listening.

MEMORIES LIKE SCARS Memories find their way into me, leave little marks. I remember telling Helena that I'd come home from France, *as soon as I finish reading Pascal*, just like it was yesterday. The Memory makes me cry, it feels like I'm sitting in an empty church all by myself imagining how it felt in the days when Pascal was a young man and the churches were filled with believers.

I remember things, I touch them up with my own happiness and sadness, using a pencil. **It was me who called myself *Monsieur Ambivalence*, not Helena.** At the time I thought of myself that way, it was a way to clarify what couldn't be understood, the only vision of I'd had of myself that made sense in relationship to my situation etc etc. We laughed about it all the time, even when making love. Near the end she'd hardly look up when I read her something from the yellow notebook. I'd become someone else to her, I wasn't myself anymore, and if I wasn't myself they weren't my words.

She took me far away *to think and to write*, which is and isn't what I'd hoped to hear at the time she said it. There's something wrong with me in the statement when I hear it said, and The Presumption when I see it written is that I was having a problem living where I was living. I do wish to write. I also wish to rest from writing, primarily to sleep and walk and eat, and her wish was that I write for myself and rest with her so that we could be together as we were not together in the country from which I've come and to which she's returned.

Toward the end, she preferred Thierry. She'd walk across the lane to his house *for things*, things being a glass of vermouth for the chicken she was cooking, red thread to mend a blouse, the newspaper of the region, a game of Checkers. Once she came back from Thierry's wearing a blue shirt with a button down collar, a dress shirt, Brooks Brothers. It was slightly used but good as new. Thierry was a good buyer, shrewd. The shirt looked a little big on her—she'd lost weight, had stopped eating bread and butter—so she gave it to me.

I've hung the blue shirt in the closet. Sometimes Helena puts it on at night and spreads her arms out wide like she's ready to go to bed.

TIME MOVES IN WITH ME   Living alone, Time has its way with me, it drags me across the stone floor or makes me sit still near the front windows. I hear it sigh and make coffee to stay awake.

For the first few days, I consciously try to free myself from myself. I don't know what this really means, but it gives me some kind of picture. Then I peter out and actually pray. I'm too shy to ask Marionette for the keys to the church—Helena always asked for me—so I pray in the petite maison. Really I do, fifteen minutes at a time, three or four times a day. I pray until I see that I'm in a place where I can't know what's happening, I'm not supposed to know, where no one other than me has ever been. It doesn't matter who left who, only that I'm left where I am, having been left alone to make the decision. At this stage, I only think of our difference: that I'd been self-taught to consider uncertainty the only thing I could be sure of, that I saw everything through the prism of doubt, of something being something but also being something else, and that Helena saw things quite differently.

I'm in my *bewilderment*, wearing a heavy plaid shirt. *Bewilderment* is my core—that I'll continue living without knowing much about my life other than it's a mystery. Then one day I add an outer ring that circles around the core—that I'm one for whom everything is difficult.

I really don't know how long I spend thinking about Helena. At first just hours pass, then days, months. It doesn't matter how much time goes by, but everything I think about since she's left has something to do with her.

AND TIME FINDS THINGS TO DO WITH ME   Sometimes I sleep late, then I feed myself, then go out to walk by late morning. I walk and walk and walk, perhaps from Tourzel to Ronzieres on the little road through the fields, then up the hill and into the village of Vodable. I walk because I'm alone, it's all I have to do.

I've given up on the terrace, if sitting quietly means that I must sit alone without the anxieties of my solitude intruding, without me wishing to be somewhere else. It's a god forsaken task. I no longer try to sit quietly in a room by myself for one hour, having stayed in the past on the terrace for longer and longer periods of time, almost until spring and the snowmelt in the Sancy, failing by not much more than ten minutes to reach the hour toward which I was striving. I've given up the idea of reading all of Pascal's

Pensees, if reading all of *Pensees* is to be constituted by reading my friend's book from beginning to end, I begin to believe that I'd mis-read Pascal, that my friend didn't mean what I thought he'd meant, that his injunction was not the injunction I thought it to be but rather an observation about men's character in general, not to be taken quite so literally. Now when I go to the terrace it's for the views, for the White Team playing the Black on the soccer field below...It's late Friday evening, the players are taking time on with such energy—and then the game came to an end and a full rainbow appears in the sky.

Sometimes I drink whisky with my friend Antonio and talk about art and movies. I wave to Jean-Claude when I see him standing at his door or out walking his poodles but otherwise we have no relationship. We've lost touch, I'm as dead to him as he is to me.

MORNING ALWAYS HAS A LESSON   The morning's so typical.

Having trouble first putting on my sock and then my shoe, for I've somehow injured my right leg while walking the rocky trail from Grandyrolles to Olloix, feeling that I will not be able to dress myself and considering my options—Simone, Genevieve in San Julien, Marionette—I'm brought to tears and a hot sweat in the cold stone house. Humiliated at first that I can't put on a simple wool sock much less my hiking boot, swearing against my fate, I'm suddenly grateful for the sock itself, for the means to have bought the sock and for the intelligence that led to the means. I swear I feel Gratitude put its arms around me and pull my sock on, first the right sock, then the left, by means of the wrought iron fireplace tool Madame Rocet's laid at the hearth.

Gratitude's the miracle I've learned in France, as the village has shown me despite my many failures—not seeking out Teradact and expressing my appreciation, my jokes with Jean-Claude, my cheese eating and wine drinking, the rich breads, the sauces I've allowed myself, the loss of the yellow notebooks in which I kept for more than six months and less than one year a record of my thoughts and feelings inside and outside, as well as the trust that they'll someday be found, the never-to-be-met goal of being able to spend an hour in a chamber contentedly by myself, the unread passages of my friend Pascal greater, I fear, than the passages I've read, Helena's leaving the village of her own free will and without me—that gratitude is my salvation whatever the situation and wherever I may be.

ONE YEAR
ANNIVERSARY, I've lived in France for over a year, living like I
AN OVERVIEW know where I'm living, living as if I have all the
time in the world, though some things have changed.

I stayed where I was because I couldn't make up my mind, because I
finally had the courage to let things go other people's way. I just stayed,
that's all, listening to what isn't here as much as what is—the rain working its way down from the roof, skinnying through the drain pipe drop-by-
drop, sounding like life itself being born. I listen for hours and hours, for
as long as it rains that is.

Teradact's niece and her husband, a quiet middle-aged couple from the Dordogne with a grown child, have moved into villa Teradact. Thierry's in a rehab clinic in Clermont-Ferrand, committed by the courts. Simone caretakes his big stone house, bequeathed Thierry by Teradact himself, a revelation Jean-Claude presents matter-of-factly as we share a cigarette by the fountain.

AND AN
APOLOGIA

I apologize to all the characters herein. It seems I did not know them as well as I should have. For instance, the one I knew best—Teradact—I knew least though he was well-written about. Robaire, if you and your art seem to be misunderstood it is all my misunderstanding and not yours. To Simone and Monica, beautiful un-subservient handmaidens, because you are so different from them you are far greater than your men could ever hope to be. To Jean-Claude, though he may soon lose his lungs to hand-rolled cigarettes and leave us bereft, I don't have the tv you gave me but I do have the knife.

AND TWO NEW
ADMISSIONS

Now that Helena's left, I've gone back to smoking, not sneaking around as I had or denying myself altogether the pleasure of sneaking exactly, thinking as I smoke that Helena might be getting reports from Simone, with whom she keeps in touch, on my activities, musing on the difference between privacy and secrecy in regard to Helena's possible knowledge.

I still read Pensees, it's the only book I have, but only by candlelight, entering the final entry, #923 yesterday in the yellow notebook:

> *People who do not keep their word, without faith,*
> *without honour, without truth, deceitful in heart,*
> *deceitful in speech; for which that amphibious*
> *animal in fable was once reproached, which held itself*
> *in a doubtful position between the fish and the birds…*
>
> *It is important to kings and princes to be considered*
> *pious; and therefore they must confess themselves to you.*

For all I desire is to give up any need I may have for power and for the need of feeling responsible for others, and to learn to concentrate with the full force of my being on such being as I have. All I want—besides the need to stay contentedly in my own chamber for at least one hour, as instructed by my friend Blaise Pascal—is to emerge from the petit maison and hear one of my neighbors say *O, it's you Monseiur Ambivalence. I see you've decided to stay in France!*

And so here I am by the grace of God, whether there is God or not, not having a God being a kind of God too to those professing not to have one, as I've noted earlier.

I'll stay here for some time, at least until next summer I think, when it's sure to be warm again, and full of thunderstorms and showers. The weather's always honest with itself wherever we are, that's why we talk so much about it.

I've started a letter to Helena. It begins:

I guess I'll bet on God like Pascal

*but I miss the sound of beef in the fields
and taking walks with you.*

    This is as far as I've gotten.

THE ACTUAL END

AMERICA, FRANCE   In light of my long standing and persistent ambivalence, but with a brand new perspective, I see that the photographs I've taken in France are overwhelmingly of places and not people, and if of people of people unknown to me, strangers who intrigued me (like the man in Egliseneuve-d' Entraigues whose nose was so enormous he should have had two faces), or people who happened to be in the foreground or background of the place and were not the actual subjects of the picture...

...perhaps this would seem to mean it takes so much time to see, that it takes up life.

Alone In France, I finally begin to let uncertainties pile up around me like bric-a-brac without thinking about sorting them out or putting them in their place or trying to make sense of them. I walk around the petit maison with whatever's in my heart and mind, with as much of the past as I can handle, in the little village in France where I make my home now. More and more it feels like I'm living in a state of grace, I think I'm finally learning to listen. Up there where all the rivers start, in the Massif du Meygal west of St. Agreve, I thought I heard Helena say that she's finished with life and that she's happy. I'm almost ashamed to say—though I accept this specific shame and am ever closer to being over it, that my situation, my condition, at the moment, is of a man who currently has no opposition or enemy other than the self but who is still tempted to see himself as a victim.

I see that at last I've reached a place where I can't imagine having a subject, and having no subject I have no object, having no object my confessor is confessing to me, my confessor and my confess-see as it were, are subsumed by the sort of nothingness I dreamed of when I came to France, the kind of awareness in which I am fully conscious of being alive but not of living a certain kind of life. Of this much I'm certain: I never want possibilities to diminish.

One morning I have a disturbing new idea: that in the future each individual will have a finite and definite space assigned to them, a certain boundary or territory in which they are allowed to conduct their spiritual life, and that Nature, that which is outside us, is also kept in certain definable areas and permitted to be what it is without human interference. That an individual would be forces to apply for access to Nature on an individual basis, perhaps by lottery, and could experience pure Nature outside the confines of his or her spiritual territories, with all the terrors and uncertainties such pure Nature offers.

For months after Helena left, I continued trying to free myself from myself, to carry on with the project of sitting quietly in a room by myself for one hour, as indicated by Blaise Pascal, though I finally petered out and began to make up my own prayers to keep myself company.

Here's one:

> I'm in a place where I cannot know
> what's happening, I'm in a place
> where no one other than me
> has ever been.

A prayer like this came to me every day I prayed. When one would come I'd say it over and over, gradually feeling better, not fretting about my ambivalence which would still come and go. In regard to Helena, I'm still not sure who left who, only that I was left here, all by myself in the village, and that I've stayed here for some time not having to make any decisions, until next season, summer I think it was, for the weather was hot and the countryside given to sudden thunderstorms and downpours that were anything but charming.

(It's possible that you can be so close to someone that you disappear and they disappear too, so that you both disappear to one another.)

I keep a picture of Helena in the room where I work, it's the last MEMORY I HAVE of her. She's picking blackberries in a field beside a small road in the Auvergne near Mont Dore and the look on her face is of a woman who's found the place she loves and who looks younger than she is because of it. *I might stay here forever*, she smiles.

We were nearing the village where we'd come to live for awhile in a small stone house, when I saw the blackberries and slowed down because I was tired of driving the car and Helena was tired of navigating, and neither of us were sure we were on the right road.

(*Who was more tired than who*? was the almost constant question between us in those days.) Helena constantly consulted the Michelin, which she balanced on her knees as I drove. She was as patient as Saint Teradact (who, I am reminded, walked the almost invisible line between the penultimate and ultimate ambivalences with such extreme dignity and skill) determined as she was to keep us on the small roads, the *green roads* she called them since they were marked in small green dashes on the map. She'd discovered the green routes somewhere in the Ardeche, as I had discovered the small blue and white enamel Michelin directional signs, usually hung high on the tallest or most prominent corner building of a village, and had become obsessed with trying to see them, as their placements were inconsistent. Often all that was left of them was an unreadable pale ghostly imprint of the name of the next village and the distance to it, part of the French publicity machine, donated to the country by Michelin to encourage travel by car, increasing Michelin tire sales undoubtedly.)

It was either late August or early September, the day before we were supposed to arrive in the village and claim the petit maison from Madame Rocet. The weather was hot and heavy, the air was trying to say something, to find the right words. I saw the blackberry vines and pulled the car to the side of the road, turning the wheels on the passenger side toward the side thorny culvert, leaving just enough room for a car to pass, as the *green roads* in Auvergne are extremely narrow. I think it was a Renault or a Ford.

The last of the blackberries hang like they're begging for mercy, at least the ones you could see, or like old people who dress in black in hot weather because they've given up the ghost and believe they've become afterthoughts. The vines themselves wound around fence posts and barbed wire that separated the farmland from the road, but you see the berries first when you're looking for them. From the road, most of the blackberries look shriveled. If there are good ones, sweet ones, they'll be hard to find, they'll hide themselves behind thorns, the last berries of the season.

Helena could hardly wait to get out of the car. She grabbed a plastic bag from the backseat, shook whatever was in it out, and walked across the culvert toward the berry bushes. I watched her from the car for as she picked the good berries, tasting them and smiling, waving for me to join her.

Finally, I got out of the car, not to pick berries, but to stretch my legs a little and drink some water, to take a little walk up the road to see what was there.

Some time went by like this, when it felt correct to be alone, when it seemed to me that Helena might be feeling the same. I did some knee bends and touched my toes, drank Volvic water from the bottle. A car or two passed by.

I walked back on the road to the place where I thought she'd crossed the culvert and called her name. She didn't answer, so I called her again.

The brambles of the berry bushes were dense and full of thorns, full of dust, malevolent. Big splashy piles of cow dung spread out on the ground like paintings hanging on the wall of an art gallery. I called her name again, *Helena*, *Helena*, but she didn't answer.

And then I saw her on the other side of the fence, sitting on a tuft of soft green grass in the sunlight. The plastic bag was full of berries and her mouth had dark streaks of berry juice along the line of her upper and lower lip. She smiled at me and I told her not to move, walked back to the car for her camera, and came back to take her picture.

This all happened years ago, as long as it's taken me to learn to do nothing, having voided the whole notion of progress in my own life, listening this very moment to the thunder beginning to parade down the valley from the Sancy, watching for the lighting that always follows the sound of thunder here. I lie still and stay lying on the now quite worn-in divan as the clock comes closer and closer to the magical time of noon, at which time all work winds down—the saws and drills and midget cement mixers are switched off—and the little village, in which one project or another is always just beginning, is completely silent and still.

At some point language is all there is, all we see and know of the world is all in our language. It's what we say that makes it a civilized world or not, a good place to live or a something like a hell. But getting rid of words is good too, we better ourselves sometimes when we give up words.

The End

A PRAYER FOR THE END OF THE BOOK

What is in you is that which is beyond you, as far as your understanding understands things; the tension of the limit, that is of understanding, is that the nature of the mind is limited, and it is good to give thanks.

THOMAS FULLER

Thomas Fuller lives in a village in rural France, dividing his time between poetry and prose. He writes poetry in small homeopathic doses when he feels like it and prose when he doesn't feel like writing poetry. Mr. Fuller's published 6 books of poems; *Monsieur Ambivalence* is the first work he's written to be classified as fiction.

COLOPHON

TYPOGRAPHY

Granjon by George William Jones,
Whitney by Hoefler & Frere-Jones

PAPER

Mohawk Superfine Ultrawhite Eggshell 80lb text and cover

PRINTING AND BINDING

McNaughton & Gunn, Saline, Michigan

DESIGN

Ingalls Design, San Francisco
Tom Ingalls and Kseniya Makarova

OTHER IF SF TITLES

Whatever Happened by Tim Reynolds
Trusting Oblivion by Michael Hannon
Tree by Brooks Roddan and Joe Goode
Bittersweet Kaleidoscope by Bill Mohr
East of West LA by Kevin McCollister
the lyrica poems, 2003-2010 by Michael Hannon
the Aphasia Cafe by Dawn McGuire
Tale of Two Heads by Sally King
Sam Haskins, Attorney, Poems 1970-1980

Founded in Los Angeles and now located in San
Francisco, California. IF SF Publishing has published
poetry, lit memoir, photography, and fine art books
since 1999.

For information about the press, please visit
ifsfpublishing.com

IF
SF
publishing